GONE

A. G. HAWKINS

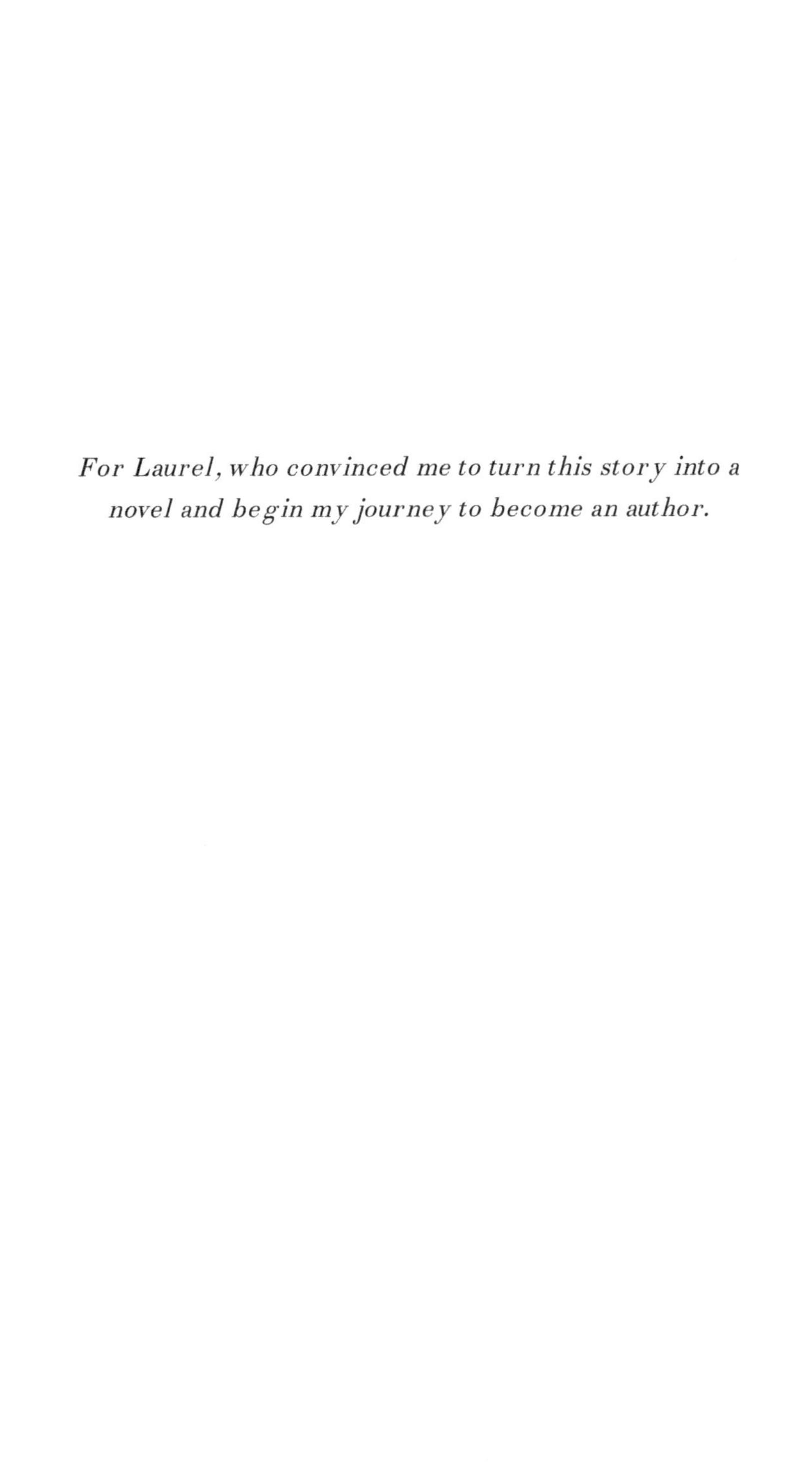

For Laurel, who convinced me to turn this story into a novel and begin my journey to become an author.

Author's Note

Dear Readers,

When you read my stories, I hope to write relatable characters. My characters go through situations, sometimes dark. For a longer list of what tropes or types of situations you may see within this story or any of my others, visit my website: aghawkins.net.

Thank you,

A. G. Hawkins

As a mother, balloons always frightened Jo. Anytime her daughter, Lulu, would pick one up, Jo imagined it popping in her mouth and lodging in the back of her throat. Her daughter loved balloons, terrifying Jo that something horrible would happen. But in the end, her fears had been unfounded. A balloon didn't steal her daughter away. Something else did.

There were several balloons attached to the terrace of the restaurant where she ate. A pink balloon became untied from the bunch. It climbed higher and higher until it became a mere dot in the sky. Soon she could no longer see it. It disappeared, much like her little girl. Tears built up behind her eyelids, and she blinked them back.

"Jo," a voice said, pulling her eyes from the sky.

Josephine turned her attention to her sister, Vivian, who sat across from her at the table. Her sister was only two years older than her, but she carried herself as much older. Her darker skin, dark eyes, and raven, curly hair all contrasted with her own straight hair, pale skin, and light eyes. People rarely believed they were sisters. It was just that she had taken after their father, and Vivian had taken after their mother.

"Hm?" Jo replied.

"I shouldn't have mentioned him," Vivian stated. She brought her hand across the table and placed it over Jo's before giving her a reassuring smile.

"It's fine," Jo lied. "Why shouldn't you mention him?"

"Well, you two haven't really spoken in what... four years now?"

"We speak once a year." Jo bristled slightly. Her soon-to-be ex-husband was not the boogie man. She could speak about him, even though it tore at her heart and made her miss everything they had before.

Spinning her spoon in her cup, Jo refused to look back up at her sister.

"Right." Vivian's voice was kind, and her hand squeezed Jo's. "Her birthday."

A sharp sigh passed through Jo's lips. In just a few weeks, her daughter would be eight.

"You know..." Vivian paused. "He... Nick, he has a girl-friend."

Jo nodded. "I know."

Just a few days ago, she saw the post online. Her husband, Nick, was not a fan of social media, but he still held his account from years ago. He never posted on it. However, he'd been tagged in a photo by a woman named Eleanor Jax. Online, Jo had seen the long post about how it was their six-month anniversary, and how she was so lucky to have Nick in her life.

Jo had stared at and studied that photo for hours. She tried to read Nick's body language and facial features. The two had been together for nearly ten years before everything fell apart. Back then, the two of them read the other so easily. Jo was sure she could still read him now. In that photo, he hadn't wanted to be photographed. His hand clutched around the glass of wine tightly, and his mouth was curved into a forced smile. What she couldn't tell was if he was uncomfortable being with Eleanor Jax, or if it was just because of the picture being taken. Not that she had any right to know. They had been separated for four years now. Nick didn't owe her anything.

"Thomas wanted me to remind you that the papers need to be signed within the next couple of days," Vivian carefully stated.

Jo let out a shuddering breath. The divorce papers. Tears stung her eyes as she recalled the papers arriving several months ago. It shouldn't have shocked her. For the past four years, their marriage had only been on paper.

Nick went through Vivian's husband for the divorce to make it easier. Thomas was a lawyer. According to Thomas, Nick said he wanted things to be fair and easy. Going through her brother-in-law helped make it that way. If Thomas was anything, he was fair.

"I know, I know. I'll sign them tonight," Jo promised. She had every intention of following through with that. She couldn't push it off much longer. It wasn't fair to Nick.

"I can come over and help," Vivian offered.

"I can sign some papers just fine on my own."

"Of course, you can," Vivian tightly smiled. She always had that look about her, as though she was prepared for Jo to have a mental breakdown. Not that she blamed her. Jo hadn't been herself in over five years. That day, when her daughter went missing, Jo had lost herself. Since then, Jo didn't know who she was anymore.

"Plus, I have Mom and Dad," Jo reminded her. Her parents had moved in with her a little while after she and Nick parted ways. They felt she needed support after everything that happened.

"Well, if you change your mind, let me know." Vivian checked her watch and then sighed. "I have to go pick up Callie from dance lessons and then TJ from his after-school science class. Are you sure you're all right?"

"Why wouldn't I be?" Jo asked. Vivian narrowed her eyes.

"No reason. Let me know when the papers are signed."

Vivian stood up and kissed Jo's cheek before leaving the back porch of the outdoor restaurant. Jo saw that Vivian had left money to pay for both of their meals. Even now, Vivian was still taking care of her.

The house was in immaculate shape thanks to her retired parents. The two of them had moved to St. Simons, Georgia many years ago, but after Jo lost everything, they moved further up north and into her finished basement to stay with her. Her father enjoyed taking care of all the outside gardening and lawn care, while her mother was always decorating for every holiday and each season as she kept the house in tip-top shape.

Jo stepped inside, and she heard her parents' small dog rushing up to meet her. Jo bent down to rub his head. He crawled into Jo's lap. Jo stood, keeping him in her arms.

"Hi, Butler," she said, bringing him up to kiss his wet nose.

"Ah, there you are," her mother, Rose, greeted. She'd pinned her hair up into a tight bun. At sixty-eight, Rose still had yet to grow a gray hair. Whenever she or her sister asked her how she pulled it off, Rose would just shrug her shoulders and tell them it was genetics. She looked her daughter over once before saying, "How was lunch with your sister?"

"Fine," Jo answered. She handed Butler to her mother and pet his head once more. "Where's Dad?"

"Out back in the garden."

Jo glanced out the large glass sliding doors that led to the backyard. They had chosen this house specifically for the backyard. It was a yard for a family, for children. She and Nick had made plans to put up a swing set and a sandbox for their daughter when she got older.

Her parents wanted her to sell the house and move back with them to the beach, but Jo would have none of it. She had to stay here. This was her daughter's home.

Jo sighed and then made her way upstairs. She bolted past the door of her daughter's room, as always. Yet today, she found herself drawn back to the closed door with painted flowers of assorted colors covering the edges and the large L painted up top. It had been her daughter's request at three years old, and her father had immediately obliged. He could never tell Lulu no.

Jo reached out toward the letter and ran her finger along the curves. Then she pushed open the door to see the room that was stuck back in time. A room that had stayed the same for five years. Every toy that her daughter had pulled out was still in its place with dust caking the top of them. Lulu's bed remained unmade, with the flowery comforter halfway on the floor. And her shoes were still askew, one beside the bed and one upside down near the closet.

While she knew she should probably clean it up and donate some things inside, she couldn't bring herself to do it.

"Lulu," Jo whispered. She let out a shaky breath as she scanned the room once more. She closed the door. Standing there for several minutes, she allowed memories of her Lulu to flood her mind. Warmth spread through her before the pain took over. She stepped back.

Right now, she needed to sign the divorce papers. It was what needed to be done. Nick had been patient with her and understanding, but it was time.

When she reached the office, Jo went right to the desk. The papers were there, not moved from this room since she received them months prior. She knew every detail inside them. She'd read through them every night.

Sitting down, Jo read through it again. Nick was being much too generous, giving her the house and alimony. She was sure she didn't deserve any of it.

As she picked up her pen, Jo felt her heart constrict. Her fingers grew numb. Even as she moved toward the first line to be signed, she couldn't do it. Something within her possessed her, and she could not sign her name.

Finally, she gave up. She would have to try again in the morning, but she wouldn't tell Vivian how she felt. Her sister would just pity her.

Jo ended up in her bedroom and glanced at the bed. Nick's side remained always made. The light blue comforter remained pulled up under the pillow. Jo slept so still without him there beside her.

Her phone rang, and she jumped. It was in her back pocket. She reached for it, checking to see who could be calling. She only ever spoke to her sister and her parents these days, having distanced herself from every other friend she ever knew. The number was unknown.

"Hello?"

"Mrs. Josephine Anderson?" The voice sounded familiar.

"Yes?"

"Jo?" She knew that voice. It was the detective from their case all those years ago. The detective had been patient and understanding, not giving up until they forced her to do so.

"Detective Morris?"

"Yes."

"What's happened?" Jo's hand came up to clutch over her heart. This was it. She was going to be told that they had found her daughter's body, and that she was dead. Morris would suck all the hope she had held for her to be returned away with just a few words. Jo held her breath.

"Jo, we found her. We found Louisa."

"Her... her body?" Jo croaked.

"No." Jo swore she could hear Detective Morris smile. "She's alive, Jo. Your daughter is alive."

ONE

SPRING 2012

"Happy birthday!" Jo's parents called in the doorway. Jo moved to the side to allow her parents to come in. They had driven the three hours from St. Simons, Georgia to be here for the birthday party. Even though they had retired to the beach, the two of them were always back for holidays, parties, and big events. They never missed an important moment with their grandchildren.

"Gran! Grandpapa!" Lulu happily screeched, running down the hallway toward her grandparents. Her grandfather, Charlie, swooped her up into his arms. He was a tall man with a big, thick beard. It had always fascinated all of his grandchildren. Lulu's fingers immediately touched the soft hair, and she giggled. "Like Santa," she said.

"Maybe I am." He winked and more giggles came.

"Where are our other grands?" Jo's mother asked as she glanced around the empty home.

"Mom, you both are an hour early. Vivian, Thomas, TJ, and Callie will be here soon because they are bringing the bounce house," Jo assured her.

"Right," her mother replied. Rose attempted to pull Lulu from her husband's grasp, but he shook his head and held her tighter. The little girl squealed in delight; she adored the attention.

Leaving Lulu in excellent hands, Jo walked around to the kitchen where her husband was. Nick worked as a free-lance writer, and Jo, who had been a teacher, was now the stay-at-home mother for Lulu. Her husband was a brilliant writer, and he got asked to write for different places all over rather often. But he always made sure to be home on weekends and never allowed himself to stay away for over two nights at a time.

The two had always wanted children. After they married, they struggled to get and stay pregnant. Over the course of their first five years of marriage, there were several losses. The years were filled with stress and sadness that they may never have children of their own. Then, by some miracle, Jo had gotten pregnant with their daughter and been able to carry her to term. Ever since then, their lives had been all they could ask for.

Nick was preparing the cake for the birthday girl. He had many talents, especially when it came to baking. Nick had iced the two-layered cake with pink frosting and decorated it with her favorite fairy characters that he had made by himself with fondant. He'd taken the time to make sure all the details were just right. Nick's skills always amazed Jo. She could hardly draw a stick figurine.

"This is amazing," Jo said with a smile. "She's going to love it."

"Oh, I hope so," Nick replied. He would do anything for that little girl. Lulu had him wrapped around her little finger.

"She will." Jo's hand rubbed up Nick's back, bringing it to the nape of his neck to play with the hair there. He turned to her, bending down to capture her lips with his own. Melting together, Jo forgot for a moment where they were. Being with Nick was like that; it always had been. The two of them could forget for a while that there was a world around them.

A clearing of a throat made Jo snap out of her moment with her husband. She still kept her hands on her husband and the smile on her face, but she turned her head to see her father standing in the doorway. Even though she and Nick had been married for nine years now, her father still was not fond of Nick. He hadn't liked him from the moment Jo brought him home.

She and Nick had met when she was 25 and he was 31. Her father had felt he was much too old for her. Charlie was shocked, when only two months later, they announced they were going to get married. They married regardless of his feelings, as Jo had been sure he would eventually come around. Plus, she knew that Nick was the love of her life. Yet, despite how long they remained together and the happy life they built, Charlie never grew fond of Nick. He only tolerated Nick for her and Lulu.

"Do you like the cake?" Jo asked her father, untangling herself from her husband. Her father grunted. "Nick did a great job, didn't he?"

"What's the flavor?"

"Chocolate and vanilla layers with buttercream icing," Nick confidently stated, but Jo knew he was nervous around her father. No matter what Nick did, it was never good enough for Charlie Scott's daughter.

"Hm," her father muttered.

"My cake!" Lulu entered the room, tugging on her grandmother's hand. Her eyes lit up as she saw the work her father had put into the cake for her birthday. Nick swung her up into his arms so that she could get a better view.

With his granddaughter in the room, Charlie smiled.

"Beautiful cake you got there, sweetheart," he told her.

"You do wonderful work, Nick," Rose said sincerely, with a big smile plastered on her face. Unlike her husband, Rose adored Nick. She knew just how great he had been for her daughter.

The doorbell rang.

"That's probably Vivian. She is bringing the bounce house," Jo said.

Growing up, Jo's older sister, Vivian, had always gone by Vivi and protested when anyone called her anything else. While their parents had given them extravagant names, they decided to call them both nicknames. However, when Vivian met her husband, Thomas, she chose to go by her full name. Thomas's family came from money and so Vivian felt she fit in with them better this way. It had stuck. Even after eight years of marriage, Vivian would cringe when someone called her Vivi. It no longer suited her.

At the door stood Vivian with her family. Five-year-old TJ rushed into the house, searching for his cousin. Baby Callie was asleep in Vivian's arms, and Thomas held the large bounce house bag. Thomas was the quiet sort. He had a wide knowledge of many things, but he rarely spoke about any of them. Instead, he'd just stand there and observe quietly. He also did anything Vivian asked of him. He spoiled her and the children rotten, but Jo wouldn't have wanted anything less for her sister.

"Out back?" Thomas asked. Jo nodded. She and Thomas got along fine, but they were never close. They just had nothing in common outside of her sister.

"Can I hold her?" Jo asked her sister, her eyes moving to her niece.

"Please." Vivian handed the three-month-old baby to Jo.

Jo sniffed the top of the baby's head and closed her eyes. She wanted another baby, but the odds were not in her or Nick's favor. They had been trying since Lulu was a year and a half. She had gotten pregnant once after Lulu, and it ended in a miscarriage.

It didn't seem fair that her sister could easily have children and she couldn't. All Jo had ever wanted was a full house. Her sister was stopping with two. She was a wonderful mother, but she didn't have that need for children like Jo did.

"You can't keep her," Vivian teased. "Where are Mom and Dad?"

"In the kitchen with Lulu and Nick."

"Dangerous," Vivian laughed.

"Yes, so please save Nick. I'll cuddle with Callie."

"All right."

Jo continued to rock the baby in her arms. She was a beautiful little thing. Her legs were long and her eyelashes were too. She already looked just like her mother. Vivian had always been beautiful. Jo couldn't recall her sister ever going through an awkward phase unlike herself. Thankfully, Jo had grown into her ears.

"Baby?" Jo turned to see Lulu glancing up expectantly at the baby in her arms with wide eyes. "Baby Callie?"

"Yes, this is your cousin," Jo replied. "Do you love her?"

Lulu nodded. "You have a baby?"

Jo frowned. "Maybe someday. Now, let's see if Uncle Thomas has the bounce house up and running, all right?"

That night, Nick read Lulu her favorite bedtime story. The little girl remained cuddled up beside him and fell asleep before he got to the fairytale ending. He kissed the top of her unruly curls. Lulu had inherited his dark curly hair, though other than that she looked exactly like her mother. People often commented how she was the perfect mix of them both.

He adjusted her on the bed and pulled her covers up to her shoulders. Then he turned off her lights and closed the door.

Jo stood right outside. He smiled. God, he loved her. He pulled her close, and the two kissed.

"Our little girl is three." Jo glanced up at him, meeting his eyes. "Can you believe it?"

"No, I cannot," Nick answered. It still felt like yesterday when he held his daughter for the first time. "Our baby girl."

"I wish we could have another," Jo said, furrowing her brows. Nick nodded. He hated that he couldn't just give that to his wife. She was the perfect mother to their daughter. As much as he would love more children, he didn't need them. He always felt like she did. Like something was missing for her.

He kissed her forehead.

"Maybe we will," he answered. "We never know what tomorrow may bring."

"No," Jo mused. He wrapped his arm around her shoulder and drew her closer. They made their way to their bedroom and fell into bed. Jo grinned as Nick peppered her jaw with kisses.

"We could always practice," he said into her ear.

"We could," Jo agreed. But she sat herself up and pulled on the sleeves of her gown.

"Jo?"

"I just... something feels off," she confessed.

Nick narrowed his eyes. He sat up next to her and touched her shoulder.

"Off?"

"I don't know," Jo shook her head. "Just... it feels like something bad is going to happen. Don't you have that feeling?" Jo did this every so often. What was scary was that, most of the time, she was right. They often joked that it was her sixth sense.

"I'm sure it's nothing, honey," Nick tried to assure her, though her words made his stomach churn. He gently tugged her back onto the bed to cuddle with him. "Today was a hectic day, darling," he whispered into her ear. "You saw your sister's baby. I'm sure your emotions are just all over the place. Let's get some sleep."

"Yeah," Jo agreed. Nick happily sighed as his wife melted into his side. They were the perfect fit, the two of them. He couldn't imagine a life without her.

Two

Early Spring 2017

Time stood still. Jo took in a sharp breath as her hand clutched tightly to the phone on her ear. *Alive.* Her daughter was alive. Blinking harshly, she tried to speak, but the words remained stuck in her throat.

"Jo?" Detective Morris's voice made her jump.

"I – I'm here. Where...." Jo could feel the sobs growing in her throat. "Where is she?"

"In Atlanta," Detective Morris answered.

"How...." Jo struggled to get the words out. "You told me she was dead."

Jo heard a sigh on the other end of the phone. "I know. All the signs indicated –"

"But she wasn't. I told you all that she wasn't. No one listened to me." Jo felt the anger growing in her chest. Even though she knew it wasn't technically Morris's fault, as she was the only detective that had tried to keep looking, she had still failed. Had they not written her daughter's disappearance off as a death, they may have found her before nearly five years had passed.

"No," Morris agreed. "No one did, Jo. And I'm sorry."

"He didn't listen to me," Jo whispered to herself before shaking those thoughts away. This was not the time for that. Her daughter was alive. That was what was important. She needed to see her. "When do I see her? Do I come to Atlanta? Is she...is she all right? How was she found?"

"She is perfectly healthy," Morris stated on the other end. "They found her at a house in Atlanta when they raided it for drugs."

Drugs. The word made Jo's stomach flip.

"But she's fine," Morris added again. "A woman that was arrested admitted to kidnapping your daughter. They did a DNA test, and they determined she was your Lulu."

"When do I see her?"

"Soon," Morris promised. "They will bring her down tomorrow."

"Tomorrow!" Jo nearly cried. "I... I can't... I can come up to Atlanta now."

"No." Morris tried to get Jo to see reason. "It's best we wait and follow protocol. They will bring her to you tomorrow."

Jo heavily sighed. "All right."

"But she's here, Jo. Your daughter is here, and she's safe. I will call you as soon as I know more."

Jo hung up the phone, and she closed her eyes. Lulu was alive. It felt surreal. How was it that her daughter had been alive all this time? But she *had* known it. Her insistence that they not give up hope had driven Nick away.

Nick. Realizing that she needed to call him, stopped her in her tracks. She hadn't heard his voice in nearly a year. Would he even answer her call?

It was a rainy day in Chicago. Nick shook his umbrella and then placed it by the door of his small apartment. He went straight to the refrigerator after the door was closed and grabbed his measly pre-made chicken and rice meal. It was Eleanor who had suggested he prepare his meals earlier in the week so that he wasn't grabbing takeout every day, multiple times a day, or eating frozen meals.

As he heated the meal, he shrugged off his wet jacket and threw it over the edge of the couch. Then he went and took the heated meal from the microwave and got a fork. After two bites, he made a face. He'd eaten the same meal for three days now, and it no longer held its appeal.

Right before he could throw the food out and order delivery, his phone rang. It was still on his kitchen counter. For a moment, he thought about ignoring it. The only person who ever called him was Eleanor, and he wasn't sure he wanted to speak with her right now.

The phone rang several times before it stopped, but a split second later, it began again. Groaning, Nick stood from his couch and walked over to his phone. When he reached the phone, he saw Jo's name on the caller id. His heart skipped a beat. He never randomly heard from Jo. Quickly, he picked up the phone.

"Hello?"

"Nick?" Jo's voice was tight, almost as though she had been crying. Worry filled the pit of his stomach.

"Jo? What's wrong? What's happened?" It didn't matter how much time had separated them both. He still loved her.

If she told him to come back, he would in a heartbeat. He would always choose her.

"It... Nick, it's Lulu," Jo said with a hiccup.

"Lulu?" He had to clutch on the countertop to keep from falling over. This was it. They had found his little girl's body.

"She's alive."

Jo's confession made Nick sway on his feet. He couldn't have heard that right. All these years and their daughter was still alive?

"Alive?"

"Yes." Now he could tell Jo was smiling on the other end of the phone. "She's alive."

"Where... how... why?" The words came out in a jumble.

"She's in Atlanta. They're bringing her home tomorrow, Nick. Well, they are bringing her here. There are more details, but you... you need to come home."

Home. He missed home.

"Yes," Nick agreed wholeheartedly. "I'll catch the first flight back. Is... is she okay?"

"They say she is," Jo told him. "Just, please come home."

Nick had many questions, but he knew he needed to get home first to have them answered.

"I'll be there as soon as I can."

Rose Scott was working on a quilt when she heard the heavy footsteps of her daughter coming down the stairs. This made her pause what she was doing and walk out into the living

room, where her daughter was now pacing frantically. Rose
was not a stranger to her daughter having these types of
panic attacks. Over the past several years, Rose had learned
to navigate them, but something seemed different about this
one.

"Jo?" Rose asked, walking forward and grasping her
daughter's hands within her own. "What's wrong?"

Jo could only shake her head.

"Charlie!" Rose called out, hoping he could hear her
through the glass door. He was always out there working.
Most days he had his earphones on, but she hoped today he
didn't.

"Lulu..." Jo finally got out. "She.... Mom, Lulu is alive."

Rose was sure she hadn't heard her daughter correctly.

"What?"

"She's alive, Mom. Detective Morris just called. They
found her!"

"CHARLIE!" Rose yelled. Then she returned her attention to her daughter. A myriad of emotions bubbled in her
chest. Their granddaughter was alive! "Where.... where is
she?"

"Atlanta."

"We should pack," Rose immediately stated. Atlanta was
only a few hours away, but she was sure they would ask them
to stay for a night or two. She wondered if she should try
to make hotel reservations or if they had already made some
other arrangements for them.

"No," Jo's voice was stronger now. "They're bringing her
here tomorrow. Well, to town. I don't know.... They're
supposed to call me later."

"I can't believe it," Rose said in awe.

"Me either. I still.... I still... she's alive!" Rose now grinned. All the heartbreak from the past five years was finally going to be mended, though she knew it was a long journey and those years missed would always hurt.

"She is. She is. Let me tell your father."

Jo entered her daughter's room once both her parents knew about her daughter returning soon. She kept her phone by her side with the ringer up as loud as it could go, afraid she would miss a call if she didn't. It all seemed too surreal, as though the world was playing a huge trick on her. Life had not been kind over the past five years. Someone had stolen their nearly perfect life from them and from there, everything else fell apart.

Nick and her relationship had been strong. They had made it through miscarriages and job losses. Once, they had nearly lost their home. But then things shifted and life became great, and they had Lulu. Losing her, though, destroyed them. Jo couldn't let go, and Nick's heartbreak made him pull away.

An inaudible sigh left her mouth. She missed him.

Jo glanced around the bedroom. It needed to be redone. The bed was much too small for an eight-year-old girl. She would need a bigger bed. She would need bigger clothes, shoes, and toys for her age.

Suddenly, it felt very overwhelming. She had so much to do and so little time. Jo didn't even know what her daughter liked anymore or what size clothing she wore. There was little she could do to prepare outside of moving the guest bed into this room. To do that, Jo had to move many things around.

She stepped further inside and lifted the shoe by the bed. Dust fell, as though the curse of the frozen-in-time room had been broken. A wave of emotion covered Jo. She watched while the dust continued to fall to the ground. It was the first item she'd dared to move anything since her daughter's disappearance. Her free hand rested against her heart, feeling its beat quicken. Her daughter was coming home.

She touched her fingers along the sparkly purple shoe. Purple had always been Lulu's favorite color. Was it now? Or would all the purple in this room need to be painted over?

Trying not to think much about it, Jo started placing things within the cardboard box that she brought upstairs to place older, outgrown items. First went the shoes. Then she headed to the closet. It was there that she froze. All the little dresses, shirts, and pants made her heart clench. Someone had stolen so much time from them. This closet held a time from when their daughter was three. She now was nearly eight. Five years stolen; five years they would never get back.

Quickly and somewhat angrily, she tore the clothes off their hangers and also grabbed them out of bins before shoving them into the box beside her. The anger came out of nowhere, it seemed, and she just allowed it to consume her. Why shouldn't she be angry? Someone stole her daughter from her and her husband, from their family. That person took Lulu away from her parents and her home. Everything they had was torn apart. Whoever had stolen her had destroyed their lives.

"Jo?" She turned to find her father standing in the doorway. He creased his brows with concern. "She's coming home," he patiently said. Walking forward, he carefully pulled the box away from her. "That anger won't help anyone."

"It helps me," Jo stubbornly stated, crossing her arms sourly over her chest.

"No, it doesn't. It eats at you, love. That pain in your chest is very real. What they have put you and your daughter through is horrible; there is no doubt about that. But only you can control how you react to that."

Jo pulled at the sleeves of her thin sweater, fidgeting with a string that had begun to come unraveled.

"You're right."

"Of course, I am. I am your father." He winked before bending over and kissing her head. "Now, why don't you let me take down this bed? I'll place it in the storage area in the basement and then work on bringing the guest bed in here."

"Thanks, Dad."

The cab pulled up in front of his home. Nick stepped out, bringing his small suitcase with him. Once he paid, he found his eyes stuck to the sight before him. His home. Had it really been four years since he had last stepped inside?

Nick took in a deep breath and walked up toward the door. He paused a moment before knocking on the door. It was getting late. It may have been best for him to stay in a hotel for the night and then come over, but he couldn't stay away. If his daughter would be there tomorrow, he needed to be here now.

It took several minutes before the door opened. From Thomas, Nick knew that Jo's parents were now living in the home. He hoped Jo would open the door, though. Facing Charlie Scott right now was not something he wished to do.

Finally, the door swung open, and he saw her. His Jo. She seemed much thinner than last time he'd seen her, and, though she had always been petite, he worried about how little it appeared she ate. Her blonde locks were in a loose braid and, like always, she wore no make-up. She was as beautiful as ever.

"Nick," Jo stated, her eyes on him.

"Jo," he breathed.

The two of them stood there apart for a moment, eyes never leaving the others. Then, before either of them knew it, they were holding on to one another tightly. It felt as though the world had come back together. And for a brief moment, they were one.

THREE

SUMMER 2012

Jo smiled and melted against her husband's mouth as he pulled her closer to him in their bed. It had been a rare morning when their daughter hadn't woken them up before dawn. She sat herself up slightly. Her eyes looked at the clock to see that it was nearing seven.

"I can't believe we're awake before her," Nick said as his lips caressed the nook between her neck and shoulders.

"Me either," Jo replied, sighing happily. "I feel like we should still be sleeping."

"Perhaps we should be," Nick said. He playfully pushed her down, climbing on top of her to capture her lips with his own. His hands ran up her sides, and she shifted beneath him before wrapping her arms around his neck. They deepened their kiss.

However, as Nick went to tug on Jo's gown, they heard little footsteps. Nick leaped off his wife and adjusted the sheets over himself.

"Morning time!" Lulu announced, opening the door. She ran toward them and jumped onto the bed before she crawled over the comforter until she was between her parents.

"Good morning, little lamb," Jo greeted. She rubbed the back of her fingers over Lulu's chubby cheek. "Did you sleep well?"

Lulu only nodded, hugging herself against her mother's chest.

"Fair today?" Lulu then asked expectantly. Both Jo and Nick met eyes over Lulu's head. They had promised they would take her to the local fair today. She had seen them setting it up the day before as they passed by in the car.

"Yes, in a little bit. It hasn't opened yet," Nick explained.

"Go get dressed," Lulu said. She was already sliding out of Jo's lap and off the edge of the bed. They watched as she ran back out of their room and into her room. Jo yawned, resting her head on Nick's shoulder.

"I guess we should get ready. She'll be relentless until we get there."

"It doesn't even open until eleven," Nick pointed out.

"Yes, but if we're dressed, we might drive around a bit and keep her entertained."

Nick cupped Jo's cheek and stroked it with his thumb. He was always so gentle; Jo never doubted how much he loved her. She grinned, and she leaned her head forward so their foreheads could touch.

"Dressed!" Lulu said, walking back into their room. Jo and Nick pulled apart and turned their gaze at their daughter. They had to stifle a laugh. She had put on her Halloween dress that was now much too small and her bright pink leggings with her unicorn rain boots.

"Why don't you let Mommy help you find something more comfortable for the fair," Jo offered, now getting out of her bed. She walked over to her daughter and took her hand in her own. The little girl looked up at her with a grin.

"Okay, Mommy."

Since Nick had the day off, he decided he would make breakfast for his girls. He grabbed the pancake mix. His daughter loved his chocolate chip pancakes for breakfast more than anything. Stirring the mixture, he made sure he added the perfect amount of chocolate chips, so there was a bit of chocolate in each bite.

As he began pouring the batter into the pan, he heard Jo and Lulu making their way downstairs. He glanced up and smiled. They were his universe. Lulu unlatched her hand from her mother's and quickly went to see what her father was doing. She beamed when she saw he was making her favorite meal.

Now Lulu was wearing a lavender dress, but not her purple shoes he knew Jo had set out the night before. It appeared Jo had not won the battle with the rain boots. Even though it was sunny outside, it seemed Lulu had insisted on wearing them. That was something Nick had to learn about parenting. Sometimes things were not worth the battle.

"Pancakes!" Jo happily said, sliding into her seat at the island.

Nick flipped the pancakes into the pan before shooting her a smile. He knew she was also a fan of his pancakes and all of his cooking. When it came to cooking, he was the chef of the family. His wife was quite useless in the kitchen, despite how hard she tried. When Jo was in charge, they often ended up eating takeout.

Once Nick finished the pancakes, he placed them on three plates with some fruit. They all remained sitting at the island. Lulu sat between the two of them. They eagerly ate the food and chatted about the day's activities. Nick couldn't help but smile. Sometimes, he felt like he didn't deserve such a wonderful life, yet here they were.

"Daddy!" Lulu said, shoving the stuffed toy into Nick's arms. "Here!"

Jo couldn't believe she'd insisted on bringing the stroller with them. Now she was stuck pushing it around the uneven ground as Lulu enjoyed running around and trying to see everything. She especially enjoyed trying all the treats that a fair offered. Jo worried they would deal with a major stomach ache tonight.

Nick placed the stuffed bear in the stroller and gave Jo a wink. He then placed his hands around her shoulders and drew her closer, as they watched Lulu run ahead of them. She was afraid of nothing.

"Should we let her ride some rides?" Jo asked. She looked at the booklet of tickets they had bought. Jo was never fond of fair rides; they made her nervous. Nick always teased her about it, calling her a Nervous Nellie. He wasn't wrong. She was, and her anxiousness had only grown as she became a parent. She found that she always worried about falling or choking or anything that could potentially harm her child.

"Let's ask her," Nick replied. "Lulu?" he called out. She turned. "Want to ride some rides?"

"Yes! Yes, yes!"

They walked over to where the kiddie rides were, as their daughter walked with an extra skip in her step. Lulu chose a ride that looked like a bunch of boats spinning in a circle. Nick stood with her in line, and Jo remained with their things. Once Nick buckled Lulu in, she giggled in delight. The brief ride spun slowly around, but it seemed exciting enough for her daughter. Lulu clapped and waved every time she saw them.

Lulu rode every ride in the kid section before asking if she could ride the Ferris wheel. Jo glanced up at the large ride. It looked old and like it could fall over any minute.

"I don't know."

"Please! Please, Mommy! Please!" Lulu begged, pulling on her arm as she jumped up and down.

Jo looked over at her husband. He shrugged, letting her know he thought it would be fine, but that he was letting her make this call. She sighed and looked back up at the large wheel. Her gut told her absolutely not, but then there was this little voice inside of her telling her she was being overprotective.

"I'll ride with her," Nick said, reading Jo's mind. He knew there was no way Jo was getting on it.

"Oh, all right. Hold on to her tightly and no swinging the seats!"

Nick and Lulu didn't need to be told twice. They rushed over toward the ride and got right into the line. It was a long line, and Jo wondered if her daughter would grow tired of

having to wait. She was only three, and she was impatient.
Jo had been wrong to wonder. They made it to the front of
the line.

The moment Nick lifted Lulu into her seat, Jo heard
her squeal in delight. Jo's chest, however, tightened. She
wouldn't relax until they were off that blasted thing. As it
spun round and round, she couldn't wait for it to end.

Finally, they were off.

"Again, again!" Lulu begged her mother.

"She did great," Nick informed her, as he bent over to give
her a quick kiss.

"I think it might be about time to leave. It's close to
nap time," Jo pointed out. Both her husband and daughter
pouted at her. Jo laughed. Most times, Lulu favored her.
However, Lulu had all of her father's facial expressions and
it was hard to say no to either of them.

"All right, all right," she said. "We can stay a little while
longer."

"Yay!" Nick and Lulu said in unison.

"But let's go over to the games now."

Lulu fell asleep on Nick's shoulder about ten minutes after Jo
had suggested they leave. Jo said nothing about being right,
however, even though she wanted to. Instead, they decided
to put her in her stroller and go over to find something to eat
for lunch. It was rare that the two got alone time. This was
about as close as it would get for a while.

Nick adjusted the stroller so they could look in on their daughter before they dug into their nachos and hot dogs.

"We'll need a bowl full of veggies tonight to balance out all the junk from today," Jo commented. She quickly swiped a nacho into the cheese sauce and took a bite. The cheese dipped down onto her chin. Nick's fingers came up to wipe it away. He would take any excuse to touch her.

"One day of junk food won't kill us," he said. "I was thinking pizza for dinner."

"Pizza! After all this?"

Nick could only smile. "What do you suggest? A salad?"

"Yes, exactly a salad, maybe with a side plate of vegetables."

Nick chuckled. When they finished, he cleaned off the table. By the time he made it back, Lulu was back awake and seemed to have all her energy back.

"Play games!" she announced.

"We should have left while she was asleep," Jo playfully stated. She unbuckled Lulu from her seat and stood. "I need to go potty. Lulu, do you want to come with me?"

Lulu spread her arms out wide before saying loudly, "No! I don't need to go potty!"

"All right," Jo said with a laugh, "I'll be right back."

Jo washed her hands, taking her time and enjoying the quiet of being alone for a few more seconds. She grinned. Today was one of those days where everything felt right.

The moment she stepped outside, she heard screams. Confused, she kept moving forward, searching for Nick and Lulu. If something was going on, she needed to be with her family.

She pushed past some people, hoping to find her husband and daughter at the same spot where she'd left them just a few minutes earlier. The table was empty, but Lulu's stroller remained beside it. She turned quickly in search of Nick and Lulu.

It was then Jo realized what she was hearing was her daughter's name being called out frantically. She spotted Nick walking around with his hands cupped in front of his mouth and calling out Lulu's name. She glanced around and saw many others doing the same. Lulu was nowhere in sight. Her heart raced. Jo quickened her steps and walked over toward Nick.

"What... what's going on?"

"She was right there." Nick pointed to the chair at the table where they were sitting. "I turned my back for one second."

"What do you mean? Where is Lulu, Nick?"

Nick's face paled as he regretfully shook his head. "I - I don't know." Jo backed up a few steps before it fully hit her.

"LULU!" Jo screamed out. "Lulu!" She turned back to Nick and asked, "Have you spoken to any of the security guards?"

"Yes, they're shutting down the park. No one in or out."

Jo pinched herself. This could not be happening. How did their daughter just disappear into thin air? The thought of someone taking her completely made Jo want to fall into a puddle of despair. But they had no time for that. She had to find Lulu. Likely she had just gone to the games, right? It was where she wanted to go.

"Have you seen my daughter?" Jo heard Nick say to a couple nearby. He was showing a picture of Lulu. The couple said they hadn't seen her.

"Check the games!" Jo called out. She rushed over to where all the games were. They were all shut down. The people were being questioned by officers. Jo felt tears sting her eyes. Her daughter wasn't here.

Hours later and there was no sign of Lulu anywhere. Nick fell into a chair and ran his hand through his hair in defeat. This could not be happening. He replayed the moments over and over in his head. They had been waiting for Jo. Lulu had been right beside him, begging to go play games. He reminded her they had to wait for her mommy. He'd lifted her and placed her into the chair beside him and kissed her forehead, telling her it would be just one more minute. The fair had been loud. From what he could remember, there had been several people walking around them, but he couldn't recall anyone being close to their table. He noticed his shoe untied and turned away from her, just for one brief moment. It couldn't have been more than thirty seconds. When he turned back around, she had been gone. Why hadn't he just stood her next to him to keep an eye on her?

Jo still stood. She tugged on her fingers and bounced her foot against the ground. He could tell that she was doing everything in her power not to cry right now. His wife was strong, but she also didn't like the world to see her emotions. He knew that tonight there would be tears, no matter the outcome.

"I think it's best you go home."

At the fair, there were now a handful of officers that had begun questioning employees.

"No, not until we have Lulu," Jo argued. "I'm not going home without her."

"Miss, we will keep searching for your daughter. You being here helps nothing. We have many people to question and a lot of areas to cover. It would be best for you and your husband to go home and take a breather. We'll call you with any updates."

"I'll search with you," Nick stated, standing up. "She's my daughter. I know –"

"Take your wife home," the officer said, placing his hand firmly, but kindly, on his shoulder. Nick realized he had forgotten this man's name. Everything felt like a blur.

He solemnly nodded to the officer's request.

"Come on, Jo," he whispered. But Jo lifted her eyes sharply to him.

"You can't seriously agree with him! Lulu is out there, somewhere! I won't leave without her!"

"They have several people searching, Jo," he whispered, trying to keep calm.

Jo blinked harshly and a few tears were shed.

"You really want to leave her?" Her voice broke. Now his tears fell.

"No," he murmured. "Never. But we have to trust they can find her, Jo. We need to listen to them."

Jo searched his face, and he tried to read hers. But it was unreadable. He knew she was angry and upset, but there were more emotions he couldn't quite make out.

"Come on," he tried again. This time, she allowed him to take her hand. "Let's go home."

Four

Early Spring 2017

Jo had forgotten how perfectly she fit in Nick's arms. As he held her, she melted right into him. He still smelled the same: vanilla and peppermint. She breathed him in and allowed a few tears to slide from her eyes. He was the only other person in the world who understood just how she felt.

The moment ended when she remembered they were no longer Nick and Jo. Nick and Jo had been a couple that faced everything together. Nick and Jo had been what others strove to be like until everything fell apart.

They were now just Nick and just Jo. Just Nick had a girlfriend. The reminder made Jo pull herself out of Nick's embrace, and she stepped back. She didn't allow her eyes to meet his.

Instead, her eyes fell over his figure. He had been working out. Nick had always been in good shape, but he was more muscular now. She looked down at his legs. Where his legs peered out from his shorts, she saw the muscular tone in them. She then looked up to his shoulders, which sat wider than she remembered them. His arms were tight in his sleeves.

"You look good," she commented, but her voice was not kind. The hurt between them was still very much there.

"You do too," he said in response. Jo loudly scoffed. Her arms firmly crossed over her chest.

"I look like shit," she nearly growled. "If you haven't realized it, the past five years have been hell." Nick widened his eyes slightly. He hadn't been prepared for her fury.

"Of course, I know that, Jo," he heavily sighed. "It's been torture for me, too."

Jo's face softened slightly. She moved to the side to offer him inside the house. He made his way in and glanced around. While he did so, she tried to read what he was thinking. Did he like the changes to their home? She hadn't made many changes, but there were a few. The most prominent was the coffee table in the living room. Jo replaced it a few months after he had left.

"Do you want to stay here?" Jo offered. "Or... I understand if you'd rather stay at a hotel."

"I was hoping to stay here," Nick answered. "Only if you're okay with it." The room fell silent for a moment. How could two people who had been so in love now be perfect strangers?

"It's your house," Jo whispered.

"Our house," Nick corrected.

Technically, Nick was right. Both of their names were on the mortgage. However, Nick had been paying that mortgage for the past four years, even when he never stepped foot anywhere near the house. Jo probably should have insisted on taking over, but she hadn't had the mental or emotional means to do so. Part of her had been hoping for him to return to her, while the other part of her just couldn't let go.

The bark of a dog made Nick jump. Butler ran in, heading right at Nick's feet. The small black and white dog sat down and eyed the new stranger. Nick gave a confused smile before bending down to pet the dog's head.

"When did you get a dog?"

"I didn't. He's my parents' dog," she explained. "They've been living here for the past four years."

"Right," Nick said. He gave the dog one last scratch on his head before standing. "Yes, Thomas told me they lived with you."

"Speak to Thomas much?" Jo tried not to sound too annoyed as she spoke. She just wanted to know how much her brother-in-law and soon-to-be ex-husband spoke to one another. What had Thomas told Nick about her? And what had Thomas not told her about Nick?

"No, not really," Nick said. "Just a few times over the years."

"Oh," Jo slowly got out. She rocked uneasily on her heels. She wanted to ask more questions, like if he ever talked to her sister. Did he send their children gifts? Because her sister never told her anything about Nick. If Nick had sent them gifts or called, she was sure her sister wouldn't have told her or allowed Thomas to tell her. Nick had been a great uncle to the children before their separation, so Jo did hope that he had kept himself in their lives at least a little.

"Nick!" Her mother's jarring voice made them both turn. Rose walked right up to Nick and gave him a big hug. She held onto him for probably a beat too long, but it didn't seem like Nick minded. He lost his family in his early twenties and had always loved Jo's mother. She had treated him like her own son.

"Hello," he greeted as the two of them pulled apart.

"Well, look at you. Do you live at the gym now?" Rose happily said.

"Mom," Jo groaned. She felt like a teenager at this moment. Rose ignored her and grabbed onto Nick's arm, leading him toward the kitchen.

"I have some leftovers. Are you hungry? You must be hungry. Such a long journey."

Jo watched as the two of them entered the kitchen. She noticed ease between them. All the years apart hadn't caused awkwardness there.

Jo had been so focused on her mom and Nick that she hadn't noticed her father beside her until he made a low sound. He just stood there with his jaw set.

"So, he came back," Charlie grunted.

"He *is* Lulu's father," Jo reminded him. Again, her father grunted. "He was a great father," she added. Though things might have been sour between her and Nick, she felt protective of him against her father. After Nick left and everything else happened, her father's dislike for Nick only grew. Her father couldn't understand what the two of them had been through, not completely.

"Perhaps," he stated. "He wasn't a good husband, though."

"You don't understand," Jo disagreed.

"I do understand. He left you when you were at your lowest. That's all I need to understand."

"But... it wasn't," Jo sighed. She opened her mouth to say more, but Nick and her mother returned from the kitchen. Nick stood awkwardly for a moment, trying to determine how to say hello to Charlie Scott. Finally, he settled on placing his hand out and attempting to give him a shake. Her father didn't budge.

"Hello Mr. Scott," Nick stated, placing his arm back by his side.

"Hi," Charlie simply said. He then turned and began walking toward the stairs that led to the finished basement. "I have some things I need to finish. See you all later."

"Don't let Charlie bother you," Rose smiled. "He's just overwhelmed by the good news. Our Lulu is back!"

"Yes, of course."

"Why don't you sit down and eat," Jo offered. "I am going to go upstairs to work more on Lulu's room."

Once Nick finished eating, he tried to offer to clean the dishes. However, Rose wouldn't hear of it. She told him to go up to the guest room and get some rest. It had been a long day. Nick felt a bit at a standstill. Just like before, in an instant, his life had changed. But this time, the news was good.

It was good news, right? His daughter was alive. His daughter was coming home. Yet, he couldn't help feeling anxious about what that meant. The last time he saw his little girl, she had been three years old. For five years, she'd been gone. She'd missed so much of her life, and he couldn't ignore the fear of what she possibly endured.

Slowly, he made his way up the stairs. The guest room was the first room to the right. Inside, there was a fold-out futon.

The guest room was small, but enough. He placed his bag on the small table and pulled out the t-shirt he always liked to wear as he slept. Though he was sure he wouldn't sleep any tonight. He felt too much anticipation of what was to come.

Wandering out into the hallway, he heard a soft noise come from his daughter's room. That was where he found his wife. She was sitting on the floor, against the wall, with Lulu's favorite unicorn in her arms. He watched her intently, wondering if he should go in and join her. Surely, they had a lot to discuss regarding what was to come.

But as he took a step forward, he couldn't do it. An invisible force telling him to stay away from Jo at this moment, that she needed this time alone.

With a sigh, he backed up and walked back to the guest room. They would have time to talk in the morning.

Jo couldn't, or refused, to sleep. She wasn't sure which one it was. So instead, she remained in Lulu's room, where she sat uncomfortably on the floor. She didn't want to get in bed and mess it up.

Her thoughts were swirling and swirling in her mind, making her mad. The euphoria that her daughter was returning had now transformed to fear. They knew so little about what had happened all those years while she was gone. Now, all she could think about was why someone would steal her child. What had they wanted with her? What if they had abused her? What if... The dark thoughts had her leaning forward and grasping for breath.

After Lulu's disappearance, Jo had fallen down a rabbit hole on the Internet, researching reasons people kidnapped children. None of them were good. She ended up researching human trafficking and growing ill. In those moments, she wanted to believe the police that her daughter was dead. At least then her daughter wouldn't have to suffer. Being stolen and taken more than likely came with something nefarious.

Searching for her phone, Jo attempted to call Detective Morris. Perhaps she had more answers for her about where her daughter had been all these years. She needed to know something. The phone, however, rang and rang. When Jo looked at her clock, she saw it was already past midnight. Unlike her, Morris was likely sleeping peacefully. She didn't have a kidnapped daughter coming home after years of mourning. She didn't have to worry about what her daughter had been through during those five long years.

When her back could no longer take the floor, Jo stood. Her back creaked, and she groaned. She placed the unicorn back on the bed. She wondered if Lulu would even remember it. For the longest time, Lulu had never slept without it.

She turned and made her way back to the bedroom. It was then that she saw the guest room door was wide open. The television was on. She peeked in to find Nick sitting up and watching some random sitcom.

"You can't sleep either?"

"No." Nick turned off the television. "I'm both excited to see her and nervous...."

"About where she's been and what she's been through?"

"So many fears," he whispered.

"Me too," Jo sniffled. Part of her wanted to rush into his arms and allow him to comfort her, but she couldn't do that. They weren't that Nick and Jo anymore. "Do you think she'll remember us?"

"I don't know. I hope so."

Nick was now off the futon and beside her. His fingers reached out slightly, as though he was about to touch her. He hesitated for a moment too long before deciding to drop his arm beside him.

"This doesn't feel real, does it?" Jo's voice was strained and just above a whisper. She glanced up at Nick, who sighed.

"No, it doesn't.... But it is, Jo. They found our daughter. You were right all along."

Jo turned her face away slightly, the weight of his words heavy on her chest. If she responded, she might not be kind. She didn't want that. The two of them had been through absolute hell. Now they needed to be strong enough for when Lulu returned to them. They may no longer be Nick and Jo, but they were still Lulu's parents. All the focus needed to be on her.

"I'm going to bed," Jo said. "Though I doubt I will sleep."

"Me either. We could..." But Nick's words faded and his head shook. "Goodnight."

Jo didn't know what time she finally fell asleep. When she awoke, the sun was rising. She sat up and immediately reached for her phone, though Morris had told her not to expect a call until around noon.

She saw several messages from her sister. It seemed she also hadn't been able to sleep the night before.

WHAT HAVE THEY SAID?

WILL THEY BE BRINGING HER HOME?

DO YOU HAVE TO GO TO THE STATION? CAN I COME ALONG?

OH, NO, I PROBABLY SHOULDN'T.

NICK ARRIVED, SAFE AND SOUND? HOW ARE THINGS BE-TWEEN THE TWO OF YOU?

I'M BRINGING BREAKFAST IN THE MORNING.

Jo yawned and placed her phone back down on the bedside table, not responding to her sister's texts. Her sister was excellent, really, but sometimes she could be exhausting. Their personalities often favored each other. One was talkative; one was not. Yet, sometimes, Jo just needed a break from her sister. Especially since Lulu's disappearance. As much as her sister did it out of love and empathy for Jo, it could feel overwhelming with how much she checked in on her.

She went to turn on the shower. While the water warmed up, she looked inside her closet, trying to decide what to wear. What did one wear to see their daughter for the first time in nearly five years?

Tears stung her eyes. Since they'd been apart longer than they'd been together, they would be practically strangers now. They had missed Christmases, holidays, birthdays, and everything in between. They would never get those times back. She would never get to watch her daughter grow from a toddler into a kid. Those moments were forever gone.

Vivian adjusted her glasses and lifted the box of pastries before walking up to her sister's door. She rang the bell and then stepped back. She was elated, of course, but she also wondered what was in store for both her sister and Nick. She had been the only witness to their breakdown, and she doubted it would easily fix everything with the return of Lulu. They hadn't spoken much in four years. Vivian just hoped her sister didn't fall down the same path that had taken her and her parents years to pull her out of.

"Ah, Vivi," Rose gladly said as she opened the door. Vivian gave a tight smile. She hated being called Vivi, but both of her parents insisted on it. It didn't matter how many times she told them she wanted to go by her full name; they never relented.

"I brought breakfast," Vivian said. "I figured today is a big enough day. No need to worry about cooking and cleaning on top of it."

Rose bent forward to kiss Vivian's cheek.

"That was sweet of you, love," she told her. "Why don't you let me take it in? Jo is out on the back porch, and I'm not sure where Nick is. I haven't seen him yet this morning."

Vivian handed her mother the pastries. She found her sister pacing anxiously along the edge and pulling on her fingers. Vivian frowned.

As she opened the sliding door, Vivian saw her sister pause. Jo gave her a nervous smile and walked over toward her. Jo was dressed in a simple blue dress with a white cardigan over it, even though it was going to be a warm day. She'd braided her hair and had it set over her right shoulder. She wore little to no make-up, making her lack of sleep noticeable around her eyes.

"I should change, shouldn't I?" Jo chewed on the side of her lip.

"No, darling, you look beautiful. Lulu will not care what you are wearing. She'll just be so glad to see you."

Jo's cheeks sunk in with worry, and she went back to pulling on her fingers.

"Who says she'll even remember me? Or Nick? Or any of us? She was only three, Vivian. She might not even want to be here."

Vivian brought her arm around her sister's shoulders. She gave a gentle squeeze and tried to calm her sister. Tears sat just on the edge of Jo's eyelashes.

"Well, I don't know," Vivian said. "But she is your and Nick's daughter. If she doesn't remember, she will quickly learn how great you both are."

"Great?" Jo let out an incredulous laugh. "Nick and I haven't been great in five years. She's coming back to a broken home. Nick and I are divorcing. He has a serious girlfriend. I don't even know if he plans on moving back here or Chicago. How will that work with custody? It's an absolute mess."

"I don't think you should focus or worry about any of that now," Vivian attempted to soothe her.

"Right," Jo said. "Do you mind just leaving me alone for a bit? I need some time to stew in my thoughts."

"Of course."

Nick spent too much time looking in the mirror, trying to make sure his hair looked exactly like it had five years ago.

With a sigh, he finished up. He grabbed the button-up shirt and placed it over his undershirt, closing each button carefully. He hoped she still liked the color purple. It was why he had chosen this particular top.

Once he got dressed, he made his way down the stairs. The moment he got to the bottom, he saw his sister-in-law was there. He met her eyes and took in a shaky breath. The last time he saw her, she had been in tears – completely and utterly heartbroken. That had been a terrible day.

"Vivian," he said, trying not to sound too awkward. He walked over toward her and thankfully, she allowed him to hug her. They had spoken a little over the years. He tried to stay in touch when he felt able. The two had been close like brother and sister at one point, and he loved his niece and nephew dearly. But it had been hard to remain in contact with Jo's family. The pain was always there.

"We've missed you," Vivian whispered to him. He could feel the tears building up. He had missed them all, too.

He quickly pulled away and looked at the large box of pastries.

"I can always count on you to bring the delicious stuff." That made Vivian grin.

"Always."

He heard footsteps coming down and walked over toward them. Jo was coming back down the stairs. He saw she was in a bit of a hurry and the moment she noticed him, she looked up.

"They'll be at the hospital in less than an hour," Jo breathlessly said.

"Hospital? Why the hospital?"

"I... I asked. They said it's just for a basic check-up. That... that she's not hurt. They want us to come and meet them there."

"We should get going. The hospital is about thirty minutes away."

"Yes," Jo agreed.

Nick reached out to grab Jo's hand, but she pulled away. It appeared she would not allow him to give her any physical support.

"Here," Vivian said, handing Jo a pastry. "You have to eat something. I'll tell Mom and Dad that you've gone. Go ahead."

FIVE

— · —

SUMMER 2012

J o was restless. It had been over 24 hours since her daughter's disappearance, and there had been no word or any inclination of where she might be. As every hour passed, she grew less and less convinced they would find her. She knew the statistics. The longer her daughter was missing, the more likely it was that they would never see her again.

She chewed on the corner of her thumb. She hadn't been able to sleep a wink. She felt completely helpless not being out there searching for her. It didn't seem right to just have to wait and see.

"Jo..." Nick tried, but she turned away from him. Deep down, she knew it had been something that could happen to any parent. How many times had she turned around for a split second? But he had been the one to do so. He had been in charge of keeping an eye on Lulu.

Jo said nothing to him about it, but from his desperate words, she could tell that he knew, in a way, she blamed him. She also knew he blamed himself. She should try to tell him he shouldn't blame himself, but she couldn't do it. Not right now. Not while her daughter was missing.

"We should be out there," Jo said. Her hands clenched into fists by her side. "We're her parents. It rained all last night. For all we know, she's out there... wet and scared!" A sharp sob escaped her.

Nick pulled her into his arms and drew her close, kissing the top of her head. He cradled her against him and rocked her back and forth.

"I know," he murmured into her hair. "I just can't believe this is happening to us."

Jo let out a helpless cry. All the anxiousness and worry that she had been holding onto was now released. She was so frightened, unsure of what to do. Terror consumed her as she thought of what her daughter was going through and how she couldn't be there for her.

After a moment, Jo pushed Nick away from her. She was between not wanting to be anywhere near him and needing him.

Her hand flew over her mouth, and she stifled another cry. She wasn't sure that she would ever be able to stop crying if they weren't able to find their Lulu. They had to find her daughter. Who was she without her?

A knock came at the door. She paused and took in a sharp intake of air before trying to quell her tears. Nick came up behind her and supportively held her shoulders. Though for his support or hers, she wasn't sure. Perhaps a bit of both.

"Come on," he whispered.

The two of them carefully made their way to the door. They knew that there were likely answers on the other side.

It was growing later in the day. Vivian had already left to go back home and her parents were on a cruise, unable to get back right away.

Opening the door, they saw two police officers and a detective. Lulu was not with them. Jo let out a low moan.

"Mr. and Mrs. Anderson, may we come in?"

Nick gently pulled Jo back and widened the door to allow them inside. They all walked into the living room. That was when Jo saw the large clear plastic bag with the unicorn rain boot inside. Her breath caught in her throat.

"Where... where did you find that?"

"Down by the Savannah River," one officer said.

"The river? That was at least a mile away from the fair," Nick said.

"We can't know for sure that this boot belongs to Lulu," the detective stated. She stepped forward. "Hello, I am Detective Morris," she explained. "I will be in charge of this case. This is Officer Jones and Officer Middleton." The two men gave her a nod.

"It looks like her rain boot," Jo said, "But these are popular rain boots; anyone can buy them at the store. What are the odds that this one is Lulu's?" She didn't want it to be her daughter's boot. Her daughter couldn't swim, and she knew how dangerous the river could be. "How would she have gotten that far, anyway? She was stolen; I know she was."

"Mrs. Anderson, why don't you sit down?" Detective Morris's voice was very kind and patient. Jo took her suggestion and sat down on the couch. Nick followed, placing his hand on her knee. Her hand then covered his because these were one of those moments where she needed him.

"Please, call me Jo," Jo told the detective. The Detective warmly smiled. She took the seat across from them and asked for the rain boot from the officer.

"All right, Jo. Can you both look at this boot and see if there are any indications on the boot that make you think it could be Lulu's? Like, say, a scratch you remember or any type of mark."

Morris handed the bag over to them. Jo tried to remember if she could recall any marks on the boots. They were pretty new, but Lulu had wanted to wear them almost every day since she had bought them.

"I... I don't know. The size is right," Jo said. "And they look kind of new. Hers..." Jo's voice broke. "Hers were new. I had only just bought them a few weeks back. But I can't... I can't know for sure."

She gave the bag to Nick, who also said he didn't know.

"That's all right. We will keep searching. This gives us an idea of where she may have been at one point. If she was taken, it's possible they traveled next to the river."

"She had to be taken. My daughter wouldn't have been able to walk that far alone."

"I need you both to write me a list," Morris said a moment later.

"A list?"

"Of names. Anyone who knows you, anyone who may have something against you, who may have wanted to take your daughter from you."

"Like an enemies list?" Nick asked, perplexed.

"I know it sounds silly, but nine out of ten times when a child is taken, it is from someone who knows them."

"We... we don't have any enemies," Jo whispered, shaking her head.

"It doesn't even have to be an enemy," Morris explained. "Just anyone you know. Everyone," she clarified. "We are still interviewing people from the fair. We've been putting your daughter's photo and description all over the Internet and on the news. Hopefully, we will hear something soon."

Six

— · —

Early Spring 2017

The entire ride to the hospital, neither of them spoke. Too much stood between them; their thoughts were with their daughter. Nick parked the car and then quickly got out before going over to open Jo's door. It was out of habit. While they were together, it was what he always did. Jo didn't even react. Instead, her hand slipped in his, like it always had before.

"What do we say to her?" She looked up at Nick. Nick turned to his wife. There had been a time when he knew all the right things to say and how to make everything right. This wasn't something he could fix.

"We just tell her we missed her and love her," he murmured.

Their steps were quick, but they felt hesitant. Neither knew what to expect when they reached their destination. A knife could have cut the nervousness between them. When they stepped inside the automatic doors, Detective Morris immediately met them. It was nice to see a familiar face.

"Jo, Nick," she greeted. Her voice was still as warm as it always had been. Nick remembered wondering how someone who dealt with such pain could remain so warm to others. He figured it must be a real gift.

"Where is she?" Jo asked, her hand tightening around Nick's. She wasn't letting go; he was glad about that.

"She's in a room, upstairs. In pediatrics," Morris explained. "Right now, I need you two to follow me. We're going to discuss where she's been and the next steps in all of this before I take you upstairs to see her."

Nick felt Jo deflate beside him. He knew how anxious she was to see Lulu and know that she was really here.

"All right," she whispered.

"Does she know her name is Lulu?" Nick asked.

Morris nodded.

"Yes, the woman who took her didn't change her name."

Nick pondered that only for a moment, because Jo's hand tightened even more around his, drawing him back to what was most important: seeing Lulu.

"Follow me."

Morris led them down a long hallway before they rode up the elevator to the third floor. She then led them around a corner and into a small office. In the small office sat a doctor who had been waiting for them.

"Mr. and Mrs. Anderson," the doctor greeted. "Have a seat." They both looked at Morris, who nodded. They sat, and Nick realized he was now the one holding onto Jo for dear life.

"How is she?"

"I met with Lulu yesterday after they found her," the doctor explained.

"And where was she found?"

"One thing at a time, Jo," Morris interrupted with a gentle voice.

"Lulu appears to be a healthy seven-year-old girl. She is a little small for her age, but nothing too concerning. I see you are petite yourself, Mrs. Anderson, so she likely gets that from you. We had her speak with a psychiatrist as well. She is very confused. The woman who took her told Lulu that she was her mother." From the corner of his eyes, Nick watched Jo's lips quiver slightly.

"So... she... she doesn't remember us," Jo whispered. Nick moved his gaze to Jo, who looked as though she might fall out of her seat. But she didn't. She was stronger than anyone could expect someone in this situation to be.

"No, but she might when she sees you," the doctor said. "It appears Lulu was loved and cared for, well... as best a drug addict can care for another. It doesn't appear any sort of physical abuse happened to her."

Nick felt a wave of relief pass over him. It had been one of his biggest fears.

"But there was neglect. Lulu hasn't been in school."

"Hasn't been in school! She's almost eight years old!" The pain was palpable in Jo's voice. She had always strived for their daughter to have an amazing education.

"Yes, and she was kept home a lot, alone. We think it might be best if we keep her here for a few days and let her adjust to you both before you take her home with you."

"No," Nick disagreed, sitting up. "She is our daughter. We have been away from her for far too long."

"I understand that," Morris spoke up. "But we need to do what is best for Lulu. She has been through something traumatic. She's just learned that the woman she believed was her mother was not her mom. She needs some time to adjust."

It surprised Nick that Jo wasn't outwardly protesting their idea of keeping Lulu for a few days at the hospital. Yet when he looked at her, he saw her chewing on the edge of her nail and she was taking in slow, steady breaths.

"Why did the woman admit to it now?" Nick asked. "Why now, after all these years? Did she suddenly grow a conscience?"

"No," Morris explained. "She got caught selling drugs in the home. She was getting arrested. When she found out that Lulu would be placed in foster care, she decided to tell the truth. Maybe it was because she cared, maybe it was because she worried we'd find out and she'd be in even worse trouble. It's hard to tell."

"I want to see Lulu," Jo finally spoke up. "We can sort all the rest of this out later. I need to see her."

"Of course," Detective Morris said. "Why don't I take you over to her? She's with the psychiatrist right now."

The two of them stood right outside the door that led to their daughter. Jo finally unlatched her fingers from Nick's and brought her hands tightly together in front of her. This was real, and it was happening. When they walked through that doorway, they would finally lay eyes on their little girl again. It felt surreal. She was nervous and anxious. Part of her felt the need to turn around and run away. But the other part of her couldn't wait to get to the other side of that door, to see her again.

The door opened, and Nick allowed her to walk in first. She felt his touch on her lower back as the two of them stepped inside. Her eyes darted around the large room. It was full of toys and crafts. In the middle was a table and that's where their daughter sat. Jo's breath hitched. Lulu had her back to them as she colored, but Jo knew it was her. She just knew it.

"Lulu," another doctor said. Jo turned toward the person and saw a female doctor in a white coat. She appeared quite young. "I am the psychiatrist, Dr. Canmore. Lulu and I have been getting to know one another." The doctor had a great energy about her that showed she was perfect to work with children.

"Hi," Jo's voice was quiet. She couldn't keep her eyes off Lulu. Despite being called by Dr. Canmore, Lulu hadn't turned to face them. Her shoulders had stiffened slightly, but she kept coloring the paper before her.

Dr. Canmore walked over toward Lulu, bending down to her level. She spoke quietly, and Lulu slowly turned to face her. The moment she turned, Jo nearly cried out. It was her little girl. Jo somehow managed to keep her composure. She gave Lulu a little wave and could feel Nick right behind her.

"Hi," Nick said.

"Lulu, this is Mr. and Mrs. Anderson. They are your parents: Josephine and Nicolas."

"We go by Nick and Jo," Nick told her. He was the first to step forward and move to Lulu's level. "Do you remember us?"

Lulu eyed Nick and then moved her eyes up to Jo. Her daughter looked so grown. Her cheeks no longer held the baby fat they once did. They had thinned out, making her look much older. Her hair had also gotten darker, longer. Even though she was sitting, Jo could tell how much taller Lulu was.

"I want to go home," Lulu answered, her brows set.

"Of course," Nick told her with a bright smile. "We can't wait to take you home."

"No," Lulu corrected him. "Not your home. My home. I don't know you."

Jo watched as Nick faltered slightly at her words, but he kept his composure about him. Her heart felt tight. Their daughter didn't remember them.

"Lulu," Dr. Canmore said with a hint of a smile. "Remember what I told you? These are your parents."

Lulu sighed again before she glanced between Jo and Nick. Jo immediately stiffened. She hoped she had chosen a suitable outfit to wear and that her daughter liked her hairstyle. Should she have worn make-up? Should she have picked different shoes? She brought her hand up to her hair and flattened it down, hoping no strays were poking up.

Lulu turned back around back to color her picture, attempting to ignore them. Pain stabbed at Jo's chest. She shook it off. She could do this.

"I brought some pictures," Jo finally said. She began digging inside her large bag to grab the album of pictures. It was something Jo had put together after the disappearance of her daughter. Generally, all of her pictures were on her phone or online, but she had decided she also needed a physical copy. It was a book that she spent many nights looking through and then cuddling as she fell asleep.

"Why don't we all move over there?" Dr. Canmore suggested. She was pointing to two couches over by the corner. Nick and Jo followed where she pointed and waited eagerly for Lulu to join them.

The little girl didn't move from the table. She kept coloring. Dr. Canmore bent over and whispered something into Lulu's ear. She glanced back over at Nick and Jo. Lulu finally stood and walked over to sit across from her parents.

Jo held out the album toward Lulu, who carefully took the album from Jo.

Jo watched her with anticipation as Lulu turned the pages. In the album were photos from the day she was born up until the day she disappeared. So many of the pictures were of the three of them. After Lulu's disappearance, she had been so glad to have all those photos together.

"Do I have a brother?" Lulu asked, glancing up from the book. Jo looked at what picture she was referencing and smiled.

"No, that's your cousin, TJ. He's a couple of years older than you."

"Do I have any brothers or sisters?"

"No," Nick spoke up then. Lulu frowned.

"I always wanted a sister," she muttered, still flipping through the pages of the album.

Jo took in a slow breath. She had wanted to give Lulu many siblings, but they had been grateful just to have her after all the heartbreak they endured trying to get and stay pregnant. But those were not things she could explain to her daughter, especially not now. Maybe one day.

"You have two cousins," Jo explained. "TJ is ten and Callie is six."

"Who are their parents?" Lulu asked.

"My sister, Vivian, and her husband, Thomas," Jo told her with a tentative smile.

"And do you have any siblings?" Lulu questioned Nick.

"I don't."

"Hm... do you have any others?" Her question was now directed to Jo.

"Just the one sister. But you also have a grandmother and grandfather. They adore you."

Lulu glanced back down at the photo album. Jo noticed she was staring at one particular picture. It was of the day she disappeared. At first, Jo hadn't wanted to print out those pictures. Part of her had wanted to delete them, but they were the last memories she had of her daughter. The photo was of just Jo and Lulu, because Nick had taken the picture. They were both eating cotton candy and staring at one another with huge grins.

"Does that look familiar?" Jo asked hopefully. Instead of answering, Lulu closed the book abruptly and then handed it back to Jo.

"I don't like it here," Lulu whispered. Her lower lip trembled, and Jo could see the distinct tears in her eyes. It was quite the reminder that Lulu was just a young child who had been through trauma. Jo wanted to swoop her up into her arms and cuddle her close, as she had when she was a small child. It was her who had been able to ease away her daughter's worries, but she could no longer do that. She had to stay back and wait for her daughter to come to her.

"We'd like to take you home with us," Nick told Lulu, leaning forward slightly. Lulu turned her face away from them.

"Mr. Anderson," Dr. Canmore broke in. "Why don't we all talk in the other room for a moment?"

When they stood, Dr. Canmore led them to a smaller room connected to the previous one. From that room, there was a large window so they could watch Lulu. She remained in the same spot where they had left her with her arms crossed over her chest and her face still turned away from them. Jo wondered if she was crying.

"Don't offer things you can't give, Mr. Anderson," Dr. Canmore warned.

"*Can't give?* She's our daughter. We will be taking her home with us," Nick impatiently stated. "No one has the authority to keep her from us."

"I understand that. But some steps need to be taken first."

"Steps?" Jo's own voice surprised her.

"Yes. They need to do a second DNA sample for one. They need to make sure she's your child."

"That makes no sense. They already connected her to us. She *is* Lulu. It is clear as day!" Nick rose his voice.

"That may be true, but we still have to follow protocol. In a day or two..."

"A day or two!?" Nick was growing more and more frustrated. Jo gently brushed her fingers over his wrist. He moved his eyes to her. For a brief moment, it felt like no time had passed between them. They had always been able to read one another so well. "I... I'm sorry."

"No need to apologize. This is all very new. Take some time and just watch her play. Don't pressure her to interact. That will come. I'll have them come for the DNA samples and we'll get that process started right away." Dr. Canmore gave them a nod, leaving them alone in the room.

"What if she doesn't even want to come home with us?" Jo asked. Nick sighed.

"She won't have a choice, Jo. She's our daughter. She will grow more comfortable with us. She will remember what we had."

"Will she? Do you?" Jo's words were a bit harsher than she intended. She dropped her hand that happened to still be on his wrist and turned away from him, so she could watch Lulu. Thankfully, Nick didn't respond to her question. She wasn't sure she could handle his answer.

The visit was too short, Nick thought, and he didn't want to tell Lulu goodbye. It didn't seem right. How could he be sure that she would still be there tomorrow when they came back? Nightmares from that fateful day plagued him for years. He thought about all he should have done differently and how, if he ever saw her again, he would never let her out of his sight.

He walked outside with Jo. She was quiet. Even though they had a little bit more time to talk with Lulu, it seemed she avoided talking to Jo the most. Nick wondered if it had to do with this woman who had taken Jo's place as a mother. Did Lulu feel like she was disloyal if she was kind to Jo?

"Why don't we go grab a bite to eat?" he suggested. Jo paused her steps, turning to him.

"I'm not hungry," she said lightly. "I'm quite tired. I hardly slept."

"Of course," he agreed.

"But she's ours," Jo then said, meeting his eyes. "And... and she's here."

"She is," he smiled. "You were right."

Jo didn't say anything in response. She did step closer toward him, bringing her hand out to touch just above his elbow.

"How did we get so lost?" she whispered.

"I don't know." It was so strange how quickly that pull had returned between them. He had felt it the moment he laid eyes on her again. How had he ever left her? How had they gotten to that dark place all those years ago? And how had he allowed it?

His phone rang, and he groaned. He pulled it out of his pocket, planning on turning it off, but he saw it was Eleanor. She was likely calling to check in on how everything was going. Jo also noticed who was on the phone. Her hand dropped from his arm. She stepped back.

"You should answer that. I'll wait by the car." Before Nick could say anything, Jo was off.

"Hello?" Nick answered with a loud sigh.

"Nick, darling," Eleanor said into the phone. Over time, her British accent had mashed with a Chicago one; some of her words still held a strong British accent, while others sounded more American. "How is everything? Is it her? Is it really your daughter, Lulu?"

"It is," he answered.

"Oh, how wonderful! What's she like?"

"She's Lulu," he simply said. "She doesn't remember us. We can't take her home, not just yet."

"Oh. Well, where are you staying?"

"At the house," he told her, "but in the guest room. We thought it would be easier for when Lulu comes home."

"Yes, that makes perfect sense. How are you doing? I could come and visit if you'd like."

"No." His answer was much too quick, and he hoped she couldn't tell. "Not right now. I think it's best we don't overwhelm Lulu. This is all very new to her."

"Right, of course. Do give me an update when you can. I miss you."

"I miss you, too."

"And I love you."

"Yes, love you, too," he rushed out. "Goodbye. I'll call you later."

"Goodbye, darling."

When the conversation was over, Nick put Eleanor's number on do not disturb.

"Sorry," Nick said as he reached his car.

"What for? You're allowed to talk to your girlfriend," Jo told him. Her words were not unkind. "How is she?"

"Fine. She was just checking in."

"That was nice of her." The two of them got into the car. "But," Jo continued a second later, "I think it's best Lulu doesn't know we're not together, not yet."

"I agree. I've told Eleanor to stay away."
"Good."

"I agree. I've told Eleanor to stay away."
"Good."

Seven

Summer 2012

The press was relentless. Every day, phone calls hounded them. If they tried to leave the house, reporters questioned them. The press would not leave them alone to sort through all that happened to them. It seemed as if their misery was the public's entertainment.

On this particular day, Nick could see the press standing outside their home. Just last night, the detectives declared their daughter had likely fallen in the Savannah River and drowned. They found another one of her rain boots, as well as the small stuffed bear she had gotten at the fair in the river. Those two items were enough to claim the river as likely her cause of death, even without a body.

The press was determined to get a statement from him and Jo, but they refused to give it to them. Their grief wasn't for others to look upon.

He blinked, and a few hot tears slid down his cheeks. He kept wondering how this could have happened to them. How could their daughter be gone? Why did he turn around, even for a split second?

Closing the blinds harshly, he turned to walk up the stairs. That was where he found his wife. Jo was standing in Lulu's doorway, clinging to the colorful unicorn that Lulu always loved to sleep with. He cleared his throat to let her know he was there.

"She can't... she can't sleep without it," Jo said with a shaky breath. "She's out there, scared... lost."

"Jojo," he tried. She spun toward him. Jojo was his term of endearment for his wife; one he'd used the first time they met. He often used it when he wanted to show her how much he loved her.

"Don't call me that," she seethed. "And she's not dead."

Nick sighed. All the evidence said their daughter fell into the Savannah River and drowned. He understood Jo's need to believe that she was still alive, and how much she needed that to hold on to. But it wasn't healthy; it wasn't right.

"She's not," she strongly repeated. "She was taken. I know it. I know it right here." Jo placed her hand flat over her chest. "I am her mother. I would know if she was dead."

Nick reached out toward Jo's hair. She stepped back, inhaling sharply at his touch, almost as though he was on fire. She then let out a low breath.

"Jo, I know we don't want to believe it, but she is gone."

"They haven't found a body," Jo reminded him. "How do you explain that?"

"They're searching now," Nick said. "I wish.... I know you're angry at me."

"I'm angry at the *detectives* for just giving up on our daughter so easily! She's been gone a week, and now they are determined she's dead. They just want a nice little wrap-up, and I am not having it, Nick. I'm not! I will fight for them to keep searching for her. I will not give up on her!"

Jo's voice broke and her chest heaved. Nick dove in then and pulled her into her arms, right as she began to cry. His wife needed to accept the harsh reality of what happened.

He hated this with every fiber of his being; he wanted his little girl back.

"I'm sorry," he whispered into Jo's hair. He cradled the back of her head, and he pressed a kiss to the top of her head. This was all his fault. "I'm so sorry."

His tears fell on Jo's hair. He hated himself.

"Don't," Jo whispered against his chest. "Please, don't."

He didn't know if she was telling him his apology meant nothing to her or if she was trying to tell him not to blame himself.

"I won't let you give up on my daughter," Jo stated as she entered the detective's office. Morris glanced up and gave Jo a solemn smile. She stood and placed her hands on the desk, bending forward.

"I am sorry, Jo, truly I am. We are not calling it, not just yet. We still are searching for her body."

Jo's cheeks turned bright red with anger.

"But you are! You should be searching for her outside of the river! Someone has my child. You all just want to call her dead!"

"We don't. We *do not*. I am pushing for more searches, but the evidence points to Lulu drowning, Jo."

Jo could feel the tears coming. It felt as though she was fighting a losing battle. No one was going to help her. Even Nick had already given up.

"Please," Jo begged, going from anger to desperate fear. "Please find my little girl. I... I can't live without her."

Morris gave Jo a sympathetic nod.

"I'm so sorry. I promise I'm not giving up. Not yet."

"I need to go over to my sister's house," Vivian said, handing the baby over to her husband. He lifted the baby into his arms and kissed her cheek. Callie giggled, reaching to grab at his nose.

"Of course," Thomas agreed. "This... well, it's a lot. Are you taking your parents with you?" Her parents had arrived as soon as they had been able to get a flight from one of their ports on their cruise. Not wanting to add more stress to Nick and Jo's plate, they were staying at Vivian and Thomas's place.

While they all got along, it did feel a little stifling with them all there. Her mother liked to 'help,' but she got in the way of the maid, who had her own way of doing things. Then her father was always out in the garden, deciding to change the set-up. Vivian's mother also wanted to talk to Thomas as he tried to work in his office. She could never ask a simple question, and Thomas was too kind, unable to ask her to leave him alone while he worked.

"No," Vivian stated. "I can't right now. Nick just asked if I would come over. He thinks Jo needs me. He said Mom will just be too much and Dad... well, you know how he doesn't like Nick."

"Right." Thomas frowned.

Vivian ran her hand through his hair, giving him a grateful smile. He'd stepped up in all of this, working from home when he could, and never complaining about her parents staying here.

"But I won't be gone long," she promised. "I love you."

This made Thomas smile.

"I love you, too. Let me know if you need anything."

Vivian kissed his cheek and quickly went to get in the car; she wanted to go before her parents noticed. They would ask too many questions and before she knew it, they would be in the car with her, heading over to Jo and Nick's house.

Thankfully, she made it out easily and arrived just ten minutes later at her sister's house. She went up to the door, only to have it immediately opened by Nick. His brow was covered in a sheen of sweat, and he held his hand tightly around the doorknob. There was redness in his eyes, giving away that he'd been crying earlier.

"What's going on?" Vivian grew worried.

"She's locked herself in the bathroom and won't come out," Nick said.

"Oh my god," Vivian said under her breath. She passed her brother-in-law and rushed up the stairs. When she reached her sister's room, she went straight to the bathroom door and knocked. "Jo, it's me. Let me in."

"I don't want to see anyone," Jo replied. She sounded calm. Vivian wasn't sure if that was a good or a bad thing.

"You can't lock yourself in the bathroom. Open the door," Vivian said, leaving no room for arguments. "You know your husband can knock this down, right?"

"Please, just leave me alone. I'm not doing anything to worry you. I just.... I needed to stay here by myself."

"Josephine, open the damn door." Vivian pushed against it.

"Leave me alone!" Jo yelled through the door.

"No, who knows what you're doing in there? Let me in."

The other side of the door went quiet. Vivian felt her heart beat harshly in her chest. She again attempted to turn the knob. She couldn't get in. Then finally, she heard the door unlock, and it opened.

Jo stood in front of her in an oversized sweatshirt and sweatpants. Her was hair tied up into a tight bun at the top of her head, and her jaw was clenched tight.

"See, I'm fine." Jo turned around and walked over to sit back on the floor in front of the tub. Vivian wondered why it was there, of all places, that her sister had decided to sit and soak in her thoughts. It didn't look comfortable at all.

Slowly, Vivian slid down next to her sister.

"Why are you in here?" Vivian asked her. Jo pressed her knees to her chest and wrapped her arms around her legs to pull them closer to her.

"It's the only place in this entire house where I can think straight," Jo answered. Vivian watched her sister rock slowly; her eyes staring down at the ground.

"And what are you thinking about?" Vivian asked carefully.

"What I can do to bring my daughter home. Whoever stole her knew what to leave by the river. Perhaps, the first shoe accidentally fell and then..."

"Jo," Vivian breathed. "Do you really think that she was stolen?"

"Yes."

"What if we hired a private investigator?"

Jo glanced up at her sister and eyed her carefully, trying to gauge if her sister was being genuine.

"Do you mean it? I hadn't even thought about...." Jo tugged on the edge of her shirt.

"I think we should try it. Don't you?"

"But how much would that cost? I guess... our savings...."

"No, you don't worry about that. I will handle all of it."

"You can't do that."

"Why not? She's my niece, after all," Vivian said. She and Thomas didn't hurt for money.

Between her job, Thomas' job, and his family money, they could easily spare some money for this if it would give her sister some peace of mind.

Jo shrugged.

"You just need to get off this cold floor, please."

That night, Jo slid into the bed, feeling a bit lighter than she had before. She spoke to Vivian on the phone, who promised her they would figure out private investigators in the morning.

"Hi," she said to Nick. The two had hardly spoken a kind word to one another in the past several days.

"Hi," he whispered back. He inched closer toward her, cupping her cheek. She turned her face into his palm. "What did you and your sister talk about?"

"She's hiring a private investigator," Jo informed him, "to find Lulu."

Nick's hand immediately slid from her face, and he sat up.

"She is?" He couldn't seem to grasp this information.

"Are you angry?" She asked, sitting up with him. He shook his head.

"No," he whispered. "I just... I hadn't thought about even trying that." He gave her a soft smile. Then he frowned. "But what if the news comes back that they believe the same thing the detectives believed? Or what if they find Lulu's body?"

"I just need her back, Nick. I can't....." She sighed. "Please...."

"Please, what? Jojo, what do you need from me?"

A stray tear slid down her cheek. Why did he need her to spell it out for him? Didn't he know what she needed? She needed him to keep fighting. She needed her daughter back. She needed not to feel alone.

Instead of saying all of that, she decided on, "I just need us to do everything in our power to find her. I won't be able to move forward if we don't."

Nick wrapped his arm around her shoulders and tugged her close. She could feel his heart beating in her ear. It thumped steadily, letting her know that he was alive. Normally, this would have made her feel safe, but now she felt nothing.

Nick was on the fence about the whole private investigator idea that Vivian cooked up. It felt fantastical. They were not fictional characters. He highly doubted that some PI was going to come in and save the day.

However, if there was a chance Jo was right and their daughter was alive, then they really should try whatever they could. Also, perhaps this could help his wife accept what had happened. He didn't expect her to get over it, but she needed to believe the tragedy. He knew neither of them would ever be okay again.

Jo was finally asleep in his arms. She rested her head against his chest, and he was too afraid to move her. It was the first time in several nights that she had fallen asleep peacefully. He wanted to make sure she got all the rest she needed.

He kissed her crown, and he gently wiped a stray hair off her cheek. Beneath his fingers, she stirred slightly. He watched as her brows knitted before she turned away from him and fell onto her pillows.

Eight

"Tell me about her," Rose eagerly asked. Her hands clasped together as Jo and Nick entered the house. Jo should have known her parents would pounce the moment they arrived. She glanced up and saw that her father was also waiting to hear about what had happened. It surprised her that her sister wasn't there as well.

"She's beautiful," Jo answered simply. She slipped off her light coat, hanging it up on the hook beside the door. Her fingers tugged on the long sleeves of her shirt, feeling a bit dazed. She didn't want to talk right now. She just wanted to prepare Lulu's room for her arrival.

"Of course she is," Rose beamed, "but what's she like?"

"She is scared," Nick said. "She doesn't remember us. This is all very confusing to her."

Rose's jaw dropped, and her eyes went between Nick and Jo.

"She'll adjust," Charlie gruffly stated. He stood by himself over by the wall. "It will take time, but she will."

"Yes, I think so too," Nick agreed.

Jo looked at all those surrounding her. She couldn't do it anymore. It was stifling. So, she rushed up the stairs and went into Lulu's room.

In the room, she was able to take a breather. In here, eyes weren't staring at her, waiting for her to either explode or have a mental breakdown.

She still needed to do a lot with this room to make it ready for her daughter. At the hospital, they had given her a list of sizes for Lulu's shoes and clothes. In a bit, she'd need to do some shopping. They had nothing that would fit her right now. She was small for an almost eight-year-old girl, and Jo realized she still did not know what type of toys Lulu liked. Lulu hadn't given them any idea about her likes or dislikes. How did she not know what type of toys her daughter liked? Or what if she was one of those children that outgrew toys early and only liked electronics? Should she try to find her some sort of tablet? Was that the mom she was?

Her mind wandered to the woman who'd kidnapped Lulu. She would know the answer to these questions. The woman knew more about her daughter than she did. She knew Lulu's likes and dislikes, and what she enjoyed doing. Jo knew nothing.

Jo sat on the edge of the bed and bounced her knees. Her eyes closed. It was all too much.

Slowly, Nick made his way upstairs. He stopped when he saw Jo sitting on the edge of Lulu's bed with her eyes closed. He knew she felt smothered with all the details. He did too. They knew so little about their daughter. Which meant there was a huge adjustment to be made in their lives.

All they had ever wanted was their little girl back, and now she was here. But they had learned quickly how many layers there were to it and their life wouldn't just go back to the way it was before. They lost everything. They would have to work together to build back their lives, but it would never be the same as it was.

He stood in the doorway, and Jo looked up at him. She sat at the edge of the bed. Taking in a deep breath, he moved forward and bent down so that he could glance up at her. His hand took hers before he gave her the tiniest of smiles.

"This will all come together," he promised her. "It's hard now, but it will. Lulu is going to remember you, Jo."

"You don't know that," Jo answered, shaking her head wearily. Her thumb moved up to her mouth to chew on the edge of her nail. "That woman stole her from us. And it's... it's not fair."

"No, it's not."

"And what are we supposed to do when you are with Eleanor? Are you going to live here in the guest room? Or... will you get a place nearby? Will you go back to Chicago?"

These were all questions Nick had been asking himself. It was hard to know which one was the right choice. Except he did know that he had no plans to move back to Chicago. He would have to stay here, near his daughter.

"I don't know," he whispered. "I will stay here, but where I'll live... I'm not sure. That can all be settled later. Unless you want me to find somewhere now, if that's easier."

Jo tightened her lips into a thin line, then her head shook.

"I think it's best you're here for Lulu, at least at first."

He sighed, relieved.

Jo pushed his hand off hers and brought her arms up toward her chest, making her sleeve slide up. Nick's eyes widened as he saw a mark on her skin. It was a dark red scar that went up and hid beneath the sleeve. Immediately, he grabbed her arm and pushed the sleeve up more.

"What are you doing?" Jo snapped at him, pushing him away and tugging her sleeve back down.

"What was that?" Nick said back, not flinching.

"Nothing." Jo stood and turned away from him. She walked over to Lulu's closet and began to shift clothing around nonsensically.

Nick realized that the entire time since he had arrived, Jo had her arms covered. She used to always wear tee shirts, no matter how cold it was outside. He swallowed hard.

"Please, Jojo," he pleaded.

"*Don't*," Jo warned. "It's none of your business, Nick. It... it was an accident years ago. Don't worry about it."

"What sort of *accident*?" he countered. He would not let this go. "One where you tried to kill yourself?"

Jo tensed, but then she scoffed.

"I didn't try to kill myself. Now, get out and leave me alone. I owe nothing to you anymore. Soon, we won't be married, just like you wanted. We'll just be two people sharing custody."

Nick's jaw remained open for a moment. He couldn't believe this was where the two of them were now.

"Why won't you tell me what happened?"

"Because there is nothing to tell," Jo quietly answered. She walked back over to him. "I'm fine. Really."

Nick reached out toward her. She kept her arm firmly at her side, making sure the harsh scar was covered with her sleeve. Her eyes wouldn't meet his. The heaviness on his chest only grew heavier.

"What happened, Jo? Please, tell me."

Her eyes shot up.

"You left *me*, remember? You don't get to know what happened after."

"That's not fair. You were the one who...." Nick allowed his words to fade. It wasn't worth the fight.

"Now, our daughter is back. We need to prepare for that." Jo went back to the closet.

"And what do we tell her, exactly?"

"About what?"

"About us?"

That question made Jo face him. She chewed on the corner of her lip. She shrugged.

"Nothing," Jo replied. "We tell her nothing. For now, we're married. It's not a lie. We still are. Us divorcing and you having Eleanor on the side would be too confusing to her."

"Yes, I agree," he said. "We'll tell her nothing for now."

"Right."

Jo took a deep breath. Though she was looking at him, it felt as if she was looking right through him. Then she walked right past him and to their old bedroom, slamming the door. It was oddly reminiscent of their last few months together before he left. All they had done was argue and yell. Many times, Jo had slammed doors in his face. Jo had been so angry at him and the rest of the world. It had been miserable.

But when he left, it didn't make it better. He felt ten times worse than when he had been there. Being away from Jo, from his entire world, had broken his heart even more.

Jo stepped out of the shower, exhausted. She grabbed her towel and brought it over her naked figure. Her eyes fell to the scar on her arm that went from a few inches above her wrist, nearly to her elbow. She stared at it for several moments. The crude scar harshly reminded her every day of her past. Quickly, she turned her arm away, so she could no longer see it. It's why she always covered it up. She didn't want to remember.

She finished drying off to then put her nightclothes on. Getting into her bed, her eyes moved over to the side that had been empty for years. Sometimes, she would wake up and forget about the past five years. Sometimes, she would wake up and think it was before when everything was happy. The heartbreak when she realized it was only a dream always wrecked her.

She ran her hand over Nick's side of the bed, or his old side of the bed. She wasn't naïve; she knew he would never sleep there again. Sometimes she swore she could still smell his scent, even though the sheets had been washed and changed hundreds of times. It was likely just her brain trying to trick her. She had never been able to move forward after Nick left. Her eyes closed.

Fear consumed her as she wondered if she would be good enough for Lulu. She was broken.

When they made it to the hospital the next morning, Detective Morris stood back at the front, waiting for them. She informed them the test results were in and that they could likely take Lulu home with them by tomorrow.

"Why not today?" Nick asked. He didn't understand.

"This is all very delicate, Nick," she explained.

"Delicate! They stole our child from us," he said. "Our child. She's *ours*."

"Nick." It surprised him to hear Jo's voice. She touched his upper arm. He expected her to be more vocal about bringing their daughter home. It was she who had fought so hard before he left, who wouldn't give up. He never expected her to be calm in this scenario. Part of him worried that the stubborn part of her had died years ago. It made him think back to the scar on her arm. What had happened there? And why wouldn't she tell him?

The thought made a shudder run up his back. Did her parents know? Did Vivian? Why hadn't they called him?

"Let's go up and see her for now," Morris suggested.

Morris's voice helped him focus back on his daughter. The scar and the past were things he could worry about later.

They went right up to Lulu this time. However, she was no longer in the large room with the psychiatrist. Now she sat in a regular hospital room. It was sterile and not at all where a healthy, young girl should be.

As they stepped inside the room, they saw Lulu sitting on the bed. The television was on with some show made for preteens. While Lulu would look up at it occasionally, she remained more focused on drawing. Nick wondered if Lulu enjoyed drawing, or if it was just something she did now that she was here. She hadn't offered him a look at her pictures.

"Hi," he said. She glanced up slightly, looking between him and Jo. Her eyes remained stuck on Jo for a beat longer. He tried to read Lulu's expression and what she might be thinking, but he found it to be unreadable. Or, perhaps, it was just because he didn't know her anymore.

"Hello," Lulu answered cautiously.

"I brought more pictures and an old stuffed unicorn of yours," Jo anxiously said. She walked up toward Lulu, handing her both. "I know you're much older now. But... you used to sleep with this every night. I didn't know...." Jo paused her words and watched Lulu closely as she examined the stuffed animal she held.

"It's cute."

Jo's shoulders loosened slightly as she gave a cautious smile. Jo pulled a chair closer to Lulu's bed and sat down.

"These are pictures of our home. More of your grandparents, who can't wait to see you. And their little dog, Butler."

Hearing that there was a dog perked up Lulu's eyes. She quickly opened the book of pictures in search of the dog. When she found him, she squealed.

"We have a dog!"

"Well, your grandparents do," Jo clarified for her. "But they live with us. So yes, you'll see him every day."

"He's so cute! Is he a sweet dog?"

This was the most Nick had heard Lulu talk. He would talk about a dog all day if it meant he could have her talk with them.

"Very sweet," Jo answered. "He loves to sit on people's laps, and he'll let you rub his head."

"Awe!" Lulu said. "And do you like him?" she asked Nick. Nick swallowed hard and nodded.

"Oh yes," he lied. "I love him." Nick hardly knew the dog. Butler seemed like an everyday dog, albeit a bit spoiled.

"That's fun. Does he like walks? Treats? Can he do any tricks?"

Jo laughed, glad to have something to talk with Lulu about. Gently, she pulled the book slightly and turned a few pages.

"Here," Jo showed her, "is Butler playing dead. You just say 'boom!' And he lies on his back, just like that."

"Cool," Lulu said, nodding her head. "When I come to your house, can I walk him?"

"Absolutely." Nick watched as Jo tentatively reached out toward Lulu's hair. It had darkened some since they had seen her last and there was a tighter curl to it now.

"I always wanted a dog," Lulu explained with a sigh. "But my mom said I wasn't allowed, because we moved too much."

Nick did not miss how Jo's face fell and paled at the same time. Her hand remained on Lulu's hair, but it had stilled.

"I... I..." Jo sputtered slightly, standing. Her eyes were clouded over with hurt, and she turned away from the both of them, pretending to look at the television. Nick felt caught between wanting to comfort her and speaking with their daughter. In the end, he decided Lulu was who needed him most.

"Well, we're glad you like the dog," he said, taking the seat that Jo had abandoned. Lulu, who seemed oblivious to Jo's upset, smiled up at him. That took his breath away. Right then, she looked just like a little three-year-old Lulu. The little girl who had adored him, who had begged for piggyback rides and extra ice cream after dinner.

"He's Grandma's *and* Grandpa's? Do they live with us all the time? Sometimes?" More questions, more wanting to know about their world.

"Um...." He didn't know. As far as he knew, they lived with Jo full-time.

"All the time," Jo answered for him. "But they do have a house by the beach and sometimes, they go there for a few weeks at a time."

"Oh," Lulu frowned slightly. "Do we ever go to the beach?"

"We can," Nick told her. "We will if you'd like."

"I think that could be fun."

Mom. Lulu called *that woman*, Mom. The word kept ringing through Jo's head as they exited the hospital. That was supposed to be her title, a title she'd cherished from the moment Lulu was born. Yet it'd been stripped from her and given by Lulu to her kidnapper. *But my mom said I wasn't allowed.* Mom. Mom. Mom.

She suddenly felt sick and bent over the bushes, vomiting behind them. Nick came up behind her, swooping up her hair before rubbing large circles on her back.

"Here," he said, handing her a handkerchief.

"Thank you," she replied, wiping her chin and mouth.

"I'm sorry," he whispered. His words were heavy, filled with so much unsaid between them. Jo wanted to reply, but she feared the anger buried deep within her might unleash.

"Let's just go," she whispered in response. "I'm tired."

Nick nodded.

They drove back to the house, and Jo stepped out. Her dad was in the front gardening. That's what he always did. He should be at the beach, but because of her, he and her mother were stuck here in this small town with little to do. She often felt guilty about it. Any time she told them to leave and that she would be fine, they insisted they wanted to stay. The truth was, they didn't trust her alone.

Entering the house, Jo walked past her mother and told her everything was fine, not wanting to delve into a conversation with her. She knew her mother would want to know every detail of their time with Lulu, but Jo didn't want to talk about what had happened and how she had been replaced. It hurt far too much. So instead, she ignored her mother's inquiries before she walked out back where she could sit on the back porch and allow the sun to warm her up for a bit.

Nick's eyes followed Jo as she walked outside to the back porch. He frowned.

"She seems to be in a right state," Rose said, her eyes on the large glass doors that led outside.

"It started well," Nick explained. "Lulu is very excited about Butler."

That made Rose smile.

"Oh, well, I'm glad about that. But then what happened?"

"Well," he said. "She called the woman who stole her 'Mom'."

"Oh." Rose frowned.

"Yeah, and Jo took it pretty badly. I mean, she tried not to let Lulu see it, but I could tell. She's been quiet ever since."

"That is tough," Rose agreed. "But Lulu will learn. She'll see what a splendid mother she has."

"She will."

"Any good news?"

"We will get to bring her home tomorrow," he said.

"That's excellent! We're dying to see her! Oh, should I call Vivian and Thomas? We could throw a little barbeque."

"I think it's best we wait," Nick said. "Just the four of us at first when she comes home. We can have Vivian over maybe a bit later, but her kids and Thomas... maybe later. It's just.... this is a lot for Lulu. We should probably handle it carefully."

"Right," Rose agreed. "You're right. I think I got a little too excited."

"I'm excited too," he said, not adding how that joy was wrapped up with overwhelming fear.

He patted his mother-in-law's shoulder and then stepped outside where Jo was sitting. She held her phone and was scrolling on it absentmindedly. When she realized she was being joined on the porch, she sighed.

"Is it all right if I sit here for a moment?" he asked her calmly.

"It is your house," she said.

"Our house," he replied.

Jo shifted slightly.

"I haven't asked.... but have you gone back to teaching? Do you work?"

"No," Jo sighed, bringing her hand up to rest on her chin. "I mean, I do some part-time work at Thomas's firm. It helps keep me busy. But after Lulu went missing, I couldn't...." Jo stared out into the distance. "But I will get a better-paying job now. It isn't fair for you to support me as much as you do."

Nick reached over, affectionately holding her wrist. "I've never minded."

She tensed beneath him before she turned away. This was when he should tell Jo that he still loved her, that whatever he had with Eleanor meant nothing. His thoughts were interrupted when he felt his phone vibrate. He looked down to see a text from Eleanor asking how everything was going.

He stood and answered the text.

ALL RIGHT. I'LL CALL YOU TONIGHT.

NINE

Nick arrived home from his trip and was relieved. It had been his first work trip away from home since Lulu's disappearance. He hadn't wanted to go, but they needed the money. The mortgage wasn't going to pay itself. While he had worked from home for a while, he made the money when he went away on those trips.

When he stepped inside his home, he found that all the lights were off. In the past, he would have arrived home with all the lights on and music playing, as Jo and Lulu would be in the middle of making something to eat or an art project. The dark was just another reminder that their life had horribly changed.

He turned on the foyer light and placed his travel suitcase by the door before glancing up the stairs. With a sigh, he walked up. But his wife was nowhere to be found. While he'd been away, Jo had hardly spoken to him. Before, when he was on trips, she'd spoken with him on the phone daily and texted him multiple times in a day, even if it was just silly memes. This time she had just texted him to be safe when he boarded his flight. She knew when he would be back home.

He made his way back downstairs, about to call her phone, when he heard sounds on the back porch. Nick turned on the light, surprised to see Jo just sitting there all alone. She didn't even flinch at the light being turned on. Instead, she remained still, staring out into nothingness.

Sliding open the door, he stepped out.

"Jo?" he whispered. She jumped slightly, now surprised. "What are you doing out here all alone?"

"I... I don't know," she murmured. She wore just a tee shirt and some sweatpants. There was a slight chill in the air, so he took off his jacket and placed it over her shoulders. His hands lingered there slightly, missing her touch.

When he pulled away, he sat down next to her.

"What if..." Nick paused, choosing his words carefully. "What if we moved, Jojo?"

Jo's head turned quickly in his direction. "Moved?!"

"We don't have to live here. I work all over the place. I often get asked to work in Chicago. We could move there. Or... I don't know, closer to your parents at the beach. We could leave this town." He hated it here. Ever since they lost their daughter, this place was stifling. Questions and inter-viewers plagued them all the time here in Georgia. They received the same looks from everyone; looks filled with pity or judgment.

Jo shifted in her chair and crossed her arms over her chest.

"We can't leave," she said. "This is Lulu's home."

"Jojo..." He reached his hand over to grasp Jo's. "She's gone."

Angrily, Jo snatched her hand away from his.

"Our daughter is out there somewhere. I can't believe you want to just give up on her!"

"I don't," he said. "But we have to listen to what's been told to us, Jo. The private investigator even said..."

"I don't care what he said. She's still out there, somewhere." Jo stood up before pacing in front of him. "Our daughter is still out there somewhere, Nick. I thought you, of all people, would fight harder for her."

"I want to believe she's out there, I do," Nick began. He slowly stood. "But I don't know what else we can do. I think it's time we put her to rest, Jojo."

"Put her to rest. What does that even mean?"

"Jo..."

"No, I don't even want to know what that means." She pushed past him and walked inside. He heard her steps going up the stairs and then the distinct sound of the door being slammed behind her.

He fell back into the chair on the porch, placing his head in his hands. Was he wrong? He didn't want to believe that his daughter was dead, but what other choice did he have? All the evidence pointed to their daughter being gone. Even the private investigator that Vivian had hired agreed. He thought after the private investigator's findings, Jo would finally believe the police and allow them to grieve.

What did Jo want from him? If they ignored what the others said and kept looking, when would it stop? When could they let go? He needed to grieve properly. Jo wouldn't allow him to do that. It was pulling them further and further apart.

He remembered the day he had sat by the river as they searched for his daughter's body. During those many hours, he had both prayed they wouldn't find her and prayed they would. One might give him an ounce of hope and the other would give him answers. They never found her, of course. There was relief in that. But the Savannah River was vast, and it was long. Just because they didn't find her, it didn't mean that she was alive.

Hot tears quickly escaped his eyelids. The past several months had been difficult. He had never known just how much his heart could break. The tears came down and covered his cheeks. He made no move to wipe them away. Instead, he allowed himself to weep for his little girl and the loss of life they had had.

After his tears settled, he got up from his seat. Walking inside, he slid the door closed. Then he walked upstairs to their bedroom. When he got there, he found the door closed and his pillow and a blanket sitting right outside the door. It looked like he would be sleeping in the guest room tonight.

Vivian hadn't expected her sister to ask her to meet her for lunch. Lately, unless she went over to her sister's house, she didn't see or hear from Jo.

Yet today, Jo entered the restaurant dressed nicely and even wore a splash of make-up. It was so unlike her sister.

Vivian stood and kissed her sister's cheek to greet her before they sat back down at the table.

"You look lovely," Vivian told her sister.

"Are you saying I don't normally?" Jo shot back. Vivian rolled her eyes.

"You know that isn't what I'm saying. I just wasn't expecting to see you all dressed up for lunch."

"Oh," Jo murmured. "Well, I guess I needed a change. And well... to talk to you about something."

"Oh? What's that?"

In the past, the two of them could talk about anything and everything. Jo was the first Vivian had gone to about every major event in her life before she married Thomas, and then she was the second person. And it was the same the other way around. Even though they were very different, they had always been close.

"Nick wants to move," Jo said, keeping her eyes downcast at the table.

"Move? Where?" Vivian asked.

A sound drew her eyes to women over in the corner who were looking at them and whispering. She was sure they were discussing her niece, and she had the right mind to walk over to them and tell them to mind their own business. However, that would just draw attention to it. Her sister had finally come out of the house.

"I don't know," Jo said. "But... he just said he wants to move. He doesn't understand...." Jo met Vivian's eyes with intensity. "We have to hire another private investigator, Vivian. We have to prove that Lulu is still alive. He doesn't believe..... *if* he believes, he won't leave."

"Jo..." Vivian breathed. "I don't think..." She paused. "You don't need a PI to keep Nick around. Just tell him you don't want to move."

"No, I want a PI to find my daughter. It's not about Nick," Jo insisted. Her fingers flew to her temple; she rubbed it in tight circles. "You think I'm losing it."

"No, of course, I don't," Vivian answered. "I don't think that at all, Jo. We will hire another PI if that's what you want. We will do whatever you want me to do." Vivian didn't know whom to believe in all of this, but she knew she wanted to support her sister. She had hoped that after the previous private investigator's information had come back, her sister would have used that to move on. But she hadn't.

"I just want my daughter back," Jo said. "That's all I want. And I don't want Nick to leave."

"Then tell him. Tell him you want him to stay," Vivian suggested. Jo sighed.

"I don't want him to stay just because I ask him to. I want him to stay because he wants to."

"She said that?" Nick asked into the phone.

"Yes," Vivian said. "Yesterday at lunch, she told me she doesn't want you to leave." Nick heard the line go silent for a moment before Vivian continued. "I probably shouldn't have told you that, but I felt like I had to. She won't."

"I don't plan on leaving her," Nick told Vivian. "I want her to come with me. I love her."

"I know you do," Vivian said. "She loves you. But I think mentioning leaving right now isn't a good idea. She needs more time. It's only been a few months."

Nick ran his hand over his face and tapped his foot against the floor. He pressed his back against the wall for support and took in a deep breath.

"I won't mention it again," he promised. "I... We'll stay here. I just want us to find some sort of normalcy. I know we won't have what we had before, but.... I miss my wife." It was the first time he said it out loud and confessed how he missed Jo. Everyone knew and understood how he missed his daughter, but they couldn't understand missing what was there.

"I know," Vivian answered. "I miss her too." She paused. There was a crash. "I have to go. TJ just knocked over his plate. I'll talk to you again soon."

Nick heard the phone line end. He placed his phone on his desk and walked out of his office. He found Jo in Lulu's room. She was just sitting there on the floor with that unicorn in her arms.

"What if we went out to eat?" Nick suggested. Jo glanced up at him. Her face was wet with tears. It tore at his heart.

"Where would we go?"

It wasn't a no. He grinned.

"I don't know. The café downtown? You like it there."

Jo contemplated this. Her head rested on the unicorn in her lap. He walked over toward her and slid next to her.

"It might be nice to get out of the house together."

"What if people stare at us?" Jo asked. He frowned. He hadn't thought about that.

"It's early. No one will be out eating right now," he said. "We'll get there and finish before the dinner rush rolls in."

"Okay," Jo agreed. Nick's heart skipped a beat.

"Yeah?"

"Yeah. Let's go. It could be nice."

Nick stood and then helped Jo up. His hand brushed along her cheek and he pulled her close, hoping for a kiss. Jo ducked her head, though, and didn't allow it to happen. She glanced up and gave him a small smile.

"I... I have to change. I'll be ready shortly."

"Okay. Sounds good."

But it hadn't been good. One reporter bombarded Jo and Nick before they could even make it inside the restaurant. Jo hadn't seen a reporter in a while. Earlier, when she went to lunch with her sister, she had seen none of them. Jo wondered if they were following Nick's car. He left the house more and, seeing them together, the reporter probably pounced on the opportunity. It was the curse of living in a small town and being their only source of entertainment as the grieving parents.

Nick convinced her to go inside the restaurant and get something to eat. They were already there, after all.

Inside, it was quiet. Only the workers were there, and they were kind enough. However, the whole time, Jo was anxious about leaving the restaurant. They would still be out there, wanting them to talk to them and snap pictures. It was so intrusive and unfair. Who reveled in the misery of two parents who had lost their child?

Jo stayed off all social media platforms and kept the television off. She didn't want to know what they said about the two of them. But Nick was always reading and getting angry. Even though it was him who suggested they stay for dinner, Jo could see the tightness of anger in his jaw.

"They don't respect anyone's privacy," Nick grumbled, looking through the menu.

"We should just go," Jo said. "Go home."

"They'll follow us there. We aren't safe anywhere."

Jo frowned.

"I won't leave this town," she said. Nick glanced up and nodded.

"I know. We won't leave. We'll make it work."

Jo reached her hand across the table and placed it on Nick's wrist, squeezing it.

"Thank you, truly. Because I can't... I can't leave."

"I know."

Ten

Early Spring 2017

J o was an absolute mess. In just a few minutes, a car would pull up in front of the house with her daughter inside of it. They said it would be best that they brought Lulu to them instead of her and Nick picking her up from the hospital. All morning, she had paced back and forth, back and forth.

She swallowed hard and walked back up to the front door, looking through the window to see that there was still no car pulling up.

Nick seemed to be less stressed, or he was at least holding it in better. He sat on the couch, his foot up on his knee and his eyes on the blank television. Jo wondered if she should try to sit by him. Yet, when she tried to move toward him, she felt held back. Her mind kept reminding her they were no longer Nick and Jo.

Taking in a deep breath, Jo turned around and saw her father standing by the window. He kept opening the blinds and peeking out before stepping back and rocking on his heels. She knew he was also eager to see his granddaughter for the first time in years.

Her mother was doing what she did best: baking. It was how she knew to solve everything. Over the past five years, Jo had eaten many baked goods made by her mother.

Finally, Jo heard a car pulling into the driveway. She rushed to the door and placed her hand on the knob, but she kept herself from turning it. She had to be patient. Lulu would be here soon.

Before Jo even realized it, Nick was standing behind her, also anxiously waiting. Thankfully, her mother and father remained in their places. That was good. She didn't want Lulu to be overwhelmed.

A knock came at the door. Her eyes moved to Nick, who gave her a supportive nod.

She opened the door and there stood Lulu, holding a small bag. Behind her were Detective Morris and a man that Jo did not recognize. Instead of even acknowledging them, Jo bent down to Lulu's level and smiled.

"Welcome home," she whispered. She reached out to Lulu, but her daughter stepped back slightly and darted her eyes around them. Trying not to show her hurt, Jo stood back up and attempted to smile. "Ready to come in? Butler is excited to meet you."

At the mention of the dog, Lulu brightened. Slowly, she stepped inside the house and her eyes darted around in search of the dog. He was sitting on his little bed by the couch, fast asleep. Jo was pleasantly surprised Butler hadn't come running to see who all the new people were. It was a small blessing because he was usually hyperactive when they had guests over.

"Come on," Nick said, offering Lulu his hand. "I'll take you over to see him."

Lulu tentatively took Nick's hand and allowed him to walk her toward Butler. Jo watched as Lulu went right up to him and bent down onto her knees. She smiled happily, rubbing the top of the dog's head.

"He's sweet."

"He is," Nick agreed.

It was then that Jo remembered she still had other people in her doorway. She turned and looked at them, shifting awkwardly on her feet.

"Um, would you like to come inside? Have... something to drink?"

"No," Morris said with a smile. "We will leave you alone to get acquainted with one another again. I will keep you updated on the case against Ms. Cook."

Ms. Cook. The woman now had a name and a face. Her picture was all over the news cycles now as the face of the woman who'd kidnapped Lulu Anderson. Jo frowned slightly as she realized this was far from over.

"Thank you, Detective Morris," Jo said, her eyes watering. "Truly. You brought our daughter home. You did it."

"Don't thank me." Morris gave her a nod before telling the other detective it was time for them to leave. Jo watched as they took off and wondered if there was something else she should have said. Should she have insisted they come inside? She felt she owed Morris so much more.

Pushing away her thoughts, Jo closed the door and walked over to where Nick and Lulu were still petting the dog. She sat down with them, and Butler perked up his ears before cuddling into Jo's lap. Over the years, the dog had become her best companion.

"He likes you," Lulu said.

"Yes, we're best buds," Jo told her with a wink.

"They always have been." Her father's gruff voice came from the corner. He still stood apart from them, trying not to intervene. She spotted her mother off in the kitchen, peeking in, but also trying not to come too close. Jo was grateful that they both were trying not to overstep until they were welcome.

Lulu glanced at her grandfather, tilting her head to one side.

"Are you my grandfather?"

"I am," Charlie replied. Jo carefully placed Butler back onto his bed, stood, and walked over toward her father. He was tall; it was where Vivian got her height.

"Yes, this is your grandfather, Lulu. He is very excited to see you again."

Lulu got up from the ground and walked over toward Charlie. She looked up and squinted her eyes.

"You're tall." That made Charlie laugh.

"I am."

"You also have a thick white beard. You look like Santa."

Charlie didn't miss a beat. Much like when she was younger, he said, "Maybe I am."

"Santa isn't real," Lulu said.

Her words hit Jo like a ton of bricks. Her daughter no longer believed in Santa Claus. They'd missed out on all the innocent years of belief, and it made her wonder if the woman had even allowed Lulu to believe. She glanced up and saw

Nick staring right at her. In his wide, horrified eyes, she saw that his thoughts were the same as hers.

"Does Butler like walks?" Lulu asked, bringing Jo's attention back to the conversation between her daughter and father. Her father still had a bright smile on his face.

"He does. But do you know what he also likes?"

"What?"

"Playing fetch."

"Oh! Can we do that?"

"In a moment," Jo answered for her father. "Why don't we go and meet your grandmother? She's in the kitchen making cookies."

"Cookies?" Lulu turned her head toward the kitchen. "That's what smells so good."

"Yes, your grandmother makes the best cookies."

Jo reached out her hand for Lulu. Lulu refused to take it, but she followed Jo toward the kitchen where her mother was waiting patiently for her turn to greet Lulu.

They walked into the kitchen, where Rose placed the cookies onto a tray. She smiled up at Lulu and offered the cookies out to her.

"Do you like cookies?"

"I do," Lulu whispered. She reached out but hesitated, glancing at Jo to make sure it was all right.

"Go on," Jo encouraged. Lulu took one and smiled as she bit into it.

"Oh, that's good. Do you make cookies a lot?"

"Sometimes. I also make pies and cakes and bread."

"Do you have a bakery?"

Rose chuckled. "No, my darling girl, I do not."

"Well, you should. This is delicious."

Jo was pleased to see that so far Lulu was doing well enough in meeting everyone in the family. She still had Vivian, Thomas, TJ, and Callie to meet, but they decided to do that on another day. Somehow, Jo had convinced Vivian to wait and not to come over today.

"Can we go outside now?"

"Sure."

Nick and Jo sat outside together, watching as Lulu happily played fetch with the dog. She would take the ball from Butler and then throw it before squealing in delight as he rushed right after it. It was quite the sight to see their daughter, here, happily playing before them.

Bending over slightly, Nick took Jo's hand in his own and gave it a quick squeeze to garner her attention. Jo looked up, curious.

"I'm sorry," he whispered, though there was so much more he should say than just those two simple words. "You... you were right."

Jo remained quiet for a moment, muddling over those words.

"No," she said, shaking her head. "You don't need to apologize. You were just listening to what all the experts said. I... I don't blame you, Nick. I never have."

He couldn't explain how much that made him calm. She didn't blame him. She didn't hate him. He turned her hand in his own, trying not to think how much he missed being able to hold her every day.

"I was a mess back then, Nick," Jo said. "I still am. All of the signs indicated that she'd died. It... It wasn't your fault."

"Jo..."

"Let's just focus on her right now," Jo said, withdrawing from him. "That's all we can do. We have to make this home safe for her."

"It will be," Nick said. "It always has been."

He heard Jo sniffle. He watched as she quickly wiped below her eyes.

"Jo..." he tried again. She shook her head, then brought her sleeves over her hands. Her eyes went back to Lulu, and she watched her as she ran around with Butler.

Nick wondered what came next. He would eventually have to return to work. While he did well for himself, work kept him sane. He enjoyed writing and being a part of the world around him. This small town had only become enough for him when he met Jo. Jo had made everything better.

But now he had left this town. He would have to move back; he would need to be here for Lulu. It wouldn't make sense to live far away. He'd hardly ever get to see her. And then there was Eleanor. Would she break up with him? And if so, would he care?

He figured that would have to be settled later in the future. Today his daughter was home. Today, they had that to focus on.

Jo was glad that her mother enjoyed the kitchen. She had made dinner for them that night. It was a simple meal with macaroni and cheese, some chicken, and broccoli. Jo knew that her mother was hoping to find something that Lulu would enjoy. When they tried to ask her what she liked, she just said McDonald's chicken nuggets. Jo wondered if they should have picked that up for dinner instead. She wanted Lulu to feel comfortable and safe here.

They all sat down for dinner together. Lulu seemed much bigger at the table than she had been before. Jo's memories took her back to when Lulu could barely see above the table, but insisted she didn't need a booster seat. When she blinked, that Lulu was gone and was now replaced with the new, older Lulu, the Lulu she didn't know.

"I hope you like dinner," Rose said to Lulu. "You used to love mac and cheese."

"I do like mac and cheese," Lulu timidly told her.

"Good."

"If you want something different, we can get it for you," Jo said.

"No, I like this."

They had full plates, and the table lapsed into an uncomfortable silence. No one knew just what to say. Lulu ate her food and asked for seconds. When Jo could no longer handle the quietness, she finally spoke.

"What do you want to do tomorrow?" Jo asked Lulu, who shrugged. "We could go to the park."

"Oh, yes. There is a park nearby with a nice big slide," Nick pointed out.

"No, there isn't," Jo said, dropping her fork beside her plate. "That was demolished a couple of years ago."

"Oh," Nick frowned slightly. "I must have forgotten."

Their eyes met. Jo felt the need to snap something along the lines of how, if he had been here, he would have known that. But she didn't. Instead, she stood and took away her nearly full plate. She found she wasn't hungry.

"Does anyone else need me to take their plate?" she offered. Everyone else said no. Jo walked into the kitchen and steeled herself. She overheard Lulu ask about other parks and Charlie tell her about the new one down the street.

There were footsteps behind her, and Jo turned to find her mother with a sympathetic look on her face.

"You're doing great," she encouraged.

"I feel so awkward," Jo confessed.

"It will take time. But it will get easier as the days go by. One day, everything will just feel like normal."

"I highly doubt that," Jo said. "She's going to need therapy. We'll all need therapy. It's just... it's not fair."

"Of course it isn't, Jo. No one ever said that it was. But your daughter is home now. You have to do what is best for her. You are her mother. And one day, she'll understand just how much you love her and what that really means."

"Perhaps," Jo sighed.

"She will."

That evening, Jo took Lulu's small bag upstairs into her room to put things up and see what needed to be washed.

Lulu remained downstairs with Nick and her parents. They were watching some princess movie that Lulu said was her favorite. Jo would have to find out again what the movie was called, then watch it so she could know what her daughter liked.

Reaching her daughter's bedroom, Jo placed the bag on Lulu's bed. Despite being asked a few times, Lulu hadn't wanted to see her bedroom yet. She insisted on staying downstairs. Jo hoped her daughter could sleep tonight; though Jo doubted she would be able to.

Unzipping the bag, Jo saw a picture frame sitting upside down. Curious, she lifted it and turned it around. Her breath caught in her throat and her body trembled. It was a photo of Lulu with a young woman. Her fingers ran over her daughter's face. She looked younger, just a little older than when she had been when Sally Cook took Lulu from them.

Sally Cook was younger than Jo. She had auburn hair and a youthful grin. In her lap, she held Lulu, who had a large smile on her face.

Jo clutched the frame tightly against her chest. Heat rose up her neck and to her cheeks, and her eyes grew misty with angry tears.

"What's that?" Nick's voice surprised her. Jo met his eyes before turning the frame around to show him.

"It's her," Jo whispered. Her chest ached as a tear slid down her cheek.

"It is," Nick nodded. "Sally Cook."

Jo shuddered at the name.

"What do I do with this?"

"Throw it in the trash," Nick said. He reached out to grab it, but Jo moved it away from his grasp.

"I can't do that," Jo disagreed. "It's Lulu's. She's kept it because...." Her words caught in her throat, and she felt a lump forming.

Nick touched her shoulder, and she didn't shrug it away. Instead, she glanced down and blinked back the tears. This woman had been the mother to Lulu all of these years. It wasn't right. She stole her, and she got to play the role that was supposed to be hers.

"You are her mother," Nick strongly stated. "You are."

"I know that," Jo whispered. "But it means nothing if Lulu doesn't see me as her mom."

"She will."

"I wish everyone would stop saying that," Jo sighed. "I need to finish unpacking her things."

"Would you like me to brush your hair?" Jo offered to Lulu as the three of them walked her into her bedroom for the evening.

"No, I can do it myself," Lulu answered. Her eyes glanced over the bedroom. Both Nick and Jo watched her carefully to see if she gave any signs of whether or not she liked it.

"Your pajamas are in the bottom drawer. Your dad and I thought that tomorrow we could take you shopping for some new clothes and toys or anything else you might need or want. We have many holidays to make up for."

Nick could tell how nervous Jo was as she talked. He wanted to reach out and grab her hand but thought better of it. Instead, he just gave his daughter a supportive smile.

"Yes, don't you think that could be fun?" he asked her.

"I have clothes."

"But you need more," Jo said. "Your dad and I got you some, but we didn't know what you liked."

Lulu walked over to the closet and looked at some of the shirts hanging up. Her lips pursed as she looked through them.

"Those look good," she answered. "Now can I go to bed?"

"Do you need a bedtime snack? Water? Help to get dressed?"

"I'm fine," Lulu said. Nick watched Jo visibly deflate.

Their old bedtime routine came with putting on pajamas, brushing her teeth and hair, and reading a book. Then there had been several times she asked for an extra story or a snack. She had used any reason to get out of bed. At the time, they had moaned about how long bedtime took. But after they lost her, they missed every part of it.

"Oh, okay," Jo said. "I'll be right down there if you need anything. We will see you in the morning."

Nick couldn't sleep. Parched, he got up from bed and walked out into the hallway. As he made his way toward the bathroom, he found Jo sitting right outside Lulu's bedroom. The door was ajar.

"Jo?" he whispered. She looked up at him, her eyes rimmed red from tiredness and tears.

"She's finally fallen asleep," Jo told him. "But she was crying earlier." Jo's brows furrowed. "Our daughter is hurting, Nick, and she doesn't want us to help her. I don't know how to help her."

Nick frowned. He moved down to sit next to Jo, moving his knees up to his chest.

"This is hard, Jo, but we'll manage it. She is our little girl. You and I would do anything for her. I know that as a fact." Jo's head fell onto his shoulder, and he didn't dare move. Instead, he just sighed and rested his head against the wall. One day at a time.

Eleven

With a shaky exhale, Jo glanced back down at the shopping list she held. According to her therapist, she needed to go back out into the world to do day-to-day tasks. She could no longer hide away in her bedroom. Her therapist said it would help her move back into the land of the living, whatever that meant.

Nick, who often did all the grocery shopping and cooking now, had written her a detailed list. It didn't have too many items on it, because he had been afraid that she might get overwhelmed. That happened now; the tiniest thing could cause her to fall into a panic attack. Sometimes an entire day would pass when she couldn't leave the bed. It was why she had agreed to go to therapy in the first place. She did want to get better.

She walked down an aisle and realized she stood where the cards and wrapping paper were. She paused. Her eyes had found a sparkly purple birthday card for a little girl. Slowly, she picked it up and opened it. The bright colors danced over the page. All Jo could think about was how Lulu would have loved this. Her innocent, childlike giggles filled Jo's head.

Lulu's birthday was just months away. On that day, she would be four years old. Her baby girl would be turning four, and she wasn't here with her. That pain etched deeper into her heart.

A flash of a pink coat moved past her, and she turned. A little girl with pigtails ran forward, laughing and turning around a corner. Jo followed her, leaving her cart and list behind. Her steps quickened as she turned down the next aisle, her heart skipping a beat. She made it to the little girl and gently grabbed her arm, spinning her around.

"Lulu!" she called out. The little girl blinked up at her and tugged her arm away. Jo immediately dropped her hand when she realized it was not Lulu. "I... I'm sorry."

"Hey lady," a woman angrily said, pulling the little girl closer to her. "What are you doing touching my kid?"

"I... I thought...." Jo stumbled over her words. Her heart raced in her chest from the adrenaline of thinking she had actually found her little girl and then realizing she was wrong. Tears formed in her eyes.

The woman and little girl walked away. She pressed her fingertips against her mouth and blinked harshly, feeling foolish for her behavior. It wasn't the first time this had happened.

She just wanted her daughter back. She *needed* her daughter back.

Jo went back to her cart and grabbed her purse, leaving the cart and her items in the middle of the aisle. She walked outside and to her car, driving to the station. There she asked directly for Detective Morris.

"You can't talk to her right now, Mrs. Anderson," the receptionist said, clearly annoyed.

"I need to." She didn't try to stop how much her voice trembled.

"Mrs. Anderson, you have to stop coming by," the man warned.

Jo felt like the dam would burst, yet again. Why wouldn't they listen to her?

"Please, just for a moment."

"Mrs. Anderson...."

"Let her come into my office," Morris said, standing out of her office door. Her eyes were filled with compassion.

The man grumbled under his breath but nodded. He moved to the side to let Jo through.

Jo walked into Morris's office and waited until she shut the door.

"Have there been any more leads?" Jo asked as chewed on the side of her thumb.

"Sit," Morris said. Jo sighed, but she did what the detective asked of her. Then Morris walked around her desk to lean over it. "We're closing the case, Jo."

"What?!"

"You know they have been wanting to close it for a while now, Jo. I've been trying to keep it open, but all the signs point to your daughter being gone - *dead*. They can't put any more resources into it."

Jo pressed her hands together tightly, shaking her head.

"No, no," she stressed. "You can't...."

"I'm so sorry, Jo. Truly I am."

"But you're not! No one is! No one is trying hard enough!"

"Jo—"

"She's still out there. Everyone has given up on her, every-one!"

Nick checked the time on the clock several times. His wife should have been home over an hour ago. The supermarket was only ten minutes away and her list had less than ten items on it. He couldn't think of a reason why she shouldn't be home yet. He hadn't thought she was ready to go, despite her therapist's recommendations. It was still much too early. Jo was drowning.

Finally, he heard the garage open. He went to open the door to help with the groceries, but Jo remained in the car. He walked out and knocked on her window.

"Not now," she said through the door. Nick tried to open it. It was locked.

"Please, Jo," he begged. He heard it unlock, and he opened it. "What took you so long?"

"There was this little girl..." Jo said as her eyes lingered on a picture of Lulu she'd put on the dash.

Nick groaned.

"Not that again, Jo. You can't keep grabbing random chil-dren." He tightened his hand into a fist by his side. "Where are the bags? In the trunk?"

"I didn't get the groceries," Jo simply stated. Her hands remained on the steering wheel.

"That's okay." He tried to remain calm, but this was getting harder and harder. He thought losing his daughter was the worst thing he would ever go through. He hadn't expected to lose his wife, too.

"I went to the station," Jo said.

"Jo..." he breathed. She went there much too often.

"They're closing the case." Her head turned toward him. "You win."

Her words hurt more than he expected them to. Did she not know how much he wanted to be wrong? That he wanted his daughter to be alive and with them?

"No one wins, Jo," he finally got out. "Let's go inside."

It took persuading her for a bit, but he got her out of the car. They walked inside and Nick told her he would order them some pizza for dinner. He placed the steak back in the fridge for another day since they didn't have all he needed to make the sides.

"Jo, now that the case is closed, do you want to move?"

"It's not over," she disagreed. "I'm not letting them give up on our daughter."

Jo grabbed a glass before filling it up with water. She took a slow sip.

"This is killing us, Jo. It's killing you. Let's move and start over."

Quickly, Jo turned to face him, her face bright red. She stepped closer to him and her body trembled with anger.

"Start over!? You want us to just give up on our daughter?!"

"Of course not, Jo. But she's gone. She's dead." The words hurt his throat and pained his heart. But he had to say them. He needed his wife to understand the truth.

"You want so badly just to forget all of it!" Jo screamed.

"No, of course, I don't," he calmly tried to say in response. "I loved her more than life itself! I would give my life in place of hers if I could."

"I wish you could," Jo spat, her jaw set. His mouth twitched at the anger thrown at him. He took a moment before responding.

"Me too," he replied. "I want us to grieve properly, Jo. I want us to have a future. I feel like there is no future anymore."

"How can there be without Lulu?" The way Jo's voice broke tore at his heart. He swallowed hard.

"I don't know," he whispered. "But if we moved to Chicago or.... I don't know, down to the beach near your parents. Perhaps we could have a new start. It doesn't mean we won't miss Lulu. She'll always be a part of us. But we can.... we can try."

"You don't understand. I don't want to try," Jo explained. "I want you to fight for Lulu. I want you to want her to come home. I want to stay here, her home."

"She's dead," he repeated. Jo's entire body clenched and the next thing he knew, he heard a loud crash as Jo threw her glass into the sink and it shattered into pieces.

Her eyes darted back to his.

"Fuck you."

Nick reeled back in shock, almost as though she'd slapped him. Jo never cursed. She was the type to say "bologna and cheese" when she got upset. It was something he used to tease her about. This woman before him was not his wife, not anymore.

Before he could say anything to her, Jo spun on her heels. He heard her feet moving up the stairs and then the loud slamming of the door, which was now a normal occurrence.

Nick didn't know how to fix this. So instead, he turned and cleaned up the mess in the sink. He lifted the larger pieces of glass, throwing them away in the trash can. Then he worked on the smaller pieces, receiving a slight cut on his finger that he hardly noticed.

When the sink was finally glass free, he ordered the pizza even though he wasn't sure if Jo would even eat anything. Usually, once she locked herself up in the bedroom, that was the last time he would see her for the day.

Suddenly and without warning, tears spilled from his eyes. He leaned forward to catch himself against the kitchen counter, and he just sobbed. His daughter was dead; his wife was pulling further and further away from him. He was losing everything.

A knock came at the door, making him stand. He wiped his cheeks, forcing himself to stop crying. Who would be over at their house right now? It was too early for the pizza delivery. He worried it was a reporter, but they usually stayed off the property and only bugged him while he was out and about. Some people tried to stir up rumors that he or his wife had killed their daughter. Though, thankfully, the police had never gone that route. There had been enough witnesses at the fair who saw them before and after Lulu's disappearance to prove they couldn't have been involved. It was just reporters trying to stir stuff up for ratings.

He opened the door to find Vivian on the other side. She was always at their house with some sort of treat in tow.

"They're closing the case," Jo said. "They are giving up on my daughter."

"Oh Jo," Vivian said sympathetically. Vivian didn't know if this was good news or bad news. All the signs indicated her niece was dead. If that were the case, then it was good news for all involved so that true grieving could happen. However, her sister was insistent that Lulu was still alive. Vivian knew her sister wouldn't believe her daughter was dead until she saw a body.

"Maybe I should let Nick go," Jo said suddenly. Vivian glanced up at her sister. Jo's eyes remained on the television and her lips were chapped. No emotion showed on her face.

"You love him and he loves you," Vivian whispered. She could not imagine a world where Jo and Nick were no longer together. They had been so in love for so long.

Jo took in a shuddering breath.

"Sometimes love is not enough."

Twelve

Early Spring 2017

Nick entered the kitchen to find Jo moving about in a hectic sort of way from station to station. She was making both waffles and pancakes, as well as toast, bacon, sausage, and eggs, cutting up all sorts of fruit, and there even appeared to be fresh muffins. Nick wondered when Jo had become an expert in the kitchen. Last he knew, all she could make were grilled cheese sandwiches, scrambled eggs, and boxed foods with simple ingredients.

"Are we having company?" he asked, making Jo pause her movements. She didn't look up from what she was doing.

"No," she answered. "I just... I..." Her lower lip came between her teeth. "I don't know what she likes to eat."

"Oh, right," he said. He walked forward, wanting to touch Jo. Instead, he just looked over the food once more and smiled. "It all looks amazing."

"Well, it's about all I can make. I'm still learning." She went back over to flip the pancakes, cursing under her breath when they were all burned.

"Hey, I'll take over here," Nick offered. Thankfully, Jo moved away to let him.

"Where is Lulu?"

"Outside with my parents," she said with a small wave. Nick glanced outside. Ah, there she was. He could see her throwing the ball to Butler and happily chasing him around the yard. "She loves that dog."

"She does," he agreed. "It's a good thing your parents had one."

"Yeah, true."

"Hey, Jo," he started. She turned and looked at him. Their eyes remained locked and the words he wanted to stay got stuck in his throat. "Um, can you hand me the spatula?" he said. She handed it to him and returned to the waffles.

When breakfast was ready, Nick went to the back door and slid it open. Rose immediately smiled up at him, but Charlie grunted.

"It's time to eat," Nick told them all.

"Come on, Lulu," Charlie called out. "Let's eat."

The three of them came inside, washed their hands, and sat down at the table with Nick and Jo.

"Please, have whatever you want," Jo said.

As they ate their food, Jo kept getting up from her seat as though she had forgotten something. Nick heard her mother whisper to her that everything was perfect and just to sit down, but Jo didn't listen. She was more of a mess this morning than she had been last night.

When Jo finally sat down for longer than a minute, she looked at Lulu and smiled.

"Would you like to go shopping this morning?"

Lulu turned her fork over on her plate.

"Do I have to?"

Jo tried to swallow the hurt and force a bigger smile.

"We don't have to today, no," she said. "What would you rather do?"

"I dunno." Lulu tugged on her hair.

"Your grandfather and I volunteer at the library twice a week. We leave today at noon. Would you like to come?" Rose brightly asked. She was always such a positive person. Nick often wondered how she and Charlie had even met and how they fell in love. They seemed so different.

"Could I?" Lulu asked, looking to Jo for approval.

"I don't see why not," Jo answered with a tight voice. Nick knew Jo wanted to spend some time with Lulu with just the three of them.

"That sounds fun." Lulu bounced in her seat and dug into her eggs.

"Then it's settled. You three can come over around one. That gives us time to sort the books before you get there," Charlie said. "And you can run to the store with your parents first." Charlie looked up, winking at Jo.

"Oh, okay."

Nick was glad that Charlie understood how important today was for his daughter. Charlie had always been able to read his daughter well. Nick was sure it was why Charlie had never been fond of him, because he had been the only other person in the world to do so, too. It had been hard for Charlie to give away his youngest daughter.

"Thank you," Nick whispered to his father-in-law. The man didn't respond, but he did give Nick a nod. It was something.

After they told her parents goodbye, Jo turned to Lulu and smiled.

"Would you like me to braid your hair before we leave?" she suggested. Lulu tapped her fingers against her thigh, shaking her head.

"I like to wear my hair down," she answered.

"Oh, of course," Jo said. She inhaled. When Lulu was younger, she had let Jo do her hair in a variety of hairstyles—well, at least what Jo could manage with her thin hair. Now, Lulu had beautiful thick hair with more curl to it. She was sure that it would braid beautifully and that she could attempt other styles. It was hard not to push, and to instead allow Lulu to come to her. Their bond had been broken by time and their loss of one another.

"Well, I'm going to run upstairs and change and then we can go."

"Where did Nick go?" Lulu asked.

"I'm not sure," Jo lied. He had taken a phone call, and Jo was quite certain it was from Eleanor. He had glanced at his phone and excused himself from the table over half an hour ago.

Jo knew she had no right to feel jealous. Right upstairs, sat the divorce papers that she still needed to sign so Nick could be free of her. But with Lulu's reappearance, everything had changed. Perhaps, if she hadn't been too afraid to sign it months ago, all of this awkwardness could have been avoided.

"Do you need anything?" Jo asked, turning on her way upstairs.

"Can I watch the TV?"

"Of course, I'll be right back."

"Are you sure you don't want me to come down?" Eleanor asked for what seemed like the millionth time.

Nick glanced up at the house, wondering what everyone was doing with him out here. He rubbed his hand on the back of his neck and sighed.

"No, it's not the right time," he told her.

"And... has she signed the papers?" Nick could hear the hint of hope in Eleanor's voice. She was careful, though, in how she asked. It was rare that she did. Eleanor had no plans to marry Nick, or at least that is what she had told him. She also never called this much before. Ever since Nick returned home, he got several calls and daily texts from Eleanor.

"No," Nick answered. "She hasn't, and I don't plan on asking her about it right now. A lot is going on. Lulu doesn't even know we are divorcing. It is a very sensitive situation that we are in. I don't think bringing it up would be a good idea."

"Right," Eleanor said. The line went quiet for a moment. He wondered what she wanted to say or ask and wasn't asking.

"It will get easier in a little while. Right now, it's just all new."

"Of course," Eleanor said. "I understand. Is there any-thing I can do to help?"

"No. We have it handled as best we can," he answered. "Thank you. I love you. I got to go." He hung up before Eleanor could reply that she loved him too. Then he walked inside the house.

Lulu sat on the couch flipping through the channels on the television.

"Ah! Jo said she didn't know where you were," Lulu said.

It was jarring to hear Lulu call them Nick and Jo. He wasn't a fan. Dr. Canmore told them not to push the titles of Mom and Dad onto her so soon. That it would come over time. He missed the way Lulu used to crawl up into his lap and cuddle close while calling him daddy. The memories hurt sometimes because he worried they would never have anything quite like it again.

"I had a phone call," he answered.

"From who?"

"Just work," Nick said.

"What do you do?"

"I write."

"You write?" Lulu squished up her nose. "Like books?"

"Not really. I get hired by people to write for them. I've done articles for newspapers, ads, stuff like that."

Lulu pressed her lips together. "Is it fun?"

"Sometimes."

"And what does Jo do? She hasn't told me yet."

"She was a stay-at-home mom when we lost you," he said carefully. He went to sit down next to his daughter. "She works part time sometimes now. But now that you are back, I'm sure she'll want to stay home with you."

Lulu seemed to ponder this. She kicked out her feet before pulling them back.

"Hm," she just said.

Nick wondered if more questions about their life were going to come, but they both heard Jo's footsteps coming down.

"I think it's time to go."

Lulu did not seem excited about any of the options at the store. Any time Jo lifted something, she would shake her head and say no.

"You don't like any of the clothes here? We could go somewhere else," Jo offered.

Lulu glared at the shirt with the unicorns on it. She wasn't giving Jo any signs showing if she liked it. It was maddening not knowing anything about Lulu.

"You can have anything you want," Nick said. "Anything at all."

Lulu sighed. Then she stepped forward and pointed at a simple purple shirt.

"I like this one," she whispered.

Jo smiled. Lulu still liked the color purple. She lifted it and handed it to Lulu.

"You want me to...?" Lulu glanced around nervously. This confused Jo.

"Don't you want to try it on?" Jo asked. Lulu blanched and took a step back.

"I don't like stealing," she whispered. Jo's eyes widened.

"Stealing? Darling, we aren't stealing anything. I just thought you might want to try it on to see how it fits. We will be buying everything."

Relief covered Lulu's features. Jo looked right up at Nick. What all had their child witnessed?

"I like this dress too," Lulu pointed out. Jo returned her attention to Lulu and looked at the new dress. It was a violet sun dress with rainbows on it.

"Let's grab what you like and then you can try it on," Jo said. She glanced back over at Nick. There was so much they didn't know.

As they continued through the store, Lulu found many more items of clothing she said she liked. While Jo was thrilled to learn more about her daughter's likes and dislikes, her mind was plagued with the innocence her daughter had lost.

After shopping, they grabbed some food and went to eat outside at the park. There was a pond nearby that Lulu asked to go and stand near. The area around it was visible, so both he and Jo said okay. Lulu went to it, leaving him and Jo alone on the bench.

When Nick looked at Jo, she was near tears.

"It isn't right," she whispered. "Who knows what that woman put our daughter through? What do we do now?" She chewed on the corner of her thumb. Nick held back the urge to pull her thumb away from her teeth. Instead, he drew his eyes back to Lulu.

"We will talk to Dr. Canmore," Nick said. "She'll know what steps to take next."

"It's just so wrong. I hate that woman, Nick. I hate her."

"I know," he mumbled. He reached out to touch her cheek. His fingertips brushed along the soft skin before she sat back slightly and turned away as though he had burned her.

"What do we do?" she asked again.

"There isn't much we can do, Jo, but show her she is safe, show her she can trust us, and we keep working with Dr. Canmore."

Jo clicked her tongue, keeping her eyes on Lulu.

"You know," he began a moment later. "She'll be turning eight soon. What do you want to do to celebrate?"

"I don't know. Vivian suggested a small party at her house. Just us, my parents, and them. But I don't know, it feels like a lot." Jo began rubbing her hands together in her lap.

"Maybe we should ask her what she wants to do," Nick said.

"Yeah," Jo murmured. "I think so, too."

Charlie smiled as he watched his wife read to the small children who had come to story time. She always enjoyed these parts of her week when she could read to the children. Losing Lulu had impacted them as well. They had clung to their other grandchildren to help, but they needed something more to help ease the pain.

Vivian was the one who suggested they find some volunteer work to do to fill their time. At first, they hadn't wanted to leave Jo home alone. However, Vivian had been right, and they needed to allow Jo to learn how to do some things on her own.

Jo kept trying to convince them to move back to the beach, but he and Rose were not willing to risk it. They had seen how far she had fallen and knew that she was still fragile. Just the thought of the past made Charlie's blood boil. How had Nick left her like that when she was so incredibly lost and broken? Charlie wasn't sure he could ever forgive him.

"Grandpa!" He heard. He grinned as Lulu rushed toward him. "Can I sit in your lap?" Charlie put down the books and lifted her into his arms. He didn't miss the hint of jealousy in his daughter's eyes as she walked up with Nick.

"Did you have fun at the store?" he asked Lulu.

"Kind of," Lulu answered.

"Why don't you go down to the floor and listen to the story?" he suggested.

"Could I just stay in your lap?"

He smiled. "Of course."

They listened to the tale while Lulu remained in Charlie's lap. He was so pleased to have her back with them. It truly was a miracle.

When the story ended, Lulu got down and rushed over toward Rose, leaving Jo, Nick, and Charlie alone. Nick rocked on his heels before making an excuse about wanting to look at some books.

Jo slid up onto the stool next to Charlie before turning to face him. She still had a youthfulness about her, even though she was now forty. It was hard for Charlie to remember how grown she was. To him, she would always be his baby girl.

"Everyone can tell how irritated you are with him," Jo said, her eyes turning to look toward Lulu and her mother.

"Hm?" Charlie pretended not to understand. Jo rolled her eyes.

"Nick, be kinder to him. He's Lulu's father."

"Jo..." he sighed.

"Look, you need to stop blaming Nick for all of it. You weren't there. You don't know the whole story."

"I know all that I need to know," Charlie stubbornly stated. "He left you all alone when you needed him most."

Jo glanced down at the ground, mulling over his words before shaking her head.

"You....you don't know all of it, Dad. I wasn't...." Jo paused. Tears sprang to her eyes. Nothing broke Charlie's heart more than to see either of his daughters sad. He sighed and conceded to his daughter's request.

"I'll try."

"Thank you. It's all I ask."

Thirteen

— · —

Late Fall 2012

"You both have been through trauma," the therapist said. "Trauma can tear even the strongest couples apart."

When Vivian admitted to Nick that Jo was prepared to let him go, he knew he had to do something. He had no plans of leaving his wife after all the two of them had been through. No, he needed to figure out what he could do to make this better. To make this right. He loved his wife too much to lose her.

"We aren't being torn apart," Nick said. He refused to believe it. He reached toward his wife, but Jo scooted away from him. "We're just...." His head shook.

"Jo? What would you like to add?"

Jo looked up slightly and sighed, shrugging her shoulders.

"I don't know," she whispered.

"Do you really want your husband to leave you?" The therapist directly asked her. Nick observed his wife. There had been a time when he could read her so well. Now, all he saw was a woman who was a stranger to him. It tore at him every day.

"No," Jo whispered. The vulnerability was easy to see. Her lower lip quivered slightly as she slumped her shoulders. "But we're not happy. We don't want the same things, not anymore."

"Jo..." he tried, but their therapist spoke over him.

"What do you mean by that?"

Jo remained silent for a long moment. The silence was deafening. But the therapist didn't let up; she kept her eyes on Jo and waited for her response. He held his breath, pretty sure he knew what she was going to say.

"Jo?" the therapist pushed. Jo inhaled.

"I don't want to give up on Lulu. He does."

"I don't want—" he started, only to have the therapist put her finger up to stop him. She gave him a gentle nod, letting him know that he would have his turn to say what he needed to say.

"Explain that a bit more for me. What makes you feel like your husband wants to give up?"

Jo licked her severely chapped lips. Her mouth contorted as she held back some tears. She looked up at the ceiling, willing the tears to remain at bay before continuing,

"He wants us to mourn and to move away from our house and this town. He wants us to stop searching for her."

"And what do you want, Jo?"

"I want her back." Jo's voice was very clear, and she met the therapist's eyes. "I want to do everything we can to bring her back."

"Like what, Jo? Can you tell me what they have not done?"

"They are just giving up!" Jo said, exasperated. "They've determined my daughter is dead. They won't keep searching! It isn't right. They have no proof."

The therapist didn't respond to Jo. Instead, she turned her attention to Nick.

"And what do you think, Nick? Do you agree with your wife?"

"I..." he sighed, pausing. "I think we should listen to the detectives and finally mourn. Jo hasn't allowed for it."

"Because she's not dead!" Jo screamed, standing from the sofa. Her eyes were wide and wild. Her face flushed red with rage. "My daughter is not dead!"

Nick pressed his hand into a fist before lifting it against his mouth.

"I wish that was true," he said between his fingers. "I really, really do."

"Jo." The therapist remained calm through all of this. "Sit down." There must have been some magic in the therapist's words because his wife did as she asked of her. She even quieted, resting back against the cushions and hugging her arms protectively over her chest. "Jo, can you explain to me why you are sure that you are right and the others are wrong?"

"Because," Jo said, her voice now strained, "I am her mother." Her finger pointed to her chest. "I would know if she was dead. I would feel it right here." She pressed her finger firmly against her heart. "I would know."

The therapist creased her brows thoughtfully and there was solemnness staring back at them both. She didn't answer right away. Nick was now learning that it was her way.

She would take everything they said in and ponder them before responding.

"That's a strong feeling," the therapist finally answered. "It's a feeling that no one else can understand but you. However, Jo, your husband is the only other person in the world who can understand the pain you are going through, and, likewise, you are the only other person who can understand his pain. Don't you see the pain that he is in right now?"

Salty tracks of tears were on Jo's cheeks. She wasn't looking at him. He reached out toward her again, grateful she allowed him to place his hand on her shoulder and didn't shrug it away.

"I just..." Jo whispered. "I don't know how I'm supposed to move on without her."

Jo didn't think the therapy was helping. It seemed like a waste of time, but Nick had insisted they go together. He wanted them to be stronger; he said. He told her he wasn't planning on giving up on her, on them.

"Christmas lights are up," Nick quietly observed as they drove through their small town. Jo's eyes searched for what he saw, and then she saw it.

The lights were strung up along the light poles and the decorations that hung.

Her heart clenched, and she wanted to vomit. Christmas was coming. Her daughter was gone. Their first Christmas without her in three years.

"Should we stop to eat somewhere?" Nick asked.

"I'm not hungry," Jo answered. It was true. She found it difficult to eat nowadays. Her stomach felt as though it was constantly in knots and her throat was closed up. The little she could get down would always leave her throat uncomfortable for hours afterward. It was difficult even to do the tiniest of tasks.

"You should eat something," Nick said. "You've lost too much weight. The wind could blow you over."

"I didn't realize the way I looked bothered you so much," Jo snapped. Nick heavily sighed. Jo knew she wasn't fair to him and that she yelled much more than he deserved, but she couldn't control it. Not really. She struggled to keep a grasp on what made her Jo Anderson. She no longer felt like that person. Not anymore.

"I'm going to get a burger," Nick replied simply. It seemed over time he had learned it was best not to respond when she snapped at him. He pulled into the parking lot at the diner and left her alone in the car as he went inside to order.

She knew exactly what he was going to order: a double cheeseburger with extra pickles, no ketchup, lots of mustard, and onion rings with water to drink. He hated soda. It was one of her first memories of when she met him and how he went on and on about how he hated the way it bubbled in his throat.

As the door of the diner opened, she looked up to see if he was already coming out. Instead, she saw him inside talking to someone. His jaw was clenched and his hands clutched tightly around the top of the bag.

When he finally stepped outside, he got into the car, placed the food on the seat behind him, and tightened his hands over the steering wheel. He didn't speak.

"What happened?" Jo cautiously asked.

"Doesn't matter," Nick answered, pulling out of the parking spot. He remained hunched over with red cheeks as they drove down the street toward their house.

"It was one of them, wasn't it?" Jo asked. "One of the reporters?"

"It doesn't matter," Nick said again.

"What could they possibly want to know now?"

Nick remained quiet for the rest of the ride home. When they arrived, he parked the car in front of the house and turned to face her.

"This is why we need to leave here, Jo. They will never let us have any peace. They will keep at us, on and on until there is nothing of us left. Don't you see that? They think we're entertainment for them. We play this new part in our town: poor grieving parents."

"You... I...." She tried to speak, but she couldn't. She didn't know what to say to him, because she knew he wasn't wrong. They would be those people for the rest of their lives. Had the therapist been right? Was it unfair of her not to help her husband in his pain?

Nick stepped out of the car and walked inside. She slowly got out and followed him. She watched as he made his plate and then he handed her the bag.

"I got you your favorite, too. I hope you'll eat it, but don't if you can't or don't want to or... forget it."

Even when she was horrible to him, he was still wonderful to her. It made her hate herself even more.

She opened the bag and placed the food on a plate. Then she walked over to sit beside him at the table. He glanced up, pleasantly surprised. It was the least she could do for him right now. She may not eat much of the food, but she could try.

"What should we do about Christmas this year?" Nick asked. He ate an onion ring slowly, almost thoughtfully.

"I don't want to do Christmas this year," she admitted. Her eyes filled with tears, yet again. She was so tired of all the tears. She couldn't believe she hadn't run out of them by now.

"I don't either," Nick admitted. "Do you think your family would understand?"

"I don't know," Jo said. She tried to think about her sister and her parents. Would they care if they didn't show up to the family breakfast on Christmas morning? It had been a big tradition each year. They always did it at Vivian's house. Her parents stayed there on Christmas Eve and then on Christmas morning, she, Nick, and Lulu would head over for Christmas morning and presents. All of Santa's gifts would be magically there (Nick would have driven them over after Lulu was fast asleep). They would fill the long day with presents and delicious food. It had always been Jo's favorite day of the year. Now, just thinking about it made her physically ill. She couldn't do it this year. Her family would have to understand.

"I think they will," Nick whispered, wrapping his hand around hers.

Jo blinked, and the tears she had been trying to hold back fell down her cheeks. Nick brought his fingers up to wipe them away. Then his hand lingered on her cheek and she closed her eyes, taking this moment in. Sometimes, she didn't realize just how much she missed his touch until she felt it again.

"We could go somewhere for the holiday. Just get away and not focus on what the day is," Nick suggested.

"Like where?"

"Anywhere," he responded. "Anywhere that's not here."

"Yeah," Jo agreed. "I think that might be a good idea."

Nick took her hand then and brought it up to his lips, kissing her knuckles.

"I love you, Jojo. I will fight for us."

Again, tears fell between the pair.

"I know."

"Where will you go?" Vivian asked her sister as they sat outside on the back porch of her large home. Her five-year-old son, TJ, was swinging on the swing set and her nine-month-old daughter was pulling up on the chair where she was sitting. The baby girl blubbered, steadying herself on Vivian's knee.

"On a cruise," Jo said. Her eyes were not on her niece or nephew. Vivian wondered if it might have been better to wait and meet with her sister later in the day, when her husband was home from work. She had taken the week off from work since her nanny was away on vacation with her own family.

Vivian noticed how it seemed to physically hurt her sister to be around her children. Jo put in an effort with them, but it was a constant reminder of what she no longer had. Vivian couldn't blame her for the pain she felt around them.

"Oh, a cruise, how lovely. Where to?"

"I don't know. Nick is planning it all out. I haven't told our parents yet," Jo confessed. "I don't know how to tell them."

"They'll understand, Jo," Vivian said.

"Will they?" Jo countered. "Dad might, but Mom...." She tugged on the messy bun in her hair. It appeared to be her signature look now. "Mom will say she understands, but she'll be upset. Christmas is her favorite time of the year."

"It doesn't matter if it upsets her. It is not your job to make sure they have the best Christmas every year. You need to focus on what you need and what Nick needs. You are the ones that have to find your way back to one another."

Jo twiddled with the drawstring on her pants.

"I just want Lulu back," Jo said in a strained voice. "She's out there somewhere, waiting for me."

Vivian ran her fingers through her hair. Her daughter was tugging on her pants, asking to be held. Vivian lifted her onto her lap and kissed her daughter's chubby cheek. The baby giggled.

"Jo, I think right now, just for a little while, you need to believe the detectives."

Jo shot her a look.

"What?! I thought you were on my side!" she breathed heavily.

"Of course, I am on your side," Vivian countered. "I am your older sister. I am always on your side. But I love Nick too, Jo. He would do *anything* for you. He loves you. Take a week to be just about you two. If Lulu is out there, then they will find her. One week won't change that."

Jo turned away from Vivian, placing her hands together and resting her chin on them. Vivian could tell that she was trying not to cry, so Vivian reached over to rub Jo's back.

"You can cry," she said. "You are safe here with me."

"I'm fucking sick and tired of crying!" Jo wept. She turned to see the baby in Vivian's lap. Her face paled slightly. "I—I'm sorry."

"It's all right. She can't talk, yet."

Jo's face crumbled. Vivian adjusted Callie in her arms and pulled Jo toward her with her free arm. Her lips pressed against her sister's tear-stained cheek.

"This all hurts so much, I know," Vivian whispered into her sister's ear. "I am hurt by the loss, so I can't even imagine the magnitude of what you feel. Please, for me, go on this trip. Cry with your husband. Laugh with him. Just be with him. Remember why you married him. Remember who he was to you."

Slowly, Jo pulled back away from Vivian and wiped her cheek.

"Trust me, Jo. You won't regret it."

Nick was the one who ended up making the call to let Jo's parents know they would not be taking part in Christmas this year and would instead be going on a cruise to the

Bahamas. He called Rose, and she took the news much better than he had expected.

"It's done now," Nick said. He slid next to Jo on the couch. Ever since the plans had begun for their trip, he noticed that Jo was allowing more physical touch between them. She also didn't discuss searching for Lulu. He didn't know if she was still doing things when he wasn't there, but she did not mention it at home.

Jo said that she wanted to stop therapy, and she wasn't sure it was helping. Nick wanted to protest, but she seemed better. Not fully healed, of course, but there were bits of his wife that he could see when he was around her now. It was refreshing.

Perhaps, on this trip, they could truly mourn. They could lay their little girl to rest. After that, they could figure out together what came next. The future still seemed dull, but he wasn't sure that would ever change. He wasn't naïve to think that they would come home from this trip as new people with bright futures. They still would not have their daughter. That weight would always be between them, but they could carry it together. They could try to find some sort of happiness in the far future.

Jo shifted to bring her knees up to her chest. She rested her head on him and he heard her breaths slow. Taking advantage of her wanting to be near him, he combed her hair with his fingers. It didn't take long, and Jo was fast asleep. Nick refused to move. He would take this time with her as he had it. He prayed he wouldn't lose it, though he was still worried about it. He couldn't be sure that this trip would save anything, but he hoped it would.

Fourteen

Early Spring 2017

Vivian checked the presents she held once more, making sure she hadn't left any back at the house. Foolishly, she allowed her children to help her wrap all the gifts, and they had made a mess. She could be a bit of a perfectionist, and she struggled to involve her younger children in the process of any sort of chore.

All five gifts for Lulu were there, as well as the pastries she had gotten for everyone. She hoped Jo wouldn't think it was too much. But this was Vivian's love language, and she couldn't help herself. She showed how much she cared by bringing things to people. Plus, she hadn't seen her niece in nearly five years. She had to spoil her. It was her job as Lulu's one and only aunt.

Vivian lifted the boxes and then struggled to close the door with her full hands. Thankfully, her father was prepared for this and was already walking out of the front door.

"You always go overboard," he said with a knowing smile. He came and took the boxes from Vivian so she could lock and close her car door.

Her father, Charlie, waited for her to be done and walked back up to the house with her. She hadn't realized just how anxious she was until this moment. She knew nothing about her niece anymore. Her niece may not even want anything to do with her. She took in a deep breath before crossing the threshold.

"Good evening, dear," Rose greeted from the doorway. She pulled Vivian down toward her level and kissed her cheek.

"Hi, Mom. Where is everyone else?"

"In the backyard. Lulu *loves* Butler."

"Right, of course."

Her father placed the boxes on the table and then turned toward her.

"Should we go outside?" Vivian asked.

"I'll go and tell them you are here. Your dad needs to start grilling, anyway."

Rose went to the sliding door, opened it, and called out for them to come inside.

Butler rushed in and began yapping at Vivian. She gave him a curt nod and bent down to pat his head. She wasn't the biggest fan of Butler. She tolerated animals, but she wasn't an animal person.

A second later, Lulu was inside. Vivian stood and her breath got caught in her throat. It was amazing. It was her. It was really her. Even though her sister had sent her a picture, it wasn't the same as seeing Lulu in person for the first time since she was so young. The little girl paused her steps at the sight of her aunt and glanced up at her, skeptically.

"You're tall," Lulu said.

"That's your Aunt Vivian," Jo said, coming in behind her.

"You are Nick's sister?" Lulu asked.

"No, I'm your mom's sister."

Lulu looked between Jo and Vivian a couple of times.

"But she's short. You don't look alike at all."

Rose and Charlie laughed.

"Yes, I got your grandpa's height and grandpa's looks.
Your mom got the opposite," Vivian explained.

"And I don't have any siblings," Nick reminded Lulu.

"Right." Lulu sighed. She then saw the large stack of
presents on the table. Her eyes lit up. "Are those for me?"

"Of course they are. Come on," Vivian said. Lulu hesi-
tantly held her hand before they walked over to the table.

"Here. I'll help you," Rose said.

Vivian stepped back, and Jo stood beside her.

"Ah, so you are going to win favorite by bringing my kid
presents?" she asked, but her voice was happy.

"Absolutely," Vivian answered.

When she heard her sister laugh, Vivian turned and saw
the first genuine smile on her sister's face that she had seen
in a long time. Part of her wanted to cry happy tears, but
instead, she wrapped her arm around her sister's shoulders
and brought her toward her.

"I'm so happy for you," she whispered to her sister. "She's
really back."

The evening had gone well. Lulu enjoyed meeting Vivian. It
didn't surprise Nick. His sister-in-law was a force of nature;

everyone liked her. She had the type of personality that drew people to her. She was an extrovert and loved connecting with everyone.

After Lulu went to bed and Jo's parents went downstairs to their little apartment, it was just the three of them left. It felt so much like the old times when they would gather after everyone had gone to bed. They'd stay up late and chat about anything and everything. Nick missed that.

Tonight, they all sat out back on the porch near the small fire pit. They didn't do much talking tonight, yet they all stayed outside for a long while. Randomly, Jo got up. She didn't announce where she was heading and disappeared, leaving Nick alone with Vivian.

"You know, I was always rooting for you both," Vivian told Nick. She sat across from him with the fire between the two of them.

"You were?" he asked her. He tried to remember that year when everything fell apart. So much of it was a painful blur. He hated to admit that he could hardly remember the parts Vivian played. All he could remember was her kindness to them both.

"Of course I was, Nick. You are family. You love Jo. I've always known that."

Nick sat back in his chair. He would always love Jo. He didn't have any doubts about that.

"Yeah," he whispered. "But it's too late for us now."

"Is it?" Vivian looked at him with so much intensity that he had to look away. Before he would say anything in response, the door slid back open and Jo rejoined them. She held cookies from Vivian's pastry box.

They sat there for a little while longer before Vivian announced she needed to go home. Long after she had left, Nick kept hearing her voice in his head over and over again. *Is it?*

They decided that the next day they would meet Vivian and her children at the park nearby. Thomas would then join in later in the day; he was still at work but would come over once his shift was over. This allowed Lulu not to have to interact with everyone new at the same time. Besides, Thomas wasn't much of a talker, so he would be the least overwhelming of them all.

Jo realized she didn't know how much Lulu had been around other children. She hadn't even thought to ask if there had been other children in the home where she grew up. She could only guess not, because Lulu never mentioned them. She also knew Lulu had never been to school.

They walked to the park rather quietly. It was a large park in the middle of their town with an older playground, well used by children for several years. Most of the playground was a dark, worn down, bluish color. Several feet away from the playground were a bunch of picnic tables where they would be meeting Vivian for lunch.

Unsurprisingly, Vivian was already there. She had brought lunch that her children were sitting down and eating. It was a pizza, a fruit tray, a vegetable tray, and some cookies. When she noticed Lulu, she smiled.

"Ah! You are here! Lulu, here are your cousins. Meet TJ and Callie."

Both TJ and Callie stopped eating to wave. Lulu watched them for a moment, remaining closer to Nick. Jo noticed she seemed more comfortable around Nick than herself and, as much as she tried not to let it bother her, it did. Lulu seemed to be settling back into this life easily, with the exception of Jo as her mother. Dr. Canmore warned that this was likely the 'honeymoon period.' As Lulu became more comfortable with them, they would see more outbursts and misbehavior from their daughter. Right now, she was just taking it all in and trying to find her place.

"Come on," Vivian encouraged. "Eat."

At that, Lulu walked over and sat next to Callie. The little girl looked up at her and smiled. Vivian made Lulu a plate, and then Nick went over to sit with the children. Jo remained back and allowed them to get to know one another.

Her sister walked over toward her and stood beside her, munching on an apple.

"Are you hungry?"

"No," Jo answered. "I ate a late lunch."

"I think he's still in love with you," Vivian said a beat later. Jo twisted her head, so that she was facing her sister.

"What?"

"Nick. He still loves you," Vivian told her.

"Don't do that," Jo said, shaking her head.

"Do what?"

"Try to play matchmaker. Nick and I are getting a divorce. We are not going to get back together. I don't know why you are so sure that we will. We won't. This... we are over and it has been over since Lulu disappeared."

"Surely, you don't mean that."

"Of course I do," Jo answered. Her sister had been fighting more for her marriage than either she or her husband had. It made little sense to her. Perhaps her sister was one of those people who believed in happily ever after to such an extent that it physically hurt her to see them break apart.

"But you love each other."

"Love was never the problem, Vivian. Love can't fix everything. Why are you so worried about Nick and me? I'm not quite sure how it is any of your business."

Vivian paused a moment before answering, "Because I love you, Jo. You are my little sister. I want you to be happy. Nick loves you more than anything. He makes you happy."

"*Made* me happy. There is a difference."

"Perhaps, but don't you wish that you two were back together? Lulu is home. You three can be a proper family now! It is all you have ever wanted. And I worry now with all of this, that perhaps you'll..."

"I'll what? Perhaps, I'll what? Vivian? What in the world are you so worried about? You, Mom, and Dad have always worried way too much about me! I can handle myself!"

"Oh, right. That's what that was four years ago, you handling yourself," Vivian scoffed. Jo angrily opened her mouth to speak, but Vivian started walking away. Jo couldn't go after her, worried that they might start a scene in front of the children. The last thing she needed to do was traumatize Lulu any further.

Jo sighed and placed her hand over her face. She moved further away from the picnic tables and closer to the benches next to the playground, needing a minute to calm herself down. Her sister was way out of line. Jo was in a much better headspace than she had been four years ago, and she had been in that better headspace for a long time now. She hated how they all seemed to treat her with their patronizing baby gloves.

"Hey." Jo turned to see that Nick was behind her. She slowed her steps so that he could catch up. Her eyes then skirted over toward the picnic table to find Vivian sitting with all three of the children. Ever since Lulu's return, she was frightened to have her out of her or Nick's eyesight for even a second. She had learned the hard way what could happen if you looked away.

"How's the picnic?" Jo asked.

"Good. The children seem to be getting along well," Nick said.

"Good."

"Why aren't you over there with them?"

Jo shrugged. "I don't know. I guess I wanted Lulu to meet her cousins without feeling I was watching every move she made. Though I'm not sure she'd notice if I was there or not, anyway. She doesn't like me."

"Why would you say that? Of course, she likes you," Nick said. Jo shot him a look.

"She hardly knows me. She hardly knows any of us. I...." She turned her head away from him. "I'm not handling any of this very well."

"What do you mean? I think you're handling it just fine," Nick said to her. "This is all uncharted ground, Jo. We have to take it one day at a time, you and me. No one expects us to be perfect."

Jo tucked her hands in her pockets before swaying on her feet. She did. She expected herself to be perfect. She wanted to be the mother she was all those years ago. It seemed she was struggling to remember who that woman had been.

"Come on, let's go back. I'm sure they'll be ready to play soon."

On the ride back to the house, Nick noticed Lulu had fallen asleep in the back of the car. He looked in the rearview mirror and smiled. She had played so hard with her cousins that it wore her out. It had been nice to see her play with them so well, to act like a kid. They ran around for hours without a care in the world.

"Look." He tapped Jo's shoulder and pointed to the back seat. Jo turned. From the corner of his eye, Nick could see Jo smiling at their little girl. She then turned back around and rested back against her chair.

"What do we do next?" Nick asked. Now Lulu had officially met all of her family members. There had been a checklist of what to do: get her clothes and toys, meet her grandparents, and meet her aunt, uncles, and cousins. But what came next? When did they announce Nick wouldn't always live in this same home?

"I... I don't know," Jo answered. "School?"

"Right," he paused. "How does that work?"

"I have no idea. I can call the district this week and see. We'll talk to Dr. Canmore. I don't know what the best answer is. Part of me thought about keeping her home and homeschooling her, at least for the rest of the year, to try to catch her up."

"Yeah," Nick breathed.

They rode in silence for the rest of the ride. Nick had many more questions, but he saved them for later. Focusing on what they would do for Lulu's schooling was enough for right now, and it didn't force the more difficult questions to come up.

Nick was caught off guard when he heard Jo gasp.

"Oh my god!" she exclaimed.

His head turned, and he saw the house surrounded by several cars. People were standing outside with cameras and microphones. He cursed under his breath. Now it began. Now they would be hounded by reporters for months on end with no relief.

He gripped the steering wheel angrily. These people were vultures. They enjoyed other people's pain far too much. Why was any of this anyone else's business outside of their own and law enforcement?

After they lost Lulu, Nick found he could no longer look at newspapers or watch the news. They had also put him off social media. All of them seemed to take pleasure in others' losses, their challenges, and their lives. So he couldn't do it. It hurt far too much, and he hurt for the other people who were being blasted all over the media.

"What do we do?" Jo whispered. He could hear the hint of fear in her voice. When Lulu had gone missing, she hadn't been as upset with the people following them around. She would always just ask them to help her find her daughter, but things were different now. Their daughter would be a part of this. Neither of them wanted Lulu to be hounded by these people.

"We try to get in the garage and shut it before getting out. Then we close all the blinds and call the police. They know they aren't allowed on our property, but they'll stay until they are reminded otherwise."

He hated how familiar he was with all of this.

Thankfully, he could pull into the garage, and none of the reporters dared to go inside. He closed it and then lifted his sleeping daughter into his arms before whispering to Jo to close all the blinds and make sure to lock all the doors. Jo nodded and rushed inside, leaving the door open for him to get inside easier.

Once he placed his daughter on her bed, he made his way back downstairs. Jo sat on the couch, holding her phone. He briefly wondered where her parents were, but then realized they may have gone to Vivian's when they saw all the reporters outside.

"The police are on their way," Jo said. She turned on the television. He glanced to see that it was on mute, but that there were pictures of them and Lulu on the screen. He felt the rage flow through him. "How do we protect Lulu from all of this?"

He rubbed the back of his neck. Then he sat down next to Jo, shaking his head.

"I'm not sure. We try to avoid them for now. Eventually, it has to die out, right?"

Jo twiddled her fingers in front of her, not quite convinced.

"I was thinking we could stay with Vivian. My parents are there now," Jo said, "but the presses would just figure that out."

"Yeah," he said.

"She's still asleep?" Jo glanced up at the stairs.

"Yes."

"At least she didn't see them. We just have to protect her as much as we can from all of this mess. Take it one day at a time."

"I agree."

"Since Lulu is still asleep, I'm going to go take a shower. What do you want to do for dinner?"

"I don't know. Something simple."

"Right, of course."

Jo left him alone with his thoughts. Nick turned up the television and turned the channel. All the major news stations in the area were covering the story. He turned off the television. They would have to figure out how to manage being in the spotlight, yet again.

FIFTEEN

WINTER 2012

Once the safety procedure presentation was over and they were free to do as they wanted, Jo and Nick went back to their cabin to place their life jackets back where they belonged. Then Jo inspected the cabin Nick picked out for them. She had not been involved in any of the planning for this, because she had told him to just do it.

In the past, she planned all of their trips and vacations down to the very last detail. It was something she had enjoyed doing, especially once Lulu had joined their family. But she hadn't had it in her to plan anything for this.

She stepped to the large window, saw the handle, and realized it was a door. She opened the door and stepped out onto the deck. They weren't moving yet, but she could still feel the ocean breeze on her skin. Jo leaned against the railing to glance down at the water below. The sun shone off the tops of the little waves, making the most beautiful, colorful patterns.

A part of her wondered what would happen if she just slipped off this deck and into the ocean. Would she find peace then? Would she see her daughter again?

Her fingers slowly lifted from the railing as she leaned forward slightly to get a better look at the ocean. She closed her eyes and could feel the waves of the ocean calling her.

An arm came around her and pulled her close, then there was a kiss on her cheek. She was brought back to reality; she shuddered. Her face turned to her husband, and she could see he was smiling.

"Isn't it beautiful?" he asked. She nodded. They stood facing away from the port, so all they saw was the ocean and skyline of the surrounding city. Soon, only the ocean would surround them. No worries for several days.

"We have dinner in a couple of hours. Would you like to walk down to the pool? Or we could go get a drink?" Nick offered.

"Or we could just hang out in here until it's time to eat," Jo suggested. Nick smiled.

"Sure. Do you like it?"

"It's very nice," Jo told him. And it was. It was a much larger room than she expected, and she wondered how they could afford it. She hadn't looked at their finances in quite some time. The two of them used to budget monthly together, and Jo had a clear view of what they had coming in and going out with the bills. Now all of that was on Nick's shoulders.

Suddenly, she felt very guilty. Her pain had put so much on her husband, who was hurting just like she was. She felt tears sting the back of her eyes. She walked up closer to Nick, cupping his cheek. His hand covered hers, and he closed his eyes. It had been far too long since they had been with one another in such an intimate, loving way.

"I love you," Jo said. "I know I don't show it as much, but..."

"Shh," Nick said. "I know. I love you too." He smiled at her and then leaned forward to kiss her. It was a simple, gentle kiss. Much like how they had kissed when they had first begun dating.

"Why don't we go walk around," Jo quickly said, changing her mind. "We can hang out in this room plenty this week. Let's see what they have."

Their first dinner was quiet. Jo was trying, though. He was seeing a side of his wife that he hadn't seen since before the summer when they'd lost everything. She smiled and held his hand. They talked about things that weren't Lulu-related. She didn't shy away or get angry at the smallest thing. Perhaps this trip was just what the two of them needed.

"More bread?" Nick lifted the bread bowl, handing it toward Jo. She gladly took it and buttered up a roll. This was also the most he had seen her eat in a long time. He was so glad.

"The food here is great," Jo said. "I can't believe we can just have anything off of the menu—and two servings if we really want it."

Nick chuckled. He had always wanted to take Jo on a cruise. He knew she would love it. The plan had been to come when Lulu was older and they could leave her with the grandparents.

They ate some more. They didn't talk much, but they looked at one another from time to time and smiled. It almost felt as though it was the beginning of their relationship. That they were just learning one another, yet again. Things would have to be slow, and Nick was fine with that. He just wanted them to find each other once more. He knew they had a very long, painful road ahead of them. He knew the hurt would always be there. But he needed his wife back. He didn't know how to survive without her.

The sun was bright, and Jo happily sighed against Nick as they sat on the deck outside. It was a peaceful moment, and they were to be on the ocean all day. Tomorrow, they would dock in the Bahamas, but for today, they were just enjoying the water.

Nick ran his fingers up her arm and she shivered at his touch. Her eyes closed, and she buried her head into his chest more. The sun warmed their skin and as they traveled further south, the air grew warmer and warmer. It was easy to forget that it was December.

Then suddenly, without warning, Jo sobbed. She didn't even know what caused it. Perhaps, feeling so safe and comfortable in her husband's arms allowed the sadness that she had been holding to escape. She hadn't even felt sad at that moment, or at least, she had thought she hadn't. But it was there, and it was strong.

Nick didn't miss a beat. He held her closer and his head hid in the nook of her neck. She heard his sob against her cheek. And just like that, the two of them let it all out. They cried and cried for their little girl into the vastness of the open air of the ocean.

Neither said a word. They both knew what the other was feeling. It was freeing to let the pain fall and hold on tightly to Nick. Her fingers dug into the skin of his upper arms and she held onto him so strongly that she worried she might leave marks on his arms. He pressed his hands firmly against her back as he kissed where her neck and shoulder met.

When their tears slowed, Jo collapsed, defeated. Nick pulled her into his lap, cradling her against him. He held her with such love and care.

"It will always hurt," he whispered into her ear. "But we will have to carry it together."

Jo nodded, unable to speak. Her hand rested on the back of Nick's neck as she held onto him like a lifeline. When Jo climbed out of Nick's lap, she cupped his cheeks and kissed him. Her lips urgently needed his, and he gratefully reciprocated.

"After dinner, let's continue," Jo said. Nick's eyes widened, knowing what she was implying.

"Okay."

They never made it off the boat on the first day it docked. Instead, they remained in bed, ordering room service and just enjoying one another. Nick ran his hand down his wife's bare back, and she made eye contact before moving up to meet his lips with her own.

This was what they needed. Not the sex itself, but the connection that had been lost for so long. Finally, they had joined as one and it had been beautiful, slow, and perfect. They had been careful with each movement, enjoying one another.

"What if we got dressed up and went to the bar before dinner?" Jo said, biting down on her lower lip. Nick sat up slightly. He slid his hand up to her neck lovingly, rubbing his fingers behind her ear and through her hair.

"That could be nice."

"Tonight for dinner, I am going to get the steak. What about you?" she asked him. He grinned.

"You had the steak last night."

"Oh, I plan on having it every night," she winked. He pulled her on top of him then and she eagerly grasped at him, kissing up his chest. "But for now, we can enjoy this," she said between breaths. "It's like our honeymoon all over again."

At that, Nick could only smile. It was like their honeymoon when they couldn't keep their hands off one another. Since the birth of their daughter, it had not been like this. They had been busy and tired. They had to fit it in after bedtimes or early mornings. But now, they could act as uninhibited as they had on their honeymoon. The difference now was that they knew each other fully. They had lived a life and tragedy with one another. It made it more intense, much deeper.

Jo was pleased with the bar, likely because it was a child-free place. Other areas of the ship didn't have that luxury. Most of the time, when they were not sequestered in their room, they were likely to see a child or two out and about. It stung. She couldn't lie and say that it didn't. Her heart always thought of Lulu in those moments.

She sipped slowly on her wine. She never liked the way alcohol made her feel and so she would only drink one glass. She had never been a fan of losing any sort of self-control. Nick sat beside her, sipping on his glass of whiskey. He looked at her with a gleam in his eyes. She smiled.

"Are you ready to head to dinner?"

Jo nodded and beamed up at Nick. He slipped out of his chair and took her hand before leading her down the path toward where they dined. As they walked down the set of stairs, a little girl ran past them, singing a little tune that was reminiscent of something Lulu used to sing. Jo hesitated, finding it hard to keep moving forward. She felt Nick hold her tightly, keeping her from falling from the ledge of the stairs.

She blinked harshly and pushed herself to keep going. She and Nick were having a delightful time; she couldn't let this ruin it. Taking in a deep breath, Jo forced her foot down to the next step. They were going to dinner and were going to have a nice time.

She felt a hot breath against her cheek and then Nick whispered, "It's okay to be sad, Jojo. You are allowed to be upset."

Those words made her turn to him and meet his own watery eyes. She wrapped her arms around his neck and pulled him close. They stood on the staircase like that for a long moment. He lovingly rubbed her back to soothe her.

"Never feel like you have to hide this from me. I want us to grieve together."

"Me too," Jo murmured. Her head pressed against his forehead. "It just hurts... so, so much."

"It does. It really does."

Nick sat back in the large lounge chair by the beach. He looked over toward Jo, who had her feet in the sand and a glass of water in her hand. Jo had insisted they stay by the beach and not go on excursions; all she wanted to do was spend the time with him by the water. He had to agree that he liked this best. Here they had no expectations, and they just got to enjoy being together.

He finally had hope for their future. He thought they now might find some sort of happiness again. He reached across and Jo smiled up at him, accepting his touch. She had a hint of redness on her cheeks from the heat.

"I never want to go back," he told her. Jo's body tensed lightly, and she dropped her hand from his before taking a sip of her drink.

"We have to," she answered, looking ahead.

"Right, of course," he replied. She looked back at him, attempting to smile.

"I'm sorry. I am enjoying this. I am. I promise."

"Me too. And don't apologize. No apologies allowed," he winked. She giggled as she moved to his lounge chair and bent forward to kiss the tip of his nose. Then he laughed as her fingers ran against the sides of his stomach. He had always been ticklish there. He brought his hands down to grasp over her wrists to make her stop, which only made her laugh and attempt to pull away.

"What? Does that tickle?" she said playfully.

"You know it does," he laughed some more. She kept trying to pull out of his grasp and move her fingers toward his ticklish spot. He let go of her wrists and then began tickling her stomach.

"Stop!" she cried out between peals of laughter. "That tickles!"

"All's fair," he whispered into her ear. She fell back. He tried to steady her, but she pulled him down onto the sand with her.

She laid beneath him and his fingers brushed the stray hairs off her face. They stared at one another, nearly breathless from their exertions. When Nick tried to get up and off of her, she shook her head, holding him more tightly.

"People are probably watching us," he said.

"Let them." She kissed him deeply before gently pushing him off her. He helped to lift her and wipe the sand off her back and out of her hair.

"We should get in the water," Nick suggested. Jo stared at the water and flinched.

"No thank you."

Nick narrowed his eyes, grinning. "You still won't go in it?"

"Are you kidding me? There are sharks and other animals in there!" He couldn't help but brighten his smile.

"Oh, all right. The showers then?"

"Or we could go back on the ship and shower there, together," she said.

"Deal."

The cruise was ending, and neither of them could face it. Tomorrow, they would be back at their starting destination. Jo felt a sense of dread as the trip came to its end. She didn't know what came next.

The trip had been great for her and Nick. But would it stay that way when they arrived back home? She wasn't so sure.

They were sitting by the adult-only pool and Nick's hand was in hers. He seemed to know that she was feeling uneasy today. She could tell by the way he didn't say much but just kept giving her reassuring smiles. He wanted to be there for her today. Again, that made her feel guilty. It should be about him, too.

"Let's walk around," he suggested. Nick stood from his seat and placed his tee shirt over his shoulders. Then he placed his hat on the top of his head. He grabbed Jo's cover-up and helped her put it on. It would be the last time she got to walk around this large ship. She wondered if they would do this every Christmas from now on.

She had honestly forgotten that Christmas had come and gone. Even though the cruise had some music and decorations for the holiday, they had been easy to ignore. On Christmas night, they had gotten room service, not leaving their room. They watched comedies on the television and never discussed what the day was, though they both knew. That was their gift to one another. They pretended the holiday didn't exist for one day.

They walked down over to an area of the deck where no one was. Nick rested his hands on the railing and brought Jo in front of him. He held her to his chest and kissed the top of her head. Her eyes looked down below, into the water, and remembered what she had felt when they first arrived. The feeling was no longer there, and she hoped it would stay away.

"Do you think you would enjoy living near the beach?" Nick asked. Jo inhaled sharply. Was that what this whole cruise had been about? Trying to get her to move away?

"I...."

"I'm sorry," Nick quickly said, as though he had read Jo's thoughts. "I didn't mean it like that. Of course, we won't move. I was only asking."

She settled back against Nick, enjoying the waves on the water and the wind against their skin. For just a little bit longer, they could forget. For a little bit longer, they could be Nick and Jo again. Even if it was just for a few more hours.

Sixteen

Spring 2017

Jo stood by the back sliding door, watching Lulu and Nick play in the backyard. Her eyes watered as she watched the two of them together. Lulu enjoyed Nick, seeking him out to ask him to play with her. Yet with Jo, she only spoke when it was necessary. No matter how much Jo tried to interact with Lulu, the girl would close up and give any excuse not to spend time with Jo.

"Ah, she's playing with that dog again." Her mother came up behind her, placing her hand on Jo's lower back.

"Yes, she's bonded with him quickly," Jo said. Her eyes narrowed slightly. "And Nick. And Dad and you." Her eyes turned to her mother. The woman stood just about an inch shorter than her.

"It'll all take time. She's bonded best with the dog. Makes sense. He doesn't have any expectations for her. He just wants attention," Rose shrugged. "Your dad and I, well, we're just the grandparents."

Jo stared through the clear window at where her daughter was playing.

"I don't... Mom, I don't feel connected to her," she quietly admitted.

"Oh dear, that will take time. You have only been around her for a week after years of being apart."

"But I'm her mother," Jo breathed. "That bond came the moment I knew she existed. I carried her for nine months and then nursed her for a year and a half. How does she feel like such a stranger to me now?" Jo caressed her belly where she had carried her child. It felt like a lifetime ago, yet she could still remember the joy she felt and how she and Nick had been so very happy.

"Because someone unfairly took her from you, Jo. They stole her from all of us. You have to give yourself some grace."

"Grace?" Jo clasped her hands in front of her. "I don't have time for grace. The focus should only be on her. I have to remain strong for her."

Rose's hand rested on Jo's shoulder, giving a gentle squeeze.

"You are strong, Jo. You've always been strong," Rose said

"I don't know about that."

"You are," Rose stated more strongly. "Now, go out there and spend some time with your daughter. You won't get to know her while you are just watching from afar."

Lulu still enjoyed the outdoors, which warmed Nick's heart. When she was just a toddler, she always spent most of her day outside. She would pick up leaves or make mud pies. Lulu had always been creative. Today she made a circle with some leaves and flowers and kept throwing the ball inside of it for the dog to fetch.

Nick was pleased when he saw Jo coming outside to join them. She kept herself guarded, however, with her arms crossed over her chest and remaining a few steps back.

"What are you playing?" Jo asked.

"Circle catch," Lulu explained. Nick didn't miss the way Jo's face lit up when Lulu spoke directly to her.

"And how do we play?"

Lulu adjusted the flowers the dog's paws had messed up and placed them back in their perfect circle.

"You see, you throw the ball into the circle and then Butler fetches it," Lulu told her. "But if you throw out of the circle, you lose three points."

"What if you make it in?"

"Then you get five points. You get an extra three if Butler gets it and then brings it back to you."

"Ah," Jo smiled. "Can I have a turn?"

Lulu tugged on a piece of her hair, her eyes turning to Nick. He knew what she was thinking; she wanted it to just be the two of them. However, Nick wanted to facilitate the relationship between Jo and Lulu. He knew how much his wife loved their daughter and how much it would mean for them to bond and get along. Once Lulu felt more comfortable around them all, she would be much happier. The bond between her and her mother had always been strong, and he knew it would be amazing when it returned.

"Go on," he encouraged. He had the ball in his hands and handed it to Lulu, so she could give it to Jo.

With a sigh, Lulu stepped forward and gave the ball to Jo.

"Here you go," she said. "Make sure it gets in the circle. Also, you have to be further back."

"Where the stick is," Nick added.

Jo stepped back to the stick and tossed the ball into the circle. It landed perfectly inside of it, but then rolled out.

"Ah, close!" Nick clapped and laughed. Lulu joined in with the laughter as she rushed over to get the ball before Butler could snatch it and claim it as his own.

"It's okay. It's hard," Lulu told Jo. "Try again."

Jo smiled down at her daughter and took the ball. Once again, she threw it. This time it stayed inside the circle. Butler rushed to fetch it and then ran it to Lulu and dropped it.

"He likes me the best," Lulu explained.

"It's because you are the most fun," Jo said.

They played the game for over an hour. Nick basked in it being the first time in years they felt like a family, even if it was only for a little while. At one point, Jo met his eyes, and he was sure she felt the same. A part of him ached to bring her closer to her and kiss her cheek, but he knew he couldn't do that. Not right now, and probably not ever.

Once Jo had learned her daughter was coming home, she wanted to update the library they had for her. Jo took most of the books that she felt might be too young for Lulu and boxed them up, having them placed up in the attic. Then she grabbed several new picture books from the local bookstore as well as some shorter children's novels.

Tonight was the first night Lulu asked for someone to read to her. Jo found Lulu looking at the books when she peeked into the room from time to time, but anytime Jo had asked her if she would like her to read to her, Lulu would just say no thank you.

She was a polite little girl. It appeared, despite everything, that she had been taken care of and loved. In some ways, though, like her education, the woman had neglected her. Lulu would need years to catch up.

"Nick, will you read me a book?" Lulu asked, picking out one of the many books from her bookshelf.

"Of course I will," Nick said. He took the book from Lulu. She sat down on the bed and patted the mattress next to her for him to join. Jo remained in the doorway. She wanted to join them, but Lulu hadn't invited her.

It was quite the sight to see, as Lulu curled closer to him. They looked like father and daughter sharing a sweet moment. For a brief moment, Jo could pretend it had always been this way.

Jo's eyes searched around the room and her eyes couldn't help landing on the framed photo of Sally Cook and Lulu that still sat on top of Lulu's dresser. The peace left Jo upon seeing it, and her lips curled in anger. It took every ounce of will not to snatch it from the dresser and smash it on the ground. How could they live with that picture, that harsh reminder staring back at them every day?

"Jo?" She looked down to see Nick staring at her, worried.

"I was just remembering what I needed to get done for tomorrow," Jo lied. "Go on and finish the book. Lulu, would you like me to come back and tuck you in?"

"No, that's okay. I prefer to do it myself."

"Right," Jo said tightly. "All right."

She pushed herself off the doorframe and walked down the hallway. She could still hear Nick reading the book to their daughter. He had always been a talented storyteller. He knew how to make the listeners laugh and exaggerate the character's expressions and enunciations as he spoke. Laughter filled the room when Nick got to a particularly silly part.

Jo paused her steps. The laughter tempted her to walk back and peer in to see the expressions on their faces and enjoy their joy. But she thought better of it. This was one of those times when she had to allow Nick and Lulu to bond by themselves.

She found herself drawn toward the office where the divorce papers still sat. As she entered the room, she chewed down on her bottom lip, slowly making her way to her desk before sitting down. Jo lifted her pen. She had read over them many times by now and knew what all it said. She didn't need to read them over again. It was time. She'd waited too long. She needed to set Nick free from her.

Jo quickly signed her name on the first line. Then the second. There were many areas highlighted for her to either sign or initial and, by the time she finished, her fingers hurt. She placed the pen down and took a deep breath. This was it. She would give them to Nick, tell him they would figure out custody, and this would be over.

Yet as she stood, she couldn't do it. Quickly, she opened the top drawer of the desk and slid the papers inside. She closed it and found the key to lock it. She would keep them there for safekeeping until Nick asked for them. Yes, that made more sense. Tonight was not the night for that.

She walked out of the office and closed the door.

"I signed the papers," Jo admitted to her sister the next day. Vivian had taken a lunch break from her work to meet her sister downtown.

"What?" Vivian breathed. "Why would you do that now?"

Jo sighed and rolled her eyes.

"Why wouldn't I? You have been bugging me about signing them for months now," Jo reminded her sister.

Vivian pressed her hands firmly against the table.

"The only reason I had been asking you about signing the papers was that you two hadn't seen each other in years and Thomas was the messenger."

"Well, I signed them now."

"And what did Nick say?" Vivian just knew this had to have broken her brother-in-law's heart. How could it not?

"Well..." Jo paused. "I haven't told him yet. I'm keeping them locked in the office desk for now. He was reading a book with Lulu. I thought it would be rude to interrupt."

"Ah, yes," Vivian said, a gleam in her eye. "You didn't want to be rude."

Jo lifted her drink and took a sip, keeping her eyes on her sister.

"What do you mean by that?"

"You don't want to give him those papers."

"Yes, I do," Jo said strongly. "We're getting a divorce. Those papers are a formality. Of course, Thomas will probably need to help us write up a fair custody arrangement after Nick figures out where he is living."

"This is ridiculous. Lulu is back. You two love one another. Stop with the dramatics, admit it to one another, and start over."

"You don't understand," Jo sighed.

Vivian clenched her jaw. She paused for a moment and then said, "I do understand. I was there that day and the days after that. Don't forget that I was there for all of it. All. Of. It." Her eyes bore into her sister, which made Jo shift uncomfortably in her seat.

"I know," Jo whispered. Her finger pressed against the bottom of her eye and she blinked harshly. Vivian knew this was to keep her from crying, but Vivian wasn't about to back down. She had been cleaning up everything for five years now, trying to keep things as close to normal as possible.

Her phone dinged, and she saw it was a message from her husband, Thomas. She smiled. He had sent her a picture from work. He was always sending her goofy pictures and silly memes. He was her constant support while she supported her sister.

"It wouldn't be fair of me," Jo said suddenly. Vivian flicked her eyes up from her phone.

"Hm?"

"If I asked him to take me back," Jo quietly told her. "You know how horrible I was to him. He's rightfully moved on. I won't be that person."

Vivian frowned. "But you are his wife."

"Not for much longer."

Vivian stared at her sister for a long moment. She had more she wanted to say about her sister's marriage, but she decided to change the subject.

"How are things with Lulu?"

"It's going," Jo replied. "She's doing okay, I guess. We meet with the psychiatrist tomorrow. She'll talk with her and then we'll all go in and talk as a family. It is a bit overwhelming. I feel a bit... stuck."

"Stuck?"

"Like I don't know what comes next. I don't know what I should be doing."

"I think you're doing just fine. It's not like there's a parenting book about this."

"No," Jo said, "there's not."

Nick hung up his phone and placed it back in his back pocket. Eleanor had called him again to check in and, as always, he gave her a small update on how things were going. She asked for pictures and told him she was glad he was bonding with her daughter. She had also asked when she could come and visit. He didn't know how much longer he could push her back. She wasn't letting up.

"Um," a voice behind him made him turn. It was his father-in-law, Charlie. He held a plate in his hand and was trying to make it to the sink.

Nick moved out of the way, suddenly feeling awkward. Had Charlie heard him on the phone with Eleanor? He didn't even know if Jo's parents knew he had a girlfriend or if they knew about the upcoming divorce. He hadn't thought to ask Jo about it, and Thomas had never mentioned it.

For the past four years, he'd been a single man and not by choice. After losing Lulu and then Jo, Nick had resigned himself to no longer having a family. The family he gained when he married Jo no longer belonged to him.

When he met Eleanor, he found comfort in having her around. With Eleanor, there was little she asked for in return. They chatted a couple of times a week, texted sometimes, and only saw one another once in a while. It was easy, and it kept him from being lonely.

"Do you love my daughter?"

The question caught Nick off guard. He paused his movements and took in a deep breath.

"I've always loved Jo," he replied. "Always."

Charlie cleared his throat and nodded.

"But you love this... Eleanor, too?"

"I...." Nick didn't know how to respond. Did he love Eleanor? Or was she just there for him? "I'm not sure how that is any of your business."

"It's not," Charlie agreed. "Will you move out?"

"Yes," Nick answered. "I'm already looking for a place to stay." That was a lie. He hadn't even thought about leaving the house. He enjoyed being here in this house with his child and wife. Sometimes it almost felt like they were back to how they used to be. Just moments, but they were there.

"Good," Charlie said. "I think you should."

Nick headed toward the living room and saw Jo standing there. She must have just arrived back from her lunch with her sister. Jo stood still, her face covered in hurt. He looked back toward the kitchen and then at her. She must have overheard their conversation.

"Jo..." he started, but Jo put out her hands to make him stop.

"Where is Lulu?" she asked.

"Upstairs in her room, playing," Nick told her.

Jo nodded. "All right."

"Look, Jo..." He tried to start again.

"I think it's a good idea," she said. "You should find somewhere else to live, but let's ask Dr. Canmore about it first."

"Right," Nick frowned. "Yes, we'll ask her first."

"Good."

It hurt more than she expected. Jo made it upstairs and to her room, quickly closing the door behind her. Nick was planning on finding a place of his own. Why was that so shocking to her? Wasn't that what they had discussed? Didn't *she* sign the divorce papers just the night before?

Jo went to sit down at the edge of the bed, and she pressed her hands against her knees. She took in a deep breath, calming her heartbeat. This was okay. *This was how it was supposed to be,* she told herself.

A knock came at her door. She walked over to the door and opened it to find Nick standing on the other side. He held a bag that Jo didn't recognize.

"Your sister dropped this off," he explained. He handed it to her and her mouth opened to speak, but he'd already gone back into the guest room.

She closed the door and opened the bag. It was just her jacket that she had left at the restaurant. She plopped it onto the bed and walked into her bathroom. Her eyes met her own in the mirror and she scrutinized her face.

She placed her hands on her cheeks and pulled the skin of her face back before dropping her arms to her side and frowning. She looked sickly. No wonder Lulu wanted nothing to do with her. She looked like a ghost, unlike Nick, who had gotten in shape and looked like a normal person. She needed to get herself together. She couldn't be a mother when she hardly kept it together.

Jo lifted her cell phone and saw she had several texts from her sister.

YOU LEFT YOUR JACKET. I'M DROPPING IT OFF AT YOUR HOUSE.

DON'T GIVE HIM THE PAPERS, NOT YET.

I THINK YOU NEED TO THINK ABOUT THE FUTURE, ALL OF YOUR FUTURES.

TRUST ME. I'M YOUR SISTER.

I DROPPED OFF YOUR JACKET.

ARE YOU IGNORING ME?

FINE, IGNORE ME.

Jo rolled her eyes and then typed her sister a message.

SORRY, MY PHONE WAS ON SILENT. THANK YOU FOR MY JACKET. AND I HAVEN'T GIVEN HIM THE PAPERS YET. I'LL WAIT A LITTLE WHILE LONGER.

GOOD, Vivian replied.

Seventeen

Winter 201

The moment they got off the cruise ship, Jo found that the high from the trip was already fading. They returned to their car in the large parking lot. Nick opened the door for Jo and then placed all the bags in the trunk.

A deep sense of dread filled Jo's bones. That sense grew and grew every hour they got closer and closer to home. By the time they drove down the street they lived on, Jo had fallen completely quiet. Nick tried to hold her hand, but she tugged it away.

"We're home," Nick whispered as they pulled into the driveway. Jo's breath hitched in her throat.

Nick opened his door before he walked over to open Jo's.

"I'll get the bags out. Why don't you go upstairs and rest?"

"All right," Jo croaked. She felt Nick's fingers brush against her shoulder, but she ignored it.

As she stepped into the house, guilt filled every ounce of her body. She had allowed herself to be happy. She had allowed herself to stop looking for her daughter. What was wrong with her?

Her feet took her upstairs, but she didn't go to her room. No, she ended up outside Lulu's room. What had she done? She pressed her hand against her mouth as she walked over toward the small, toddler-sized bed. She sat down and grabbed her stuffed unicorn. It still smelled like her daughter.

She rested against the pillow and closed her eyes. She hated herself.

Nick didn't know what had happened. They'd been home for two days now and Jo still hadn't left their bed. She wouldn't talk to him; he didn't understand. The two of them made some headway on their cruise, and he had thought they were heading toward some sort of closure so they could become a couple once again.

The gifts Jo's family left for Christmas sat in their living room untouched.

Feeling unsure of what to do, Nick sat down on the couch next to the presents. He ignored them and turned on the television. Lazily, he flipped through the channels, hoping to find something easy to watch. As he landed on the local news, his finger paused on the buttons. On the screen was a picture of him and his wife stepping off the cruise ship. Jo still wore a small smile on her face, with her arm around his waist.

"This Christmas, the Andersons left the loss of their daughter behind as they went on a Bahamian cruise. I

don't know about you, but do you think you could go on a cruise just months after the loss of your child?"

Nick shut off the television before standing. He threw the remote onto the couch out of anger. How dare they? These small-town reporters were relentless and ruthless, finding anything to use against them. Was this town so dull that their only entertainment was them?

If Jo saw this, it would kill her. He debated unplugging their cable just to make sure she didn't come across the story.

His hand ran through his hair as hot tears stung his eyes. The local press would never leave them alone. Every year, they would be the talk of the town. The grieving parents.

Taking a deep breath, Nick decided to go upstairs and check on his wife. He stepped into their bedroom to find her curled up away from the television. Nick was relieved; it didn't seem she'd seen the segment about their vacation.

He climbed into the bed beside her and brought his arms around her, pulling her close. He kissed the corner of her lips. She didn't move.

"I think being here is too hard for you, for us," Nick carefully said. Jo's shoulders slumped, but she didn't reply. "On that cruise ship, we could grieve, but we could laugh too. We found a bit of ourselves again, Jojo. Here, it's too hard," he said again. "Here, the memories suffocate us."

"I knew it," Jo whispered under her breath. She turned onto her back. Nick sat himself up slightly. Jo's eyes searched his face as she clenched her jaw.

"Knew what?"

"You did take me on that trip to try to get me to move away," she growled beneath her breath.

"No... Jojo...."

Jo swung her feet over the edge of the bed and she turned away from him. Nick moved closer, kissing the spot where her skin was bare.

"I love you, Jojo. I want the two of us to be happy."

"Happy?" Jo stood quickly, making him nearly fall forward. Nick caught himself with his hands and adjusted himself so he wouldn't fall off the bed.

"We aren't happy, Nick! We will never be fucking happy again. Don't you see that?"

Nick's eyes narrowed. "Why can't we ever be?"

"Because someone took our daughter from us! How can you be so stupid?" she threw back in his face. He didn't know what to say.

"I'm not happy," he said, defeated. "But I had moments of happiness with you on that cruise, Jojo. We can't just sit here in this purgatory for the rest of our lives." There was a hint of anger and impatience in his words.

"You don't understand," Jo cried, pressing her hands against her face and leaning forward slightly.

"I do," he disagreed. "I lost her, too."

"But..." Jo hesitated, turning to face him. "But I forgot her."

"What?" he breathed. Jo blinked, and a flood of tears slid down her cheeks.

"I.... I forgot her," Jo repeated. The tears continued. Nick's heart softened, and he cupped her cheeks, rubbing the tears away gently with his thumbs.

"What do you mean?"

"There were moments when I... I forgot her," Jo whispered.

"Oh, Jojo, no," he murmured. He inched her face up slightly so that she had to look at him. "You did not forget our daughter just because you were happy for a moment. You love Lulu with every ounce of your heart, Jojo. Lulu would not want you sitting alone in your misery. That isn't what our little girl would want."

"I.... I don't know anymore," Jo admitted, shaking her head. "I.... I don't know."

"Shh," Nick soothed. "I'm here." He dropped his hands from his wife's cheeks and brought his arms around her, drawing her against his chest. He just held her there for several moments, not saying a word.

Now that she admitted to him how she was feeling, he understood her actions more. He didn't know how he could fix this for her or them. What he knew was that they should leave. Being here made it harder for them both. His wife especially struggled with being here, and that was clear. He had seen parts of her return while they were away. That was how they would heal. They had to get out of this town.

Eventually, he convinced her to join him on the bed. She curled up against him and he was grateful that she was allowing it. They had a few more days before he had to go back to work. Perhaps, during those days, he could figure out what he could do to help his wife see they needed to move.

Vivian walked into her sister's home, unsurprised to see the presents still piled against the wall in the living room. Her sister hadn't even responded to her New Year's text, nor had she answered any of her phone calls. Her parents had called her earlier that morning, insisting that she go over because they also hadn't heard from Jo. This was Vivian's role. She didn't mind it. Though if it weren't for Thomas, she wasn't so sure she'd be able to manage her home life while also trying to keep tabs on her sister.

The key remained in her hand as she stepped further into the house. She found Jo sitting on the couch with a large blanket over her lap, eating popcorn. Nick was nowhere to be found. Jo glanced up.

"You can't just use my key whenever you want," she said with a sour face. Vivian raised her brows.

"I can when my sister doesn't respond to my texts or phone calls or Mom and Dad's," Vivian said pointedly. Jo just rolled her eyes, taking another handful of popcorn and eating it. "Where is Nick?"

"At work," Jo shrugged. "He left yesterday."

"He couldn't take more time off? How long is he away?"

Again, Jo shrugged.

"Surely he told you," Vivian said. She walked over to the couch and sat down next to her sister. But she only sat at the very edge. Jo had the couch covered in bags of food and some clothing that Vivian did not know if it was clean or dirty.

"I'm sure he did." Jo took another bite of her popcorn.

"Did your trip not go well?" Vivian asked. She didn't mention the news segment about the cruise, hoping Jo hadn't seen it.

"It went fine," Jo said.

"Are you going to keep being like this or tell me about your cruise with your husband?"

Jo placed the bowl of popcorn down next to her, and Vivian didn't miss how when she moved, it spilled over slightly; small pieces falling in between cushions. She shivered at the mess her sister made no attempt to clean up.

"We actually had a good time," Jo told her. "We enjoyed being with one another. The beaches were beautiful."

Vivian smiled. "Oh good!"

"And now..." Jo paused. "My...." She shook her head, deciding not to say it out loud.

"And now, what? You've realized how much you need your husband? You two are going to go to therapy? You're going to move away? Start anew?"

Jo frowned. "Oh my god! He has you in on it too! For heaven's sake. Did he send you over to talk me into moving, because it's not going to work?! I am not moving!"

"No," Vivian said steadily. "He hasn't spoken to me since the day you two got back from your vacation over a week ago to tell me you got home safe. Unlike you, who never said anything."

"Oh." Jo visibly deflated. She brought her knees up to her chest. "We've been arguing since our return. So I think that's why he went back to work."

"What have you been arguing about?"

"Moving. He wants to. I don't. I *won't*."

"You don't have to sell your house, Jo. You could just leave for a little while. This town is small, and it's like being under a microscope. I still have people stopping *me* when I'm out and about. I can't even imagine what it's like for you or Nick."

"At least they still remember her. At least maybe if they see something, they'll know and tell us."

Vivian took her sister's hand, surprised at how cold it felt despite the warmth of the room.

"I'm sure they will," she just said. Her eyes remained focused on her sister. She knew there had to be more she could do to help her. "Would you like to come and stay at my house for a few days? I hate to think of you here all alone."

"I'm fine," Jo said. "I have stayed here plenty by myself. It's a safe neighborhood."

"Okay. Well, at least let me get you something real to eat. Popcorn is not a meal," Vivian told her. She stood and picked up the bowl. Then she took it into the kitchen. It hadn't been cleaned in days.

She placed the bowl on the counter and looked for some food. She found nothing. She would need to order something. She quickly called the Chinese place down the road and placed an order before cleaning up the kitchen.

"You didn't have to do that," Jo said when she entered the kitchen twenty minutes later. "I was going to."

"I know you were. Our food should be here shortly."

"You're staying for dinner?"

"Of course I am," Vivian said.

When the food arrived, Vivian put their food on plates and set the table. She didn't know the last time her sister had a proper meal. But as they ate, she noted how her sister barely ate anything.

"Come on, now. Eat." Vivian pushed her plate closer toward her.

"Don't you have children you can baby instead of me?" Jo bit back.

"Fine, starve," Vivian quipped. Something about her tone or, she didn't know, her words, made Jo's lower lip quiver. Vivian immediately apologized. "I was only joking."

A few tears slipped from Jo's eyes. "I... I think I might be pregnant."

"Pregnant?" Vivian asked. She knew just how much her sister had wanted to be a mother and how much she had wanted to have a little brother or sister for Lulu. Vivian also knew right now her sister was not ready for another baby.

"I don't know, not for sure, anyway. And if I am, it's still very early," Jo sniffled.

"What did Nick say?"

"I haven't told him."

Vivian frowned. "You should call him, tell him, and ask him to come home."

"I can't be pregnant," Jo cried. "But then again, we weren't careful on our trip. We never just got pregnant before, so I didn't even think—"

"Shh," Vivian attempted to soothe, as she saw her sister getting close to hysterics. "Now, you don't even know that you are. Why don't you let me run to the store and get a test?"

"No. I... I can't do it."

Vivian chewed on her bottom lip.

"Okay. Well, how about we go back to your couch and watch a movie? I'll call Thomas and tell him I'll be back later."

"You don't have to babysit me. I'll be fine."

"It's not babysitting." Vivian rolled her eyes. "I am spending time with my sister. I want to spend time with you. Come on."

Jo awoke a bit disoriented in her room. She couldn't remember what time she went to bed. She turned to one side, reaching out her arm and remembering that Nick was out of town. Her head pounded, and she groaned. She perked up when she heard a noise in her bathroom. Grabbing her blanket, she wrapped it around herself and tiptoed toward the noise as her eyes searched for anything that could be a weapon.

However, as she stepped closer, she saw her sister digging through her cabinet in the bathroom.

"What are you doing?" Jo hissed. She had forgotten her sister spent the night in the guest room the night before. She ended up staying late and just decided it would be best to stay instead of driving that late.

"I know you have some," Vivian flippantly said, digging in the cabinet.

"Stop going through my private stuff!" Jo growled, pulling on her sister's shoulder to tug her away. Vivian didn't relent. It wasn't her style.

"Ah ha!" Vivian grinned. She lifted a box of pregnancy tests. "You were trying before Lulu went missing. I knew you'd have tests."

"They're probably expired," Jo said. She had zero desire to take one of them.

"They're not," Vivian said as she read the expiration date. "Now, take one."

"Why?" Jo sighed

"Because you think you might be pregnant. This will let you know for sure."

"I doubt I am," Jo said. "I'm only a few days late and.... and I don't get pregnant easily, as we know."

"Take it," Vivian stubbornly said to her. She forced Jo to hold the box. "I'll be right here in your room."

As the bathroom door closed her in the room alone, Jo glanced down at the box. She looked back at the door. She could easily lie, say she took it, so her sister would just leave her alone. However, there was a part of her that wanted to go ahead and take it. The whole *was she* or *wasn't she* was making her feel as though she was losing it.

She opened up the box and pulled out one of the tests. Taking the test brought back all the memories before she got pregnant with Lulu. She couldn't even count how many there had been, how many hopeful tests she had taken hoping to be pregnant.

Once done, she set the timer and placed it on the edge of the countertop. Then she walked outside the bathroom and sat by her sister, giving her the phone with her timer on it. The next three minutes felt like a lifetime. When it finally went off, Jo jumped.

"Want me to check?" Vivian offered. Jo nodded.

Vivian slid off the edge of the bed and walked into the bathroom. She came back a moment later. She gave Jo a solemn smile.

"Negative."

"That's good," Jo simply said, though the feeling in her chest said differently.

"Jo—"

"No, really, that's fantastic."

"It's still early..." Vivian tried.

"I didn't want to be pregnant. This is good news."

"Are you sure?" Vivian didn't sound convinced. "I can stay today, and we can eat ice cream and cry if you'd like. When will Nick be home?"

"Honestly, I'm fine," Jo lied. She lied a lot lately. Not maliciously, but because it was easier. "You should go home. Don't you have to work today?"

"It's a Sunday," Vivian reminded her.

"Right," Jo sighed.

"When is Nick coming home?" Vivian asked, yet again.

"I told you; I don't know." She had been told. She re-membered Nick kissing the top of her head and promising he would be home by a certain date. It was just that she couldn't remember what that date was, and she found she didn't care.

"I can call him," Vivian offered.

"Don't," Jo said sharply. "I don't need you being the go-between Nick and myself. I'll talk to him when he gets home. He'll be home soon enough."

"Oh, fine," Vivian sighed. "Are you sure you don't want me to stay with you today? The nanny is at my house, and Thomas can handle anything else that is needed."

"No, I just want to be alone. I should probably clean the place."

"Okay," Vivian said. "If that's what you want."

"It is."

Once she was alone, Jo allowed herself to cry. She hadn't expected to be torn up about not being pregnant. Now would not have been a good time to have a baby. She still wanted her daughter back. That pain was all-consuming. Would it even be right to bring a baby into this world right now with the way she and Nick were? With the loss of Lulu?

But it hurt her nonetheless. It was also a harsh reminder that the odds were that she wouldn't have any more children and that Lulu had been her only chance at motherhood.

She curled herself on the bed and let the tears fall. Then she heard the door being unlocked and quickly sat up. She wiped her cheeks with the tips of her fingers before rushing to the bathroom to hide the evidence of the test and wash her face.

"Jo?" she heard Nick call from downstairs.

"I'm up here!" she yelled from the bathroom. She scrubbed her face, hoping Nick wouldn't notice any of the signs of her crying.

When he entered the bathroom, he gave her a soft smile.

"I missed you, Jojo."

"I... I missed you, too," she whispered, not quite meeting his eyes.

"Did anything exciting happen while I was away?" Nick asked as he kissed the top of her head. Jo met his eyes in the mirror and smiled.

"No."

Eighteen

Early Spring 2017

"But I want to go to school," Lulu said, as Jo and Nick were explaining the plans for her homeschooling until the end of the year to get her caught up.

"You do?" Jo asked.

"I've always wanted to go," Lulu answered.

Jo looked at Nick, who shrugged, before turning back to their daughter.

"Well, you will go next year," Nick told her. "But right now, your mom is going to teach you. This is what we and Dr. Canmore think is best for your transition into school next year, since it's all very new to you."

Jo gave Nick a grateful smile for his support in this matter. She honestly wasn't quite ready to send Lulu to school. She knew her daughter needed to have as normal of a life as possible and make friends, but she couldn't bear the thought of sending her to school for several hours without her supervision. Wild thoughts of someone snatching her child away, yet again, always plagued the back of her mind.

"Oh okay," Lulu sighed. She glanced up when she saw her grandmother enter the room. "Where's Butler?"

"Still sleeping, my dear." Rose smiled. "He likes to sleep with your grandpa. The two of them nearly kicked me off the bed!"

Lulu giggled. She looked at Nick, who laughed along with her.

"Does he snore?" Lulu asked.

"Who? Your grandfather or Butler?"

Lulu pondered this before smiling widely and asking, "Both."

"Well, they both do. It gets quite loud at night," Rose admitted with a wink. "I tell you what. Why don't you go downstairs, grab Butler, and take him outside for a little bit?"

"Can I?"

"Of course," Rose said. "Maybe that'll get your grandfather up and moving, too. He's always been a bit of a night owl that doesn't like to wake up in the morning."

Lulu jumped up from the table and rushed downstairs.

"Will you go outside with her?" Jo asked Nick. "I need to start the laundry."

"I can't," Nick answered. "I have a meeting I need to get to."

"A meeting?" Jo asked. "I thought you weren't going back to work until after Lulu's birthday."

"I'm not," Nick quietly answered, his eyes falling to the table.

"Oh," Jo said as it hit her. He was going to look at apartments. "Well, Mom, can you sit outside with Lulu?"

"Dear, I can't. I have to start getting ready for the library. And I'll have to wake your father. I doubt he'll even notice

Butler leaving the bed. She can play outside by herself. You have a fence and a locked gate. She is nearly eight years old, Jo."

Jo shook her head. "I'm not letting her play outside alone."

"Jo, she's got to have some independence," her mother tried. Jo hated the way her mother spoke down to her. Her hands slammed against the table.

"She will not play outside alone," Jo nearly yelled.

"I... I think Jo's right," Nick cut between her and her mother. "We've already lost Lulu once. It's not worth the risk."

"Right," Rose awkwardly replied.

Lulu was back upstairs with Butler a second later and Jo stood from the table. She would have to do the laundry later and watch Lulu herself.

"Let me see it, darling," Eleanor's voice came through the phone. Nick turned the phone's camera so that Eleanor could have a better view of the apartment building he was looking at today. He didn't have many options in this small town in Georgia. He could go right outside of town and find plenty of homes or apartments for rent, but that would take him at least thirty minutes from Lulu. This was about his only option only ten minutes away.

"I know it's not much," he said to Eleanor as he walked up toward the building. He was meeting someone to show him around in about ten minutes. The apartment had seen better days.

He and Jo had lived here for a year after they had first gotten married. The apartments held a special place in his heart. They were a reminder of early love and happiness. Their very first fight had been right back in the courtyard. He couldn't remember what they'd fought about, but he could remember their make-up afterward.

"It's, um, quaint," Eleanor said, drawing him away from his memories. He turned the camera back to him.

"You're always good about finding the positives in even the worst situations."

"Couldn't you buy a house?"

"I probably will in time," he told Eleanor, "Once the divorce is finalized and we have all of that figured out. But for now, this is my best bet."

"Do you want to bring your daughter there to visit?"

It was a good question. Did he want Lulu to stay here? As he walked inside, he saw a lot of older people. It didn't even seem to be a family-friendly establishment. He double-checked the name to make sure it hadn't turned into a retirement community.

"It will do," he told her. "I'm sure the inside is better than the outside. I'll call you after I see the apartment. Goodbye."

"Au revoir," she said. Nick hung up the phone. He saw a man walking up toward him as his eyes scanned over the lobby. It wasn't terrible. Just dated.

He reached out and gave the man a shake.

"Would you like me to show you the apartment?"

"Yes, please."

"Your mother wasn't trying to step on your toes this morning," Charlie said as he sat down next to Jo on the bench outside.

"So, Mom has you doing her apologizing now?" she asked.

While there had been benefits of her parents living with her over the past four years, sometimes they did not outweigh the negatives. She was a grown woman, but they often treated her like a child. Jo always felt like she had to remind them she was an adult. It was why over the past year she had tried to convince them to move back to their home on the beach. She didn't understand why they insisted on staying here with her. Their grown daughter did not need her parents to take care of her, not anymore. She wasn't the same woman from when they came to stay with her all those years ago.

"No," Charlie said. "But don't be so hard on your mother, all right? She only cares about you and Lulu. She would never suggest anything if she thought it meant Lulu wouldn't be safe."

"I'm not letting her play outside by herself," Jo said quietly.

"I'm not telling you that you have to," Charlie replied. "I'm just saying, don't be so hard on your mom."

Charlie stood and patted Jo's back, making her huff. Her father slipped back inside, leaving Jo outside alone to watch Lulu. It's kind of how she preferred it, not having to further converse with anyone.

Jo used to enjoy talking to people. Now, she reveled in the quiet.

Once, there had been friends. Her group of friends had lived nearby. They did playdates with the children and girl nights out, but after she lost Lulu, her friends disappeared one by one. When Lulu was gone, Jo hid away. Even when some of her friends tried to reach out, she ignored their attempts.

She ended up getting a new phone number, only letting Nick, her sister, and her parents know what it was. She'd also told the station, in case they ever found out anything about Lulu.

So if any of her old friends had tried to reach out after finding out Lulu was alive, she wouldn't know. She knew two friends had come by the house and left small gifts. She hadn't answered the door. Her mother relayed the messages with the gifts. Jo knew she should take the time to contact them back, but she didn't know what she would say.

"Lulu," Jo called out, standing. "Come on, we should go inside and get something to eat."

"Can we go somewhere today?" Lulu asked, walking inside with Butler. "It's boring just staying here all day, every day."

Jo brought her thumb up to her mouth to chew on the edge before walking over to the front window to peer outside. Reporters were over in the neighbors' yards, just waiting to see the girl who had been found.

"Not right now," Jo answered. She hated feeling like a prisoner in their own home. Right now, it seemed the only safe place for them was the hospital where they met with the therapist. If they tried to go anywhere else, reporters bombarded them.

"You are never any fun," Lulu pouted. Jo opened her mouth to speak, but found she didn't know what to say. Lulu just ran up the stairs, leaving Jo all alone to stew in her thoughts.

"Do you really think that's where you should live?" Eleanor asked over the phone. Nick kicked a rock that was in front of him and shrugged his shoulders.

"It's not that bad," Nick explained. As he walked toward his car, he saw a man with a camera who snapped a quick picture. Before Nick could tell him off, the man had already disappeared. Who knew what would show up in the papers now with that picture?

It didn't matter. He didn't read the papers or watch the news. As far as he could tell, Jo didn't either. They were especially careful around Lulu to protect her from all of it.

"You don't even have a kitchen," Eleanor said.

"There's a kitchen," he disagreed.

"With no stove? And just a tiny little fridge?"

"It's enough for me," he argued. "I'll get a microwave. I travel a lot with my job."

"Do you think Jo will be okay with you bringing your daughter there?"

Nick stopped walking and thought over Eleanor's question.

"She won't have a choice, now will she?"

"Have you two even discussed what custody will look like? Does Lulu know, yet?"

"No," Nick simply answered. He made it to his car and got inside. His free hand rubbed at his temple. He still had many details to figure out.

"When will you tell her?"

"I'm not sure," Nick said. "But I signed the lease and put down the deposit. I can start setting up the apartment in a week. I guess we'll figure it out then."

"And you'll ask Jo about the divorce papers?"

"Yes," Nick replied sternly. He was glad Eleanor couldn't see him right now. The pain was etched on his face. "I will."

"I'm not sure that was the right way to say it," Vivian said to her mother as she sat with them at her house. Callie was singing a song at the top of her lungs, adding to Vivian's headache that she had woken up to. Thomas was off at work, and TJ was at school.

"Your mother is just trying to help your sister see how overprotective she's being," Charlie stood up for his wife. "I told Jo as such."

Vivian rolled her eyes. Why was she always the one in the middle of all these relationships?

"I think she has every right to be protective. Lulu hasn't even been home that long. Give her time to adjust. I doubt she'll follow Lulu to college. It'll all work out."

Rose wrung her hands, unsure.

"Mom, truly, it'll be all right," Vivian continued. "Just give her some space, please. Why don't you both stay here for a little while or, I don't know, go to your house?"

"We can't leave Jo," her mother said, shaking her head.

Vivian rose a brow before chuckling. "Mom, you do realize you're acting just like Jo is with Lulu? You criticize her for not letting Lulu out of her sight when Jo is a grown woman and you won't leave her side."

"It's different," her mother protested.

"It's not."

"Vivi is right," Charlie said, earning a side eye from Rose.

"Mom, it's time for you to let Jo figure it out. She's an adult. Plus, Nick is back."

"For how long?" Charlie countered. Vivian sighed.

"He won't leave. Lulu is back. He is a wonderful father," she reminded her father. Charlie made a discernable face and tutted his tongue.

"I guess," Charlie said.

"He won't," Vivian strongly stated. "He will stay here with Jo and Lulu."

"And his other woman?" Rose asked.

"What about her? You know Jo and Nick are getting a divorce. We can't do much about that, but be supportive. I am glad Nick is going to be back here. I, for one, missed him."

"Yes, I did too," Rose had to agree.

Charlie just huffed.

"Dad, be nice," Vivian said. Then she turned to Callie, who had begun her next set of songs. "Darling, please, can you find something quieter to do while we're talking?"

Callie paused before answering, "No."

Vivian's headache only grew.

Jo heard the door open, and she busied herself with the dishes. There wasn't much to do. She'd been cleaning all day. Being stuck inside made her focus on all the little details of the house. Lulu didn't want to spend much time with her and so she was often alone if everyone else had things to do.

She lifted the clean plate and grabbed a sponge to wipe it, yet again.

"How was the apartment?" Jo tried not to sound too curious. She wanted to act as though this was no big deal. And it wasn't. The two of them were no longer a couple. They only shared a child together.

"It was... an apartment," Nick simply said. He entered the kitchen and grabbed a drink from the refrigerator.

"Yeah, I know the ones you are talking about," Jo replied. They had lived in them when they first got married and it was a dump *then*. She couldn't imagine now, fifteen years later, how they would look. Yet, some of her best memories were of that place. She grinned, thinking about the time they accidentally caused a hole in the wall trying to hang up a picture.

"You know," she began a beat later, "we could sell this house and each get a modest house in another smaller neighborhood. Maybe even a duplex. You live on one side, and I live on the other."

"No," Nick said with a shake of his head. "This is Lulu's home."

"I could always move out. I am looking for a job," Jo told him. She worked part time, but she knew it was past time for her to find a full-time job to support herself and Lulu. It wasn't fair to keep relying on others to take care of her.

"I'm not sure that's a good idea," Nick disagreed. "Lulu just got back. I think you should stay home with her until she settles in. Maybe in a year, but for now, I personally would like you to stay home."

Jo frowned.

"I'm not telling you what to do," Nick added. "If you want to go to work, then fine, but I think deep down you agree with me. One of us needs to be at home as she adjusts and it should be you."

"Lulu doesn't even like me," Jo said.

"She likes you."

"She doesn't." Jo took a deep breath. "She doesn't, not at all."

"What about homeschooling her?"

"I'll homeschool now and start working when she starts school in the fall," Jo explained. "Maybe I can find something that works within the school hours or even go back to teaching. I don't know...."

"All right," Nick replied. "If that's what you want."

"It is." Jo set down the plate that was extra clean now and tapped her fingers against the counter. "You could live..." She paused, realizing that was not a good suggestion. Nick had a girlfriend. It would be awkward if he brought her here, in this house. "Never mind. I'm sure you will spruce up the place. The apartments have a pool, right?"

"Yup."

"I don't even know if Lulu can swim."

"We'll teach her," he promised.

"Yes, or hire someone who can." Then she made a face. "Is the pool clean at the apartments?" This made Nick laugh.

"No, I don't think we'll be letting her swim there."

For a moment, the two of them met eyes and the laughter between them was like it had been before. Jo thought of how much everything had changed and for a moment, her heart ached for the time before they lost everything.

"Oh, you're home!" Lulu was running down the stairs. "Can we go for a walk? Can we take Butler?" she asked Nick directly.

"I don't know..." Jo began.

"Yes," Nick answered, causing Lulu to jump up and down and clap her hands. "Go, get his leash." He turned to Jo. "I already checked. No one is out there right now. She's getting antsy from being here all the time. I won't let anyone bother us."

Jo slowly breathed in before nodding. "All right. I trust you."

The two of them walked down the street on the sidewalk while Lulu led Butler on his leash. It was late afternoon, and Nick kept his eyes peeled out for any reporters or cameramen. They were being left alone, though he noted some neighbors looking between blinds or from their front porches.

"When I was a little girl, did we have a dog?" Lulu asked.

"No," Nick answered.

"Why not?"

"Well, your mom had to take care of you and I had to be away from work a lot. We did discuss getting one when you were older," he said.

"Oh. Why don't I have any brothers or sisters?"

Nick had not been expecting the hard-hitting questions. He sighed before adjusting Lulu's hand within his own and continuing down their path.

"We wanted to have more children," he honestly answered, "but we weren't able to have any more."

"Oh."

They turned the corner to be accosted by a man with a camera, who stuck it nearly in Lulu's face. Immediately, Nick lifted her and pushed the man away from them.

"Lulu!" the man called out. "What's it like being home? Can you tell us about the woman who took you?"

"Leave my daughter alone," Nick warned. He pivoted around and told Lulu to hide her face in his shoulder. They rushed back to the house with Butler running by Nick's side. He went through a neighbor's yard, hoping it would deter the reporter from following them.

When they finally reached the house, Nick placed Lulu down and closed the door behind them, glad to see they hadn't been followed. His chest heaved up and down with the adrenaline. Jo stood in the foyer with her hands on her hips, concerned.

"What happened?"

"There was this guy with a camera. Daddy yelled at him!" Lulu explained. She giggled and ran off behind Butler to take off his collar. Nick noticed the way Jo's expression flickered between joy and hurt at Lulu calling him Daddy.

Then it hit him. His daughter had called him Daddy for the first time in five years.

"What happened?" Jo then asked.

"A reporter," Nick groaned. "I pushed him away, picked Lulu up, and rushed back here."

"They are ruthless," Jo said. "Come on." She waved him toward the kitchen. "Let's get you something to drink. You look flushed."

They went into the kitchen, where Jo prepared him a large glass of ice water. She placed it down in front of him and took a seat.

"They won't leave us alone," Jo said.

"They won't," he agreed.

"Perhaps we could go somewhere?" Jo suggested. "Just for a week; Lulu needs a break from all the craziness here."

"But where would we go?"

"Go to our house!" Rose called out from the living room. Nick didn't even realize that his in-laws were back at the house. He heard his mother-in-law's footsteps and soon saw her in the doorway between the kitchen and living room. "You both should go down to the beach, go to St. Simons. It's beautiful there. You can take Butler with you."

"Won't someone be staying there?" Jo asked. Then she turned to Nick to explain, "They use it as an Airbnb most of the year now."

"Not this week. It's free and I'll block the dates. You guys could celebrate Lulu's birthday there. We'll be upset about missing it, but it would be better than being harassed every time you leave the house."

Nick looked at Jo, who asked, "What do you think?"

"Sure, why not?"

"Then it's all settled. You can leave as early as tomorrow. It was just cleaned today."

Nineteen

Spring 2013

Nick felt as though he was living in some sort of limbo. He went to work, came back home, fought with his wife, slept in the basement, and then repeated it every week. He couldn't remember the last time he and his wife had spoken to one another in a way that wasn't rude. Even if he tried, he would get back a snappy retort. It didn't even seem worth it.

Their daughter's fourth birthday was drawing close. He needed to find a way to talk with his wife to discuss what they should do that day. She kept herself locked upstairs most of the time. It was rare to see her out and around the house and even rarer to see her outside. She had stopped therapy. She had stopped talking to her sister and her parents.

He made his way up the stairs and knocked on the bedroom door.

"Come in," Jo said. He pushed the door open to find his wife sitting on the bench by the window. She held a book, but it didn't appear that she was reading it. He wondered what she did locked up here every day. He wasn't even sure that he had seen her eat anything in weeks.

"Are you leaving again?" she asked, placing the book beside her. He walked closer to Jo and took a seat beside her on the bench. She was hardly recognizable. She'd lost too much weight and the bags beneath her eyes were dark. Was she even sleeping?

"No," he whispered. "I was wondering what you wanted to do for Lulu's birthday." Jo glanced down at her fingers, picking at the skin in her nail beds—though they were already shredded.

"Oh."

"We don't have to do anything, but I thought...."

"No, we should do something," Jo agreed. "But just us. I don't want you inviting my family."

"Is there a reason you aren't talking with them?" Nick asked.

Jo shrugged. "There's nothing to say."

Nick wanted to ask more about it, but decided that now was not the time. That could be sorted out later.

"I was thinking we could go out to eat and then down by the park she liked. Just a day to honor her and remember her."

"That could be nice," Jo whispered.

"I didn't know if we should buy some toys to donate to a shelter or somewhere in honor of her, too," Nick also suggested. That made Jo smile slightly.

"I think that's a good idea," she said. Jo rested her head on Nick's shoulder. He breathed the scent of her in, grateful for this rare, nice moment between the two of them.

Nick knocked on his sister- and brother-in-law's door. Thomas answered. If Nick were, to be honest, he'd say he was a bit dull. He was a good guy, don't get him wrong, it was just that he didn't seem to have much of a personality. Perhaps there was another side Vivian saw; the two of them appeared to be happy.

"Hi, Thomas," he greeted. "Is Vivian home?"

"She is," Thomas answered. "But she's upstairs getting ready for a girls' date with some of her friends," he added.

Oh right, Nick thought. *Other people had lives.* He sometimes forgot what it had been like before his daughter went missing. Before there had been friends and get-togethers. He sometimes forgot that Vivian and Thomas's lives still went on outside of them.

"Can I help you?" Thomas offered.

"No, but could please ask Vivian to call me when she has a chance? I want to talk with her about Jo. But no rush."

"Okay."

"Thank you, Thomas."

Nick made his way back to his car. As he was opening his door, he heard Vivian calling out for him. He paused with his hand on the door handle and looked up to see her rushing out toward his car.

"Is everything all right?" she asked, breathless.

"Yes, I told Thomas that it wasn't an emergency," Nick answered. "You're busy; I don't want to take up your time."

"No, it's okay. I don't have to meet my friends for another hour. What's going on?"

Nick knew he shouldn't have come here. It wasn't fair for him to put Vivian between him and Jo. It was just that she seemed to be the only person who cared whether or not he and his wife survived.

"Nick, what is it?" Vivian pushed more, crossing her arms over her chest.

"I just... I don't know what to do anymore," he admitted.

The corners of Vivian's mouth curled downwards.

"I know. She's been worse lately," Vivian said. Nick was glad that he wasn't the only one who had noticed. "Do you think it could have anything to do with when she thought she might be pregnant? Maybe that messed with her head?"

"What?" Nick breathed. "Pregnant? When did she... when did Jo think she was pregnant?"

Vivian's jaw dropped, and she took in a long breath.

"Oh, I assumed...." Vivian paused. "I thought she told you. I didn't know."

"No," Nick was curt. "She didn't tell me."

"Nick, she probably just didn't want to upset you and—"

"No, it's fine," he quipped. "I.... I should go. Have fun tonight."

"Nick...."

Nick got into the car, closed the door, and turned on the engine before he could hear what else Vivian had to say. He wasn't angry with her. It wasn't her job to tell her everything that happened with Jo.

It had to have been a while back; they hadn't made love since the cruise. Why didn't she tell him?

He hardly realized he had made it home until he pulled into the driveway. Jo's car was still there in its spot, like it had been for months.

Nick stepped out of his car and locked the door before heading inside. He needed to speak with his wife and find out why she was hiding things from him.

When he walked inside the house, the anger deflated. He found Jo in the kitchen icing a cake and beside the cake sat a number four candle and unicorn sprinkles. Lulu's fourth birthday was in just two days.

"Hey," he mumbled.

"Hi."

"You're making a cake?" he asked. He moved up closer toward Jo and rested his head on her shoulder. For the first time in forever, she didn't tense when he touched her.

"I thought it might be nice," she whispered.

Nick smiled. "It is nice. Lulu would have loved it."

"I... I think so too," Jo nodded. She put down the knife and picked up the purple number four. Nick watched as she carefully sat it in the middle of the lopsided circle cake. Jo had never been much of a baker.

Jo making the cake this year felt bittersweet. For one, Nick knew that Lulu would have loved this cake just as much, even if it wasn't extravagant. She would have been excited about the sprinkles and the icing that her mother had taken care to put on top. It was also bittersweet because Jo, who had stayed locked up for months, was putting so much care into this cake that their daughter would never see.

He straightened up and pressed a kiss on the top of Jo's head. She turned, surprising him, and cupped his cheeks. Her hands were cold. He brought one of her hands to his lips and kissed the tips of her fingers.

"Will you make some figures for the top?" Jo asked him. "I found some fondant at the store."

"You went to the store?"   He couldn't believe it.

"Just for a few things," Jo said. She pulled out the fondant and handed it to Nick. "I thought maybe a unicorn and a rainbow."

"Sure."

Jo remained at his side while he formed the items with the fondant. He took time and care, as though Lulu would be inspecting them after he was finished.

"It's perfect," Jo whispered when he placed them on the cake.

"She would like it," Nick said quietly.

"She would *love* it." Jo melted against his side. He brought his arms around her and held her close. They remained there for several minutes, looking at the cake.

Jo shuddered, and she slowly pulled away from Nick, leaving him feeling bare. He watched as his wife headed back up the stairs. He waited for the distinctive sound of the door shutting behind her, but it never came.

Curious, he followed her path up the stairs to find their bedroom door wide open. Jo was going through the dresser in search of something. When Jo realized he was at the door, she stopped what she was doing.

"I don't know what to wear for her birthday," she admitted.

"Wear whatever you wish," Nick said.

She turned her head to face him.

"Will you sleep in the same bed with me tonight?"

"Of course."

Waking up on her daughter's birthday, Jo felt heavy. She turned onto her back and glanced up at the ceiling. She didn't know if she could do it. How was she supposed to live in a world without her daughter?

A hand came over her stomach and she turned to see Nick lying beside her. He held his head up on his other hand and his eyes were on her intently. She shuddered slightly.

"We don't have to do anything today," he whispered to her.

"We do," Jo disagreed. "It's her birthday." As she said it, a hot tear slid down her cheek. Nick's fingers moved from her stomach up to her cheek to wipe away the tear with the pad of his thumb.

"And we can celebrate that however we want," he reminded her.

Jo turned slightly to face her husband. He hadn't shaved in days and so he had hair covering his cheeks and chin. Her fingers reached out toward it. He used to never let it grow, but since Lulu's disappearance, he went long stretches between shaving it.

"I know; I need to shave," he lightly chuckled.

"No, I like it," Jo said. "Don't."

"All right. If that's what you'd like."

"I would." She felt her throat closing up from the tears and Nick seemed to notice as well, because he placed his hand behind her neck to draw her into his chest. She let out a low sob.

The two of them remained like that for a good while until their stomachs growled and the bright sun filled their room.

"I could go and grab us some food?" Nick offered.

"No, let's do as we planned. Lulu deserves that."

It was a warm day, and Nick regretted putting on a sweatshirt. He pushed up his sleeves and sat down next to his wife on the bench. They said little between them, but they were together. It was one of those moments when Nick felt hope again. If these moments could keep happening, then he could believe that he and Jo would be okay one day. He could believe that she still needed him and wanted him.

"Let's go for a walk," Jo suggested.

He stood. There was a path around the playground and up through the trees in the back. It was a simple path so that families could take their children for a small hike to tire them out. Lulu had always enjoyed going on the hike, searching for rocks and leaves. Sometimes she would even find the odd bug or two. She had never been afraid of little creatures.

"I've been thinking," Jo said as they turned a curve on the path. "That we should hire another private detective."

Nick stopped walking.

"What?" he breathed.

"It's been nine months since her disappearance. The police and the detectives have clearly given up. It's time we tried again."

Nick tightened his jaw. Jo slipped from his hold, and she tugged on her fingers. He could see the nervousness in her body and how she shifted uneasily from foot to foot. He had been foolish to have hope for their future. She was slipping further and further away.

"Jojo," he carefully stated. "Our daughter is gone."

Jo's shoulders tensed. Her back straightened, and she dropped her hands to her side.

"Yes, she was taken from us," Jo bit.

"Honey," he breathed, stepping forward. "We have heard the facts of the case. She died that day in the river."

"No!" Jo yelled, harshly. "No! She's not dead! Our daughter is not dead!"

"I wish that was true," Nick said.

Tears made their way down Jo's cheeks, but she didn't make any effort to wipe them away. Instead, she creased her brows and her cheeks turned dark red.

"Why is it so easy for you to give up?"

Her words pierced through his heart.

"Give up? I would never."

"She's still out there. I know it." She hit her hand against her chest. "No one believes me. *No one.*"

"Jojo...."

"We should just go home. This was a bad idea."

That night, Nick slept in the basement again as usual. They had finished this basement for Jo's parents when they came to visit, but they hadn't stayed with them since Lulu's disappearance. Anytime they came for a visit, they stayed with Vivian. It was probably better that way.

Rose called him today to check in on him. He was grateful for her. It was nice to have someone who cared about him as much as she did. She never made him feel like just a guy who married her daughter. No, she made him feel like he was her son.

He couldn't sleep. He needed something to drink. So he grabbed his robe and made his way upstairs to the kitchen. He pulled down a cup to pour some water into it.

As he walked past the garbage can, he noticed the top was slightly ajar. He pulled it aside to adjust the top. That was when he saw that the cake he and Jo had so carefully decorated had been torn into pieces and thrown inside. The unicorn's head had been pulled off and smashed. His heart clenched. It was becoming harder not to give up.

Twenty

SPRING 2017

"Wow," Lulu said. As they drove over the large bridge that led onto the island of St. Simons, she stared out the window with large, wide eyes.

"Yes, your grandparents have a house right on the beach," Jo explained with a smile. She couldn't stop watching as her daughter took this all in. Based on her response to seeing the water, it was clear she had not seen the ocean in the years that she was away. They had brought Lulu a few times when she was a small child, but she wouldn't have remembered that now.

"Will we get to play on the beach?"

"Yes," Nick said. "But it might be a bit cold for swimming."

"That's okay," Lulu replied. "I don't mind the cold."

They came to the other side of the bridge, and Jo had to look at her phone for directions. She hadn't visited in over five years. Every year since they'd moved into her house, her parents tried to get her to come with them for a week in the summer, but Jo always refused. She hadn't been able to leave the house. This was her first vacation since she and Nick had gone on that cruise four and a half years ago.

"Um, take a right," Jo said. Nick pulled into the right lane and that's when Jo realized her mistake. "Wait, I meant left."

Nick looked up at her with a gleam in his eye. She had always been terrible at giving directions.

"Sorry," she told him. He just shrugged and then tried to get over to the left lane. It was impossible, so they had to go down a road to turn back around.

After a few wrong turns, they finally made it to her parent's place. It was a small but quaint house.

"Why is the house so high up?" Lulu asked, pointing to the stairs that led up to the front door.

"For flooding reasons," Nick explained from the trunk of the car as he lifted out all their luggage.

"It floods?" Lulu's eyes widened.

"Don't worry. It won't while we are here. We will be safe," she promised. "Come on, let me show you the house."

It made Jo happy to see Lulu so eager to see the house and to be on this vacation with them. Perhaps this was just what they needed.

When they entered the house, the beachside décor accosted them. Jo had forgotten how her parents went overboard with all the decorations. Every wall of the house had photos of the beach. But it was nice, not too tacky.

Right up front was an old picture of their family. It was her last time here at the beach. The entire family had come down that summer for the week. In the photo, Vivian was visibly pregnant with Callie, TJ was in Thomas's arms, and Lulu was held between her and Nick.

She stared at the photo for a long minute before Butler's bark reminded her to finish the tour of the house.

The house had two bedrooms, each with a queen bed and a pull-out couch in the living room. When they had all last visited, her parents had insisted they all stay in the house. She recalled how crowded it was. They had been on top of one another. On the last night, Vivian announced they were staying in a hotel.

"Where should I put the bags?" Nick asked.

"Um.... What room do you want? I'll sleep on the couch. You can have one room and Lulu can have the other," Jo told him.

"Don't be silly. You have your parents' room. Lulu can have the guest room. I'll sleep on the pull-out couch."

"Nick, your back," Jo disagreed.

"Remember when we all slept on that couch when your parents insisted we all stay here?"

Jo laughed. "I do."

"I think I can handle it by myself," he winked.

"Oh, all right."

She then found Lulu standing at the back door, looking out the window and at the ocean with her fingers on the glass as though she could almost feel the waves.

"Why don't we take her down to the beach first," Jo said, pointing to their daughter. "It's been a long drive. We should probably stretch our legs."

"Yes, that sounds like a fantastic idea."

Lulu's giggles filled the air as she stepped forward, tipping her toes in and allowing the waves to crash over her feet before running back to the sand. She did this repeatedly, and Nick worried about her toes being cold with the nip in the air.

He held her shoes in one hand, while his other kept Butler on his leash.

Jo kept a suitable distance between him and her. It was something he quickly noticed. She was there with them, but made it clear that she was not with him. It was probably better that way, so they wouldn't confuse one another about what they were. They did plenty of that before they split up.

"There are no reporters here," Jo said over the sound of the crashing waves.

"No, there's not," Nick replied with a smile. "We can go out and do things."

"Yes," Jo agreed. Then they lapsed back into silence.

Thankfully, most of their silence was short-lived. Lulu was much chattier than she had been before they arrived at the beach. She kept running up to them and asking them an odd question here and there about the beach and what they would do while they were here. She seemed thrilled that they had come. It made him wonder if this was the first vacation she could remember. The first one she'd had since she'd been stripped away from them.

"Should we walk down to the pier to get something for dinner?" Nick asked as the sun started to set, and it grew chillier outside.

"I... I'm not sure what places allow a dog," Jo said, tugging on her fingers. "I know some do, but..."

"We could always leave him at the house."

"Right." Jo nodded. "All right. Let's take him back, put on some warmer clothes, and walk down to the pier. That sounds fun."

Thankfully, it was right before Spring Break season and so the college students had not yet overcrowded the restaurants. They found a place to eat easily. For a moment, they felt like a proper family, much like they had before they lost Lulu. No one recognized them, because even though Jo was sure others had seen them on the news, to the casual observer they just looked like any family going out for dinner.

Lulu ate every bite of her grilled cheese and French fries, showing that their time out on the beach had worked up her appetite. Jo munched on her sandwich but found that she was jealous of Nick's fried shrimp.

"Come on, have some," he encouraged, reading her mind. He slid his basket toward her and Jo took out one.

"Oh, I'm definitely getting this next time," Jo said.

She reveled in this moment, knowing that this week might be their only one like this. When they returned, they would have to discuss what the future held for them. But for right now, they could just enjoy being the family they once were. For a while, they didn't have to remember all the dark details that had led to their demise.

"Are you sure you want to sleep out here?" Jo asked as she handed Nick some more blankets from the closet. "We could... I mean..." Nick noticed the way her cheeks blushed.

"I'll be fine," he promised. He took the blankets and sheets, ready to make up the bed for him to sleep on that night. Butler had already claimed the edge of the bed, and he had to ease the sleeping pup off to place the sheets over the mattress.

"Today was a good day," Jo commented.

"It was."

"I think she's happy."

"I think so, too," Nick said.

"I just hope she'll always be happy with us," Jo added. "Not just when we're on a vacation."

"She will be."

"I hope so." She took in a deep breath. "Good night, Nick."

"Good night, Jo."

Nick finished making up the bed and then grabbed his water before lying down. It was only nine o'clock. He turned on the television and searched for something to watch.

About an hour later, he heard a door open. He looked up to find Lulu walking down the hallway, yawning. She paused at the end, surprised to find Nick on a bed in the middle of the living room.

"Is everything all right?" he asked her.

"I couldn't sleep." Lulu climbed up onto the chair next to him.

"Ah, probably all the excitement. Why don't I get you a snack?"

He got off the bed and walked into the small kitchen to search for the snacks Jo had brought with them. He found some crackers and brought them back to Lulu. She gratefully took them before tilting her head to the side.

"Why are you sleeping out here and not with Jo? Aren't you married?"

"Oh, I snore a lot," he simply said. Nick was not about to be the one to tell her the truth, not right now and not without Jo's input. "So I decided to sleep out here so your mom could sleep better while we're on vacation."

"Oh," Lulu said. It seemed to be a good enough explanation for her. She sat on the chair next to the sofa bed and munched on the crackers. "Is that me in the picture over there?" Lulu asked, pointing to the large family picture up front.

"It is," Nick smiled.

"And my cousin, TJ? Aunt Vivian? Uncle Thomas? Grandma and Grandpa?"

"Yes, the whole family."

"Where is Callie?"

"Your aunt was pregnant with her," Nick explained.

"Oh, right. Did we come here a lot?"

"We came a few times," Nick said. "The first time was when you were eight months old. You cried a lot." Nick smiled at the memory. At the time, he and Jo were spent. They had not expected Lulu to be so difficult just because she wasn't in her own home or bed.

"Did you get angry at me?" Lulu wrinkled her brow.

"Oh no, not at all. We just took turns walking you outside, back and forth. It was the only thing that calmed you down. Then we waited another year and a half before coming back. You liked it much better that time."

"Oh," Lulu said, biting down on her lip. "Where did you get my name from?"

At that question, Nick smiled.

"You were named after my mother, Louisa," he said.

"So my full name is Louisa Anderson?"

"Yes. We decided to call you Lulu for short. Louisa felt like such a big name for a little girl."

"And where is Grandmother Louisa?"

"Sadly, she passed away a long time ago. But she would have loved you, Lulu. She and your grandfather both."

Lulu chewed on the side of her lip.

"I wish I could have met them."

"Me too."

"Well, I should probably go back to sleep," Lulu said with a yawn. She placed the wrapper on the table beside her. "Will we come back here again?"

"I'm sure we will," he promised. That made Lulu smile brightly.

"Good! I love it here." With that, she skipped back to the room. He waited until she shut her door to lie back down. Then he turned off the television. It was probably best that he tried to go to sleep. He was sure she would be up early, ready to start her day. He would need his rest.

The crash of the waves was a wonderful sound to wake up to. Jo happily turned onto her back before raising her arms as she yawned. She smiled and sat herself up before walking over toward the window of her parents' bedroom. It looked right out to the ocean. It was a gorgeous day outside. The sun was already up high and she could see a young couple walking along the beach with their dog.

Jo grabbed her robe off the chair by the window and threw it on. As she walked out into the hallway, she saw that Lulu's door was still closed. Nick, though, was up. He had already tucked his bed back into the couch, with the blankets neatly folded. He sat at the kitchen table on his laptop. Whatever he was doing appeared to be important because he was staring intently at the screen as his fingers typed quickly on the keys.

"Work?" Jo questioned. Nick glanced up from his laptop and nodded.

"Yes. Just a small job," he answered. He typed a few more keys before hitting a button with his mouse and shutting his laptop.

"Do you miss Chicago?" Jo then asked, walking over toward the kitchen to start the coffee pot. She didn't care for the taste of coffee, but she enjoyed the smell. It was something they had started when they married. Jo would make it and he would drink it.

"No, not really," Nick said. "I like the city, don't get me wrong. But Georgia is home."

Jo cocked her head slightly at his words. Nick had not grown up in Georgia or anywhere, really. He moved around a lot of his life. They met because he had joined the Army and ended up at Fort Benning. Nick had only planned on spending a few years in the Army. When they met, he was already finishing up his last weeks. He ended up staying in Georgia to be with Jo. It made Jo wonder if he meant Georgia was his home or her and Lulu.

"I bet you miss Eleanor," Jo said. She knew she was walking on a thin tightrope now. Asking about Eleanor was none of her business. She justified it by telling herself that they would all need to get along for Lulu's sake. It was best she played nice and didn't allow herself to sound or be jealous of her.

"Yeah," Nick simply replied. He stood and walked to grab himself a coffee mug.

"What... what does she do?"

Nick stiffened slightly. Then he filled his coffee pot with the warm liquid before turning toward her and taking a sip.

"Flight attendant."

"Oh, that's interesting. Domestic or international?"

Nick's brows furrowed. He appeared to contemplate whether or not these questions were genuine.

"International," he said. "She's from England."

"Oh," Jo replied, surprised. She had not realized that Nick was dating someone from another country. "I had assumed she was from Chicago. Silly of me, I guess." Jo chewed on the inside of her lip. Nick had always loved the idea of traveling around the world. It seemed Eleanor was the perfect fit for him. Unlike her, who had him move to her small hometown in Georgia, where they rarely went anywhere else.

"Have you... met anyone?" Nick asked her. At that, Jo laughed.

"No. I don't...." Just thinking about going on dates seemed overwhelming. "No."

It grew silent. The only sound was the waves outside. Jo started breakfast to fill the void. She hoped Lulu would wake up soon so they would have something else to focus on than one another. This was the most time the two had been alone since before Nick left. It was bringing up too many feelings and too many words that they still hadn't spoken.

"I was thinking," Nick then began, "that when we return, I should start moving into the apartment building. It's probably best that we explain to Lulu soon how we are getting a divorce. The sooner we start, the easier it'll be for her."

A lump formed at the base of Jo's throat, but she still managed to get out, "Right, of course. We can tell her after we get back."

She forced her mouth into a tight smile. She grabbed the eggs out of the refrigerator and began breaking them into a bowl. One thing she had learned about Lulu was that she loved scrambled eggs, which worked nicely because it was one of the things Jo could cook.

Again, the room fell silent. Thankfully, she heard Lulu's door open, signaling that she was awake. Jo had just finished making the eggs and scraped them onto a plate, setting them down on the table.

"Oh, eggs! Thanks, Jo!" Lulu eagerly said. She sat down and ate.

"You're welcome," she replied. "After you eat, I thought we could go for a walk on the beach. How does that sound?"

"Great!"

Today their daughter was eight. It felt surreal. For years, the two of them had celebrated their daughter's birthday without her. But not today. They made sure the day was all about Lulu. All she asked for was to spend the day outside at the beach. It was a simple request.

Nick was sad he wouldn't be able to make her a cake. The stove at the beach house didn't bake evenly; it needed to be replaced soon. Instead, they let Lulu pick out a cake from the local grocery store. She chose a cake with a beachy theme.

"Happy birthday!" Nick and Jo said together. They brought out the cake to the back porch after their simple dinner of hotdogs and macaroni and cheese, per Lulu's request.

"I love cake," Lulu said.

"You get that from your mom," Nick said with a wink toward Jo. Even though the sun had begun to set, he could still see the blush on her cheeks.

"Who doesn't like cake?" Jo replied with a simple shrug. "But have you enjoyed your birthday? You are now eight years old!"

"Eight," Lulu said. "I didn't know when my birthday was before...." She then frowned.

Anger ran through Nick and his face flushed with warmth. He clenched his fists by his side in an attempt to keep his anger at bay. Today was supposed to be a joyful day for Lulu, but he was finding it hard not to be angry at the woman who'd taken her. The birthdays they should have had together could never be returned. His daughter missed out on just as much as they had.

"Did you not... celebrate ever?" Jo carefully asked. Nick and Jo's eyes met over Lulu's cake. They still had much to discuss during their therapy sessions.

"We did," Lulu shrugged. "But she told me my birthday was in the summer."

"Oh," Jo said uncomfortably.

"But I'm glad I know my real birthday now," Lulu smiled again. "And I know my name is Louisa. I'm learning lots."

"We are too," Jo said. She reached out to touch Lulu's cheek. Lulu's smile brightened.

"What about presents?" Nick asked. Lulu glanced up, and Jo moved to the side so she could see the pile she'd hidden behind the chair.

"For me?"

"Of course! It's your birthday."

"Oh yes! I love presents."

DID YOU TELL HER?

Nick read the text from Eleanor. He quickly typed back.

YES.

HOW'D IT GO?

FINE.

He kept his words short because he didn't feel like Eleanor needed to know every detail of his conversation with Jo. He knew Eleanor was ready for him to get the divorce papers and be back out of the house. Eleanor was patient, but even she had her limits. It had to be difficult knowing he was living with his soon-to-be ex-wife and playing family with her.

"Daddy?" His head jerked up from his phone to find Lulu holding a sandy ball that they played with at the beach. Butler was beside her, sitting patiently.

"Yes, my darling girl?"

"Can we go outside to play?"

It was only him and Lulu at the beach house. Jo needed to run to the store to grab a few more groceries to last them for their final day and a half at the beach house.

"Sure, why not," Nick said. He grabbed his shoes. Then he helped Lulu place the collar on Butler. The dog was always over-excited when someone put on his collar. He would move around, making it difficult to buckle.

They stepped outside onto the back porch and went down the stairs that led to the path that would take them to the beach. As he reached the bottom stair, Nick heard his phone ringing. He sighed. He'd left it on the kitchen counter.

"Stay right here," Nick said. "I'll be right back."

Nick rushed up the stairs and grabbed his phone from the counter. He turned to see Lulu running toward the beach. His heart raced. He placed his phone in his pocket and rushed after her.

"Lulu!" he yelled. She was still running. Lulu turned a curve, making it difficult for Nick to spot her.

"Where is Lulu?" He heard a voice behind him. He turned slightly to see Jo following him. He didn't know when she had gotten home or how she had known that he was running after their daughter.

"I... that way," he just said, pointing ahead. Jo had run track throughout school. So before he knew it, she had rushed straight past him. He followed quickly behind. He'd already lost sight of her.

They found Lulu a moment later sitting on the beach, holding Butler in her arms, breathless. Nick's body relaxed. Lulu was okay.

"He escaped!" Lulu explained.

"You cannot run after a dog!" Jo yelled at her. "You are not allowed to be out of our sight!" Nick went to place his hand on Jo's upper arm to try to let her know she was being a bit too harsh. It was an innocent enough mistake.

"I didn't mean..... I just was trying to keep from losing Butler...."

"You don't run away like that!" Jo was furious, but Nick could hear the real fear in her voice.

"You're mean!" Lulu snapped back, standing. "My mom would let me go out by myself all the time. She was much nicer than you are."

Nick watched as all the color drained from Jo's face, just to be replaced with bright red.

"She's not your mom! I am! I am your mom! She stole you from me!" Jo nearly screamed.

"All right," Nick stepped in. "This was all an honest mistake. Lulu, why don't we go back to the house now, okay?"

Lulu made a face at Jo before accepting Nick's hand. He looked at Jo, but she turned away from them both and started walking in the opposite direction.

When he got Lulu back into the house, he saw Jo walking up the path to the house. Her arms were crossed tightly over her chest. He made sure Lulu was content on the couch and went outside to meet up with Jo. She looked defeated.

"Jo," he said at the top of the stairs. She looked up at him, her face flushed. Her steps were harsh as she walked up each stair.

"Why weren't you watching her?" Jo angrily asked. Her chest puffed out.

"I had to run back to grab the phone. I just turned around for a second –"

"Yes, like you always do." Jo's words were cold.

"Jo...."

Jo let out a loud breath. Her eyes scanned over to the sliding door to find Lulu sitting on the couch. Her body deflated slightly.

"Not here, not now," Jo then said. "We'll... we will hash this out later. But not right now. Not right now."

"Jo..."

"Not now."

With that, Jo disappeared into the house. Nick watched her move past their daughter and go back down the hallway to her parents' bedroom. The good week was over.

That night Jo stood in the doorway of Lulu's room. She felt immense guilt for how she had reacted to her daughter. She hadn't meant to blow up at her; the fear had taken over and she couldn't control herself. Not that she allowed that to excuse her behavior.

"Hey," she said in the doorway. Lulu sat up in bed.

"Hey." Lulu scooted back slightly in her bed and tugged nervously at the comforter. The guilt grew in Jo's chest.

"Can I come in?"

"Sure." Lulu chewed on the edge of her lip.

Jo walked inside her daughter's room before sitting down on the edge of the bed. She sat there for a moment, not remembering what she wanted to say. She couldn't mess this up.

"I am sorry for yelling at you. I shouldn't have done that," Jo said. She reached out and touched Lulu's shoulder. "I was worried and I just... well, I overreacted."

"It's okay," Lulu said. Her eyes moved down to stare at the comforter.

"No, no, it's not okay. I should not have acted like that, Lulu. I love you and was scared I might lose you again, but that doesn't give me the right to yell at you like that. It won't happen again." Lulu nodded. "How did you feel when Butler got away from the collar?"

"Scared," Lulu answered, glancing back up at Jo. "I was worried I was going to lose him."

"I understand. And that's why you followed him, right?"

"Yes," Lulu said. "I didn't want to lose him."

"That is how your father and I felt when you disappeared five years ago, Lulu. We searched everywhere, but we couldn't find you. We lost you. It was horrible. I still worry every second of every day that we'll lose you again."

"I won't go anywhere," Lulu said with a small, shy smile.

"Good," Jo said. "We are so glad that you are back with us. We are trying really hard to be what you need. I know this is all new and difficult for you, but I want you to know that we love you, Lulu. We want you to be happy with us."

"I am happy with you," Lulu told her. Jo's breath caught in her throat.

"You are?"

"Yes. You and Daddy are nice. And you make me feel safe. I'm glad you found me. I wish I had always been with you both."

Jo's heart leaped in her chest.

"Me too."

Lulu leaned forward and brought her arms around Jo's neck. The hug was quick, but it was a hug. Jo had to blink to keep from crying. As they pulled away, she smiled at her daughter.

"Would you like me to read you a book before bed?"

"Yes, please."

"Perfect."

Twenty-One

Summer 2013

Today was the first anniversary of Lulu's disappearance. When Nick woke up, he wanted to curl to his side and go right back to sleep. He doubted he could face the day. A low sob escaped his lips, and he pressed his fist against them. The pain was unbearable.

Sliding his legs to the side, he sat himself up. He wasn't sure how he was going to make it through today, but he knew he needed to go to Jo. They may not have spoken for weeks now, but they needed one another today.

He got up and made his way to the small bathroom in the basement. He grabbed his toothbrush and glanced at his face in the mirror. With his free hand, he scratched the beard that had started to grow. He went longer periods between shaves now. The beard made him look nearly unrecognizable, but he liked it that way. He could leave his house without being bombarded.

The reporters had died out. Other people from town hadn't been stopping them either. After they had their field day about their cruise excursion, the stories began to peter out.

However, whenever he was out and about in the neighbor-hood, he still received sympathetic looks from people as they passed by. Yet with his beard, when he was alone, no one knew it was him. He could hide under the radar.

Once he had brushed his teeth and put on a shirt, he made his way up to the main level of the house. It remained untouched, with no sign of Jo. Not that it surprised him; it was rare that he saw her out of their room. She just remained up there most of the time, hiding away from the world. He didn't know what else to do to bring her back into the land of the living. It seemed she didn't want to join.

Since she wasn't on the main level, he walked up the stairs. He reached the top of the stairs and to their bedroom door. Part of him wondered if she'd locked it, but she hadn't. He easily turned the handle and opened the door. His eyes fell to the bed where Jo lay turned away from him.

At first, he thought she was asleep. He debated leaving the room and letting her sleep. Because if she could sleep through the day, she should. Then he heard the sobs and his heart broke.

With a solemn sigh, Nick climbed into their bed. He brought his arms around his wife, and her sobs grew louder. She turned into him and he pulled her closer. Her soft locks of hair brushed against his face, and he took all of it in. He hadn't held her for so long. His lips caressed the top of her head as he stroked her shaking back. He closed his eyes before the tears fell down his cheeks.

It surprised him when Jo glanced up from his hold. Her eyes were searching his and then she sat up slightly, kissing him. He melted against her, grasping at the back of her neck as her fingers tugged at the fabric of his shirt to pull him on top of her.

Her fingers slipped down to the edge of his top before she tugged it up and over his head. He brought his hands back down after his shirt was off and pulled at Jo's top. She sat up and allowed it.

No words were said between them. They just cried and loved one another. It was slow and patient, each one taking comfort in the other as they made love. Even when they finished, Jo kept her arms around Nick to hold him close to her, not letting him go. He felt her warm tears against the nook of his neck.

He didn't know how long they remained like that, but eventually, Jo pushed him off of her and then got out of bed, walking to the bathroom. He heard the shower turn on and decided he would join Jo. Nick waited a moment before sliding out of the bed.

As he walked into the bathroom, he found Jo standing outside of the shower, curled up away from him. He stepped behind her, wrapping his arms around her bare stomach and placing his head on her shoulder. Her body tensed beneath his touch.

She spun around, shoving him away.

"What are you doing?" she seethed.

"I thought...."

"That," she pointed toward the bedroom, "was just comfort, Nick. Go away!"

Nick stumbled back slightly, hurt by her words. Not saying another word, he left the bathroom, grabbed his clothes, and went back downstairs.

The hot water sprayed against Jo's skin. She didn't reach for the soap or shampoo, only allowing the water to soothe her broken soul for a moment. She struggled to find the energy to do anything anymore. Her heart constantly ached and her body mourned for a life it once had.

Jo remained in the water until it turned stark cold. She grabbed her bathrobe and placed it over her soaking body, not taking the time to dry herself off with a towel.

Stepping into her bedroom, she found Nick was no longer in there. She was glad. She didn't have the energy to talk with him right now.

Her eyes fell to the window, and she saw the overgrown garden in the backyard. Once there was a time when the garden had been her pride and joy. She would spend hours outside with Lulu running around as she worked on making the garden perfect. That had been before. Now it had sat neglected for a year.

Suddenly she felt the need to go out to her garden. With little thought, she made her way downstairs and outside. Her bare feet walked on the grass, and she headed straight to the gardens. Her hands dug into the soil and she tugged and pulled against the plants on the ground.

With each one she lifted out, she threw it to the side. Then she grabbed another and another, determined to tear them all out of the ground.

"Jo! What are you doing?" Nick called from behind her. She ignored him. The garden needed her tending.

The next thing she knew, he was holding onto her shoulders. "Oh my god," he said beneath his breath. "You are soaking wet and you've cut yourself. Come on, let's go inside."

Jo wanted to argue with him and draw away from his grasp, but she was too tired to do so. She allowed him to stand her up and lead her back inside. He sat her down at the kitchen table. It was then that she saw the cut on her chest. She hadn't even felt it as it happened. But now, she could clearly see the four-inch scrape against her skin.

"Here," Nick said, pressing a cloth against her chest. "It looks superficial," he added a moment later. "I think we have some antibiotic ointment in the cabinet above the microwave that I can put on it."

Nick made sure she was holding the cloth over the cut before he stood up to search in the cabinet for the ointment.

"I'm fine," Jo said as he tried to place some of the ointment onto her skin. She stood up and pulled the robe tighter over her frame. "I don't need your help."

Nick let out a disbelieving chuckle. "Right, you're fine," he bit.

Instead of saying something else, Nick left Jo alone in the kitchen.

As Jo went to grab herself a glass to pour water into, she heard Nick turning on the television. It was an odd sound. The television in the living room hadn't been on in months. The two of them never spent time in that room and if either of them watched television, they watched it on their own in their own rooms.

She turned on the tap to get her water and then took a sip. She hadn't realized how parched she was until that moment. She took a few more sips.

"Dammit!" Jo heard Nick yell. She rushed toward the living room where she saw what he was watching. It was a commercial about a special that night.

"Tonight, please join us as we discuss the death of Lulu Anderson. One year ago, she went missing only to be presumed dead from drowning in the Savannah River. In tonight's broadcast, we will discuss ways to protect your children from drowning."

Nick stood up and walked over to the front windows, looking out. He groaned.

"They're out there," he told her. His finger angrily pressed against the glass, pointing toward the reporters across the street.

"We'll just stay in." Jo shrugged.

"It isn't right," Nick growled. "We deserve peace and quiet today, not to be hounded by those... those vultures!" He reached up and shook his fist.

"They'll get bored," Jo said. She had learned to block all those people out.

"No, they won't. They will hound us, hoping to get a story or for us to speak," Nick disagreed. "This... this is why we need to move."

Jo met his eyes, her jaw set. "I'm not moving."

Nick hit his hand against the edge of the couch, making Jo take a step back.

"Right, it doesn't bother you because you never leave this damn house. You just stay inside, all day long. You don't even live! You do absolutely nothing."

"And what is there to live for, Nick?" she countered.

"Me," he answered, pointing to his chest. "You could live for me. Or your sister. Your parents. Your niece and your nephew. Any of us."

Jo crossed her arms in front of her while tapping her foot.

"You just want me to give up," she said.

"You already have given up, Jo," Nick sighed. "You gave up a long time ago."

"Maybe you should go," Jo said as she turned away from him. Nick narrowed his eyes.

"Go? Away for the day? Off on a work trip?"

"No, leave. You've been wanting to move away," she stated.

Nick's face fell slightly. He blinked harshly and walked toward her.

"You really want me to leave?" The pain in his voice shot through her heart. He tugged on her upper arm. She turned to him, her stomach flipped as she saw sadness clouded over Nick's face. The old Jo would have wrapped her arms around him and told him she was wrong and that she loved him and needed him. Instead, her eyes pierced directly into his.

"Yes."

Nick stepped back as though someone had slapped him.

"You've wanted me gone for months," he said, hurt. Then his hand curled into a fist. "It's why you didn't tell me about possibly being pregnant."

"What?" she asked. "What are you talking about?"

"You didn't tell me because it thrilled you not to be stuck with me any longer."

"Vivian," she whispered beneath her breath when she realized how he knew. Then she looked up at him. "I didn't tell you because I wasn't pregnant. What would the point be?"

"I'm your husband. If you thought you might be pregnant, you should have told me. But you don't care about me or anyone anymore, do you?"

"God, Nick, it had nothing to do with you," she fought back. "I wasn't pregnant. You were gone on a work trip. There was nothing to tell you."

"There was *everything* to tell me," he said in response. "You are my wife. We have always gone through our journeys together, but that moment was when you decided to cut me out."

Jo's head shook vehemently. "It wasn't that big of a deal," she disagreed.

"We always said we wanted more children. How was that not a big deal?"

"Because I wasn't pregnant. You were gone. How would me telling you any of it, change anything?"

"Because then you would have let me in, like you used to, Jo."

Tears stung Jo's eyes. She took in a shuddering breath. Trying not to let the tears spill, she glanced up at the ceiling. As she blinked, it made a few of the tears fall.

"Jojo..." Nick's voice softened. He lifted her chin, gently forcing her to look at him.

"I didn't tell you, because it would just confirm what we already knew.... I can't give you more children, Nick. There will be no more children."

Nick attempted to bring her closer to him, but she shoved him away. She didn't need his pity.

"All I have ever needed was you," he whispered, his voice tight. "Losing Lulu has destroyed us, Jo. She was our everything. But we can have a future. Please, don't give up on us."

Jo hugged herself tightly.

"I'm going back to bed."

Nick felt his body tremble and watched as his wife went back up the stairs. He then fell back against the cushions of his couch before allowing himself to crumble. Around them, the rest of the world was moving on. They stayed stuck here in this purgatory, and he wasn't sure there was a way to escape.

His phone rang. He looked down to see his mother-in-law calling. He was confident she had tried to call Jo multiple times already today but knew she hadn't answered it. Her parents had driven up a few times to check in on her when he was out of town and she wouldn't respond to their calls.

"Hello?" he croaked. He hadn't realized how much his throat had closed up until he attempted to speak. He wiped his eyes with his fingers and took in a deep breath.

"Hi," Rose kindly said. "How are you both?"

"We're..." Nick paused, his eyes moving to the staircase. "It's tough."

"I know it is, dear," she said. "Would you and Jo like us to come up for a few days? Or you two could come and stay with us?" While Nick appreciated their offer, he knew Jo wouldn't want either.

"I think it's best if it's just us this week," he answered.

"Right, of course." The line fell silent for a brief moment.

"Thank you for calling though. I'll let Jo know I spoke with you," he then said.

"Thank you, Nick. Please, let us know if you need anything. We love you both."

"We love you too," his reply was automatic. He hung up his phone.

That was when he noticed a few messages from Vivian. He slid open the messages to see that she had texted both him and Jo in a group text.

I'M COMING OVER AROUND TEN OR ELEVEN AND BRINGING DOUGHNUTS.

NO ARGUING. I'M COMING.

SEE YOU BOTH SOON.

He clicked the button to darken his screen and set the phone down. He had no reason to reply to his sister-in-law; either way, she would show up. He knew her well.

Standing up, he turned off the television before going to make sure he had tightly shut all the blinds. He didn't know why the reporters kept coming by. They had yet to make any sort of comments to them. Only once had they spoken to the reporters, and that was when they were still searching for Lulu. They gave their plea to anyone who had any leads to let them know. After that, they avoided them.

As he turned around to walk back into the living room, he was shocked to see Jo standing at the bottom of the stairs. She had put on some leggings and a loose t-shirt. Her hair was still wet but drawn up into a tight bun.

Her eyes seemed empty as he walked toward her. She looked right through him. He opened his mouth to speak and then closed it.

The surrounding air was heavy. He missed the times when he could be near his wife and feel full and happy. It felt as though those days would never come again. It felt as though the world was ending and that no matter what happened between them, he would lose her forever soon. As he attempted to grasp at straws to save them, he found it was futile. No happily ever after stood on the other side of their grief. It would swallow them whole if it hadn't already.

"I don't want to lose you," he whispered.

Jo stepped off the bottom stair and walked right past him. He held his breath as he followed behind her, twisting his wedding band around his finger. What was she doing? This was the second time today she had left their bedroom. He watched as she opened the refrigerator door and pulled out some leftovers. She placed the food on a microwave-safe plate before heating it. Then she sat down to eat.

"Jo?" He tried, yet again. She inhaled sharply. "Jojo?" He hated the desperation in his voice. It was like she was on a sinking boat and he was forcing himself to sink with her. He knew he would sink with her if that's what it came to. He loved her that much.

The fork dropped onto Jo's nearly full plate, making a loud dinging sound. She stood, taking the plate to the sink to scrape off the food into the disposal. His eyes were still glued to her. What was she doing? Why was she acting as though he wasn't even there?

Once she finished cleaning off her plate, she left it in the sink. She then turned to face him. Now her eyes bore into him, making him uncomfortable. He shifted on the soles of his feet and cleared his throat.

"Jo?" He tried once more.

Her eyes cut toward him as she clenched her hands at her sides. He saw a brief moment of hesitation on her face, showing that whatever she was about to say, she debated saying it, even if only for a split second.

"It's your fault," she said, her words dripping with venom.

"What?" Nick breathed.

"You're the reason our daughter is gone. You're the reason we lost her."

All the air was sucked out of the room, and Nick had to grasp for the chair in front of him to keep from falling over. Jo stared at him in contempt before opening her mouth and saying,

"I hate you."

Twenty-Two

Spring 2017

The drive back from the island to their small town was nearly silent. Jo was still furious at Nick for what had happened the other day. She had a lot she needed to say to him and she was sure he did, too. Right now, they had to play it kindly between the two of them, with Lulu in the back seat. Thankfully, she didn't seem to notice the tension between them.

For one, Lulu was exhausted. Their week had worn her out, and she slept part of the ride. When they had to stop for food, she happily told them what she wanted to eat and then chattered on a bit about what fun she'd had.

Jo kept looking back at her and smiling. Lulu was finally acting comfortable around them. And finally, Jo felt a connection with her little girl. It wasn't as close as it had been before her disappearance, but the connection was there. It could only grow stronger over time.

They would have therapy in a few days, and Jo was excited to tell Dr. Canmore about their growth together as a family. They would need to take more trips like this, perhaps in the summer. It would be fun to let Lulu go back to the beach when the weather was warmer and she could enjoy the water more.

But then Jo remembered that there would be no more trips like there had been this past week. No, they would no longer be a family soon. She and Nick had to get their argument over soon so that they could discuss how they would tell Lulu he was moving out.

Jo rubbed her temple. It shouldn't hurt as much as it did. She and Nick had been separated for four years now. Four years with only brief interaction. She had already signed the divorce papers. The sooner Lulu knew the truth, the better it was going to be for her. It was only fair. They would make sure she was well loved. They would come up with a good agreement that made sure Lulu got to see them both. Jo had no doubts that they could co-parent well together.

"Do you need to stop for something to eat?" Nick asked, his voice laced with concern. Jo dropped her arm to her side.

"No," she told him. "I'm fine. Plus, we're close to home. I don't think we need to make any more stops."

"Right," he agreed. They had already stopped more than necessary.

They continued on their journey and, twenty minutes later, they were at the house. Excited to tell her grandparents all about their trip, Lulu jumped out of the car, taking Butler with her. As Jo looked up, she saw her parents standing in the doorway. She wondered just how long they had been waiting for their arrival.

"Jo," Nick said, placing his hand over hers.

"I know," Jo whispered. "We can talk about it tonight. Once we get Lulu in bed for the evening and my parents have settled down, let's meet out back and just hash it all out."

"I don't want to fight with you, Jo," Nick told her. "I know I screwed up, but I... I don't want to fight." He bowed his head, tapping his fingers against his thigh. "I'm sorry I turned my back," he added.

She took in a deep, harsh breath. "You shouldn't have done that."

"I know, and I have already punished myself enough about it," he said. "But I don't want to argue with you, Jo. I don't want to end this with a fight."

Jo studied him for a moment before determining how she wanted to respond.

"I don't either," she whispered. "Why don't we...." But a knock on the glass cut her off. She turned and grinned when she saw Lulu standing impatiently at the door.

"Are you two coming inside? Grandma and Grandpa made pizza! From scratch! Did you know they could do that?"

Jo carefully opened the door so she could talk to Lulu better.

"I knew they could do that. It's really yummy. Your daddy and I will be inside in just a moment. All right?"

"Okay!" Lulu skipped back up toward the house. Jo watched her enter the home, and then she turned back to Nick.

"Tonight."

"Right, tonight," he agreed.

Jo got out of the car. She walked to the back to grab some blankets and bags that she could fit into her arms before she headed toward the house. Nick also got out of the car, but he was taking his time. She could tell he was trying to keep the distance between them.

When she walked inside, she could smell the pizza. It smelled heavenly.

"Ah! Jo! Honey, how was your trip?"

Nick carried the bags into the house, placing them by the front door. He heard lively chatter in the kitchen. It made his heart swell. He had missed that happiness in this home. At one point, he thought this house would always be full of sadness.

He peeked around the corner to see Jo sitting at the kitchen table and Lulu beside her. Lulu was talking about a million words per minute, explaining to Rose and Charlie all about their trip. She was allowing Jo to touch her shoulder, and Jo was smiling brightly.

His girls.

The thought filled his head before he even had a minute to realize it. His smile faltered. Then he stepped back. It was probably best that he took all the luggage upstairs and begin a load of laundry.

As he lifted the first bag, he heard a knock at the door. He sighed. It was probably some reporter who had noticed they were back home. Part of him wanted to ignore it, but he worried Jo or Lulu might open the door and be accosted by the vulture, so he decided he would do it.

Opening the door, his jaw dropped.

"Eleanor," he said. "Um, what...."

"Well, you said you were returning today from your holiday. I haven't seen you in weeks; I thought I would come by to see you." As always, she looked perfect from head to toe. He wasn't sure he had ever seen her without makeup. She kept her dark locks cut into the perfect bob right along her jawline. Not one hair was out of place. She wore a nice, form-fitting blue and white dress and blue heels.

"But..." he sputtered. What on Earth was she doing here? And could he get her to leave before anyone else noticed?

"Daddy! Come eat pizza!" Lulu said as she ran toward him. She paused when she saw the woman at the door. Her eyes widened in wonder and she tugged on Nick's hand. "Who is that?"

Eleanor bent down to Lulu's level and smiled.

"Hi there, Lulu. I'm Eleanor. I'm your daddy's-"

"Friend," Nick broke in, shooting Eleanor a look. She widened her smile.

"Right, friend."

Lulu eyed the new visitor carefully. Nick noticed the look of uncertainty on Lulu's face and the way she hid slightly behind Nick's back.

"You're his friend?" she asked again. Her eyes narrowed in on Eleanor. Eleanor only smiled brighter.

"I am."

"Let her join us for pizza." It was Jo who spoke, standing near the kitchen and looking over. She crossed her arms protectively over her chest with an unreadable expression on her face. "It would be nice to get to know your friend."

"Great," Eleanor exclaimed. "I do like pizza."

Nick knew this wasn't a good idea, but there was no way to stop it from happening. He felt increasingly uncomfortable. This was not how they were supposed to meet Eleanor. This wasn't how any of this was supposed to go at all.

"Come on then," Jo said with a tight smile.

"My grandma and grandpa made it from scratch. Have you met them before?" Lulu cocked her head to the side slightly.

"No, I haven't," Eleanor answered.

With a deep breath, Nick attempted to smile. Jo turned into the kitchen and Lulu ran after her, leaving him and Eleanor alone. He wanted to tell Eleanor then it might be best if she left, but Rose had already come out to greet the new guest.

"Oh, how nice to meet you, Eleanor." Rose was her usual bright self, reaching out to give Eleanor a handshake. However, her eyes did give way to how uncomfortable it was that Eleanor had just shown up out of the blue.

"It's nice to meet you, too," Eleanor said.

They went into the kitchen, where Charlie sat at the table. He gave a tight nod but said nothing. Lulu scooted her seat closer to Jo's and continued to eye Eleanor suspiciously.

He and Eleanor sat across from Jo and Lulu, while his in-laws sat at the ends of the table. As Eleanor sat beside him, he felt her fingers linger on his thigh. He gently pushed it away and grabbed a slice of pizza.

"So, Eleanor, how do you know my daddy?" Lulu asked.

"We met in Chicago," Eleanor answered.

"Chicago?" Lulu squished up her nose. "When were you in Chicago?"

"Well, darling," Nick began, "with my job, I travel a lot. I just haven't since you returned home. But I will have to soon."

"Oh," Lulu murmured. "For how long?"

"Not too long," he promised. Lulu ducked her head slightly, taking a bite of her pizza.

"So, Eleanor, what do you do for a living?" It was now Rose's turn to do some interrogating. Nick should not have been surprised. Rose always wanted to know everything. He remembered the first time he came home to meet her and Charlie. He had been asked so many questions that it nearly made his head spin.

"I'm a flight attendant," she answered. "I fly internationally."

"That sounds fun," Rose said. "Do you enjoy it?"

"Very much so."

"But that would be a tough job with children, wouldn't it? Traveling from country to country often. Do you spend a lot of time in any one place at any time?" Rose met her eyes.

"Um, well, I don't have any children," Eleanor said. "I don't plan on having children, but I do spend time in Chicago every few months. I consider it to be my home base."

"Oh?" Rose said. "But your accent sounds European?"

"Well, yes, I am from England," Eleanor told her. "Right outside of London. But, since I have begun traveling, I found I feel most at home in Chicago." She smiled at Nick. He cleared his throat.

"Lovely. What is your favorite thing about Chicago?"

"I think that is enough questions for right now," Jo interrupted. "Why don't we focus on this delicious pizza?"

"Yes," Nick agreed.

"I had a birthday," Lulu told Eleanor. "I'm eight now. How old are you?"

"Thirty-five," Eleanor answered.

"Cool. Jo is forty. My dad is forty-six," Lulu informed her. "Grandpa, how old are you? Grandma?"

"It's not nice to ask a lady her age," Rose replied with a smile.

"I'm seventy-two," Charlie answered at the same time.

"Ah. Are you the oldest of us all?"

"Yes."

"That means Grandma is older than Jo and younger than you. So somewhere between forty and seventy-two."

"That's right. You are my clever granddaughter," Rose said with a wink.

"Well, as fun as this has been," Jo said, standing up. "I think it's time to clean this up and Lulu should probably bathe and get ready for bed. It was a long week."

"I'm not even tired...." Lulu disagreed. "And it's only six."

"Yes, but by the time you take a bath and get changed and do some reading, it'll be eight. Come on."

Lulu sighed but did as she was told. Nick took the opportunity to stand. He was not about to be left in this room alone with Jo's parents and Eleanor.

"Come on Eleanor, why don't we go out front and we can talk?"

"Oh, okay."

He grabbed their plates and took them to the sink. "I'll clean this when I get back," he told his mother-in-law.

Part of him worried that this was a bad idea. Even though he didn't see any of the vultures outside, there could be someone looking from afar. The papers would have a field day with this.

"Why are you here?" he immediately asked when they were no longer within earshot of anyone at the house.

"I missed you," she said simply. "You weren't replying to my messages about coming to visit, so I thought, why not?"

Nick grunted under his breath and ran his fingers through his hair in frustration. "This isn't a good time, Eleanor. We haven't even told Lulu that we are getting a divorce or that I am moving out."

"When are you going to?" Eleanor asked. "How long can you keep this ruse up?"

"Not much longer," Nick answered. "We were planning on discussing that tonight."

Eleanor let out a low whistle. "Ah, well, that's good."

"You should leave," Nick said. Eleanor stepped back.

"Leave? I only just got here."

"Eleanor, I'm in the middle of getting to know my daughter all over again. Jo and I are..."

"Yes. *Jo*," Eleanor said, crossing her arms.

"She is Lulu's mother. Jo will always be a part of my life, Eleanor. Do you have a problem with that?"

Straightening her shoulders, Eleanor's mouth twisted into a crooked, uneasy smile.

"Of course she will, Nick. But I am staying here for now. I've missed you."

"Where are you staying?" It was clear to Nick that Eleanor had no plans of leaving anytime soon. He needed to decide if he was going to assure her of his love or end this.

"At a hotel about twenty minutes away. I took a cab here," she explained.

"Well, why don't you let me take you to your hotel? We can talk for a bit there."

"Okay."

Jo watched from the upstairs window as Nick and Eleanor talked. It was hard to read their body language from so far away, and she also knew that it wasn't very kind to peek in on their private conversation. She told herself it was all right because she couldn't hear a word of what they were saying.

"Jo?" She turned around. Despite all of their growth, Jo still hadn't earned the title of mom. She tried not to let it bother her that Nick got his title, but she had not.

"Yes, Lulu?"

"Will you read me a book?"

"Sure," she softly smiled. She closed the blinds in the guest room and followed Lulu to her room. Lulu's hair was still wet from her bath, and she wore the new pajamas they had picked out for her birthday.

"Will you brush my hair first?"

Jo's heart nearly burst. It was the first time she had allowed that. She happily took the brush from Lulu before Lulu climbed up into her lap. Jo sprayed her daughter's hair with detangling spray, brushing through sections of Lulu's hair.

"Can you braid it?"

"Absolutely," Jo said. She split the hair down the center and then did two French braids down each side. Lulu got up, when she finished, to look at it in the mirror.

"Oh! I love it!" Lulu gushed. "You braid really well."

"I'm glad you think so," Jo said. "Now, do you want to pick a book?"

Lulu walked over to the bookshelf and chose a book from it. As she picked one up, she turned to Jo.

"Why did that Eleanor person come to our house tonight?"

Jo's shoulders tensed.

"I'm not sure," she replied. She knew she needed to be careful with how she approached all of this. It didn't matter how she felt about any of it. This was going to be her daughter's future. She trusted Nick that the person he chose to be with was safe for their daughter. So she had to grin and smile through it all, even if she felt the woman was a bit vapid. The last thing she wanted to do right now was share her daughter with another woman when she had just gotten her back. But that was how it had to be.

"She was nice," Lulu said. "But... I like you better."

Jo laughed at that. "Well, she's not replacing me. I'm still your mama," Jo winked. Lulu happily smiled.

"I know! And I'm glad."

Jo touched her chest, feeling so full. "Good. I am glad, too."

The hotel Eleanor stayed at was right outside of town. It took closer to thirty minutes to arrive there. He pulled up and parked. Then he debated on whether or not he wanted to go to her room. It was likely best if he didn't.

"Come on," Eleanor said as she stood right outside of the car.

He opened his door and walked over to her. His hands rested on her shoulders and she smiled, moving closer to give him a quick, chaste kiss on his lips.

"I missed you," she said.

"And I missed you," he answered quickly. "But I think it's best I go back to the house. If Lulu isn't asleep yet, she'll want me to read her a book. And if she is, Jo and I are supposed to talk. I can call you in the morning. We could do breakfast?"

"That sounds nice," Eleanor agreed. "Will you bring Lulu? She's adorable."

"Probably not," Nick said. "This is still all very new for her. I think it's best we do this slowly."

"Right, of course. Well, I'll see you for breakfast."

"I'll pick you up at seven," he promised. He kissed her crown. "Sleep well."

"Good night."

He climbed back into the car and waited until Eleanor was safely inside before pulling out and heading back to the house. His mind was swirling with thoughts. He hoped Jo knew he hadn't invited Eleanor to their home. He would never have done that without consulting her. The last thing he wanted to do was overstep in that way.

He still couldn't comprehend why Eleanor thought it was a good idea to show up at their house without asking. Though he guessed he really shouldn't have been shocked; Eleanor loved surprises. For his last birthday, she had planned a trip to New York City without even consulting him. He always told himself that she was fun and carefree, and it was why he dated her. But that wasn't a good thing when it came to this new life with Lulu. Eleanor couldn't be like that when he had a daughter.

When he reached the house, he found that someone had already cleaned the kitchen up and there was no sign of Jo's parents. He walked upstairs in search of Jo. It was time for them to talk.

Lulu sat awake in her room looking through a book. She glanced up and smiled at him. He smiled back.

"Where's your mom?"

"I don't know," she answered with a yawn.

"All right. Goodnight, sweetheart."

"Goodnight, Daddy," she said.

He then made his way over to the master bedroom. The door was closed. He raised his fist to knock but then decided against it. Jo obviously didn't want to talk to him. So he went into the guest bedroom where he was staying.

There was an envelope sitting on the chair. Lifting it, he opened it. It was the divorce papers, signed.

Twenty-Three

She said it. Nick had known it was how his wife felt, but she had yet to say it out loud. He stumbled slightly on his feet, stung by her words. She hated him; she blamed him. He blamed himself, too. He had been the one watching Lulu when she went missing. That guilt had weighed on him every single moment of every single day. But somehow, Jo saying it out loud, killed him.

"I know," Nick whispered. He could feel his fingers losing their grip against the chair. He unlatched them and ran his hand over his face. "I know it is my fault."

"It is!" Jo screamed. "It's all your fault! You were supposed to be watching her! You were supposed to protect her! I will *never* forgive you!"

Nick swallowed hard. "Jo, I know...."

"I hate you!" Her words were filled with bitterness. "I. Hate. You. You have been wanting to leave, so leave. *Now*. I don't want you here anymore."

"Jo, certainly you don't mean that!" An exasperated Vivian rushed into the room. Nick had forgotten all about her coming over. The front door must have been left open or perhaps, Vivian heard the yelling and used her key to step inside.

"I do." Jo's eyes hadn't left Nick.

"Now, don't say something you'll regret," Vivian said, stepping toward her sister and reaching out toward Jo's upper arm. Jo shrugged Vivian away angrily and turned toward her.

"You stay out of this, Vivian! It's none of your business!"

It would have been smart for Vivian to walk away right then. Nick had seen his wife become someone he didn't recognize over the past year. Vivian had seen it too, but she hadn't been the brunt of it when she was like this. But Vivian did not walk away from arguments. No, she walked right into them. She was not one to back down.

"It is my business," she disagreed. "I am your sister. Nick is your husband. I think you need to take a breath and go calm down. This is not what you want, not deep down."

"Oh, fuck off!" Jo yelled at her sister. "You think you know more than me?! You get to have your perfect husband and your perfect kids and your perfect nanny. It isn't fair. I was always with my daughter and I lost her. You leave yours with a nanny all the time!"

"Hey now," Nick broke in, seeing the hurt on Vivian's face. "Your sister has been nothing but kind to you and me."

"Just leave! All of you leave! Vivian, go back home to your perfect little life, and Nick, go on and leave! I don't want any of you here anymore. I want you all to leave me the fuck alone!"

Vivian stepped backward. She placed the doughnuts on the side table and then rushed outside of the house. Nick remained for a moment, watching as his wife breathed heavily. Then he turned. He walked toward the stairs. Before he reached the first step, he heard a loud crash. Quickly heading back toward his wife, he saw the plate from earlier was now smashed on the kitchen floor.

"Jo! Be careful!"

"Go!" she screamed back. He was about to speak when he felt himself shake his head and turn around. It wasn't worth it.

She was shaking. She couldn't even recall how she had managed to break the plate in front of her. Her head was pounding from all the yelling. Deep down, she knew she had been horrible to both her husband and her sister, but it was what had to be done. She needed to free Nick, and she needed her sister to just leave her alone.

Carefully bending down, Jo grasped at the larger shards of porcelain. She placed them in a pile next to her. Then she grabbed a large shard and turned it over in her hand. She didn't know what came over her, but she swiped it over her palm. She looked at the blood seeping from the cut, mesmerized. She stood and grabbed a cloth to put over it.

Trying not to think much of what she'd just done, she went back to cleaning the mess on the floor.

Nick already had a job starting in Chicago in two days, so he immediately booked a last-minute flight that would allow him to leave in a few hours. If Jo no longer wanted him here, he would leave. She knew how to contact him if she changed her mind. But he was sure that she wouldn't. They were done. She made that abundantly clear.

He searched for his suitcase and found it in the guest room closet. He grabbed it from the closet shelf and brought it down. That was when he saw Vivian's car still parked in the driveway.

He placed the suitcase back on the bed before going downstairs and out the front door to Vivian's car. When he reached it, he knocked on Vivian's window. She jumped. As she turned, he saw she was crying. Nick couldn't recall ever seeing his sister-in-law cry in the past.

Vivian rolled down the window and looked at him.

"You can't leave her, Nick," she cried.

"She didn't mean it," Nick said to her, frowning. "She loves you and thinks you are a great mother."

Vivian sniffled. "She loves you, too. She just...."

"Hates the world?" Vivian nodded. "I have to leave, Vivian. My being here hurts her. I have to go away for a while, for her sake."

"But for how long?"

"I don't know." He nearly cried thinking about it; leaving Jo and not being with her. "Will you keep me updated on how she's doing, please?"

"Yes."

"I–I'm sorry," Nick said. "I wish things...."

"Just let us know where you go, please. We love you, too."

Vivian then rolled up her window and pulled out of the driveway. Nick watched before he went back inside. He saw his wife sitting on the couch with a cloth pressed against her palm, making him wonder if she had accidentally cut it when picking up the broken plate.

"I don't have to go," he tried, hoping for her to change her mind. But she didn't answer him. She just sat there, quiet. He stood there a moment longer before giving up and walking back upstairs to pack his bag.

Jo remained silent on the couch as Nick packed. She could hear bags being zipped and drawers being opened. Part of her ached to go upstairs and beg him to stay, but she didn't. They'd lost one another so long ago. It made no sense to ask him to stay with her.

About an hour later, Nick came downstairs. He had multiple bags with him. He had packed to be away for a while. She kept her eyes away from him, knowing that if she looked at him, she would break. That couldn't happen.

From the corner of her eye, she could see Nick searching for a picture to take with him. He picked a few up as he carefully made his decision. Finally, he took one of the most recent ones of Lulu. He glanced toward Jo to see if she would say anything. She didn't. It was as much his as it was hers.

Then he went and stood in the doorway, the picture tucked beneath his arm.

"My flight leaves at 5. I'll be in Chicago. You know how to contact me if you need me," he said. His voice was constricted, and he held tightly onto the doorknob.

Jo swallowed hard.

Nick stood there for another moment before turning the knob and walking out of the house.

Immediately, the house felt still and quiet. Jo stood, her heart racing in her chest. Everything was crashing all around her. She made her way to the window that looked out at their driveway, where she could see Nick placing the bags in the trunk of his car. She briefly wondered what his plan was to get his car to Chicago.

Nick turned, and she quickly hid so that he couldn't see her, but she could still see him. He was looking up at the house. Pain was etched all over his features. He remained in that spot for several minutes before finally turning around and getting into his car.

Jo moved back to her original spot and watched as Nick drove away. She kept her eyes on his car until it disappeared around the corner.

He was gone. It was likely he wouldn't return.

She felt empty. She felt cold. She let out a heartbreaking scream.

Nick stepped onto the airplane, taking his seat. At first, it didn't feel real. He traveled on planes often. It was something he did for his work. But the moment he sat down, it hit him. He had left his home. He was sure Jo wouldn't ever ask for his return.

His fingers pinched the bridge of his nose as he leaned forward in his chair, trying to control his heart rate. *This was what Jo wanted. It's what she asked for.* If she no longer wanted to be with him, then he would give her that. He couldn't handle being the cause of her pain.

Pulling his phone out of his pocket, Nick checked to see if there were any messages. He prayed for some from Jo, but there were none from her. He did have one from Vivian, though.

WE WILL MISS YOU. PLEASE KEEP IN TOUCH. DON'T STAY AWAY TOO LONG.

He quickly typed a message back.

WATCH OVER HER. GIVE TJ AND CALLIE MY LOVE.

Then he turned his phone off. It would soon be time for the plane to take off. Once he arrived in Chicago, he would need to find a hotel to stay in. He hoped the one he had booked a few nights out would have space for the next couple of evenings until then.

He still had many things he needed to figure out, like his car and where he would stay in Chicago. Jo would have to talk to him soon, if only for them to discuss what came next.

As the plane drove down the tarmac, he closed his eyes. He wasn't sure he was ready to say goodbye, but he hadn't been given much of a choice.

Twenty-Four

— · —

Spring 2017

"So," Eleanor said, glancing around the small town as they drove down the streets. "This is where you lived before you moved to Chicago?"

"It is," Nick said, nodding.

"And, you liked it?" Eleanor squished up her nose before quickly changing her demeanor and giving a fake smile. "I mean, it is quaint. I just.... You seem more like a city person, Nick. Do you think you'll be happy living here after being in Chicago for so long?"

"This is my daughter's home," he answered. "And I lived here much longer than I lived in Chicago. Plus, I'll still travel with my job."

"Yes, I can see how traveling could help," Eleanor agreed with a nod. "Of course, you'd want to be here with Lulu."

"It's a good town to raise children in," Nick explained. At least, it had been, he thought. This *was* where their daughter had been stolen away from them. It was also where he and Jo fell apart. They moved here because Jo's family lived here and she grew up in the town. He wanted to make her happy. Over time, he easily adjusted to the small town life. It wasn't his top pick, but with Jo and Lulu, he had been more than happy.

"Did you and Jo discuss the plan for Lulu last night?" Eleanor asked.

"No," Nick answered. "She was in bed when I got back."

Eleanor frowned. She tapped her fingernails on the console between them.

"But," Nick added, "she did sign the papers. They were on the bed when I got back yesterday evening."

"Oh, Nick! That's so great! You can finally move forward. She's been holding on to them for so long now," Eleanor said. It felt much more final now that he had told Eleanor Jo signed them. Part of him regretted saying it the moment he said it.

"They are signed now. All I have to do is get them to the lawyer once we've discussed what happens with Lulu. I'm sure more papers will need to be signed."

"Right, of course, but this is good news, Nick! I'm staying until the end of the week," she then added. Nick glanced over at her.

"What? All week?" He wanted to ask why in the world she thought it a good idea to remain here all week. He stared at her with wide eyes. How would he explain this to Jo? Or Lulu?

"Yes, well, I figured I could see Lulu a few times, but not overwhelm her or you or everyone. But I am her daddy's girlfriend. It's probably best she knows me and gets comfortable around me."

"Eleanor," Nick began, ready to tell her he didn't agree. However, when he saw the hopefulness on her face, he conceded. "We will take it one day at a time. You don't think you'll get bored here?"

"I'm staying outside of the town. That area has much more to do."

"It does," Nick agreed. "As long as you're sure."

"I am."

"Where is Daddy?" Lulu asked, walking into the kitchen where Jo was cleaning up their breakfast. Her parents had already gone to the library for the day. They rarely worked on Saturdays, but Jo wondered if her mother hadn't convinced her father to leave them alone today after the appearance of Eleanor the night before.

"He went out for a bit," Jo simply answered. She closed the dishwasher and turned it on. "He said he will be back by lunchtime."

"Oh," Lulu said. "Is he with Eleanor?"

Jo stopped in her tracks. "I don't know, maybe."

"Because they are friends?"

"Yes."

"Why do they have to spend so much time together?"

Jo did not want to be answering such questions, so instead, she decided to change the subject. All questions about Eleanor would go through Nick. Jo wanted nothing to do with any of it. She turned to Lulu and smiled. "Why don't we take Butler out back? Play a bit of fetch?"

"It's raining," Lulu pointed out, looking to the back door. Jo turned to look. How had she missed that?

"Oh. Want to play a game?"

"Like what?"

All the games they had in the game closet were either much too young for Lulu or likely too old. She walked over to it and opened the door. There was Monopoly, but that game took hours.

"Ah, checkers?"

"What's that?" Lulu asked innocently.

"You've never played?"

Lulu shook her head.

"Oh, it's easy. I'll teach you," Jo told her with a smile. "And when we start school next week, we'll do a lot of learning with games like this one."

"I can learn with games?"

"Yes, absolutely you can."

"Cool!"

Jo felt lighter. Her relationship with Lulu was already organically growing. Their moments were no longer filled with awkwardness at all times. Finally, they were at ease with one another.

Vivian received the text from her sister at seven the night before telling her that Nick's girlfriend, Eleanor, had come to the house. She wanted to go over right away, but her husband convinced her to wait until the next day. He suggested they could all go over and vet her together. Thomas had a way of knowing when to keep Vivian from intervening.

"Have you let Jo know we're coming over?" Thomas asked as he placed Callie in her seat.

"Not exactly," Vivian answered, blushing.

"Vi..." Thomas said, looking at her. "Why wouldn't you?"

"Well, Jo knows that I'll want to come over and talk about it all," she shrugged.

"Yes, but we're bringing over the children. Do we even know if the girlfriend is still there?"

"I don't know," Vivian said. "But Lulu enjoys her cousins, so I think it's okay."

Her husband hesitated, but he got into the front seat. Vivian grinned; she almost always got what she wanted. Thomas tended to be a pushover who would do almost anything to make Vivian happy. Only from time to time did he step in and say something.

"You're a good husband," Vivian squeezed his knee.

"I guess so."

When they arrived at the house, they had to run to the front door as the rain was starting to crash down. Callie cried because she hated being wet, and TJ rolled his eyes at his sister.

Vivian waited for her sister to open the door, deciding not to use her key. Jo eyed them all when the door swung open.

"You didn't tell me you were coming," Jo said.

"Surprise," Vivian said. "We thought since it's a rainy day, it might be fun for the children to spend some time together."

"Sure. Come on in." Jo widened the door, and both children ran in toward the kitchen. "We were playing checkers."

"Fun." Vivian and Thomas stepped inside. "Well, Thomas, why don't you take over the next game so I can talk with my sister?"

Vivian kissed Thomas's cheek before he obediently walked away and toward the kitchen to be with the children, leaving Vivian and Jo alone.

"So, is she here?" Vivian quietly asked, her eyes scanning around.

Jo laughed. "No. Why would she be here? She's staying at a hotel right outside of town."

"Oh, right, of course, she would be. I guess it would be strange for her to stay at your house."

"It would," Jo agreed.

"What is she like?"

"I don't know. Stylish?"

Vivian made a face. "Stylish? What on earth does that mean?"

"She looks stylish," Jo simply answered. "Maybe a bit vapid."

That made Vivian raise her brow. "Vapid?"

"Into herself," Jo said. "She seems nice enough, I guess. I wouldn't have gathered her as Nick's type, but-"

"Because she's not," Vivian said, interrupting. "You are."

Jo didn't respond to that. She kept her eyes on the children playing at the kitchen table. Then she added, "And Nick is out with her right now."

Vivian's face fell. "Oh."

"I mean, she came all this way."

"And how long will she be staying?"

"I don't know," Jo said. "She didn't tell us. Maybe she's told Nick. It isn't my business."

Vivian pursed her lips in thought. "Did Nick invite her?"

"I don't think so," Jo said, "though I can't know for sure. But I don't think he would. We had planned on discussing what came next last night before she showed up."

"I don't think he would either."

"I.... I gave him the divorce papers."

Vivian took in a sharp breath.

"You did?"

"Well, I left them in his room where he'd see them when he arrived. It was time. He has her, after all. I won't stand between that."

Vivian mulled on this information for a while. She couldn't believe it. This was the end of Nick and Jo. She had thought that time would heal all wounds. When they found Lulu, she was sure that would happen even faster. Her heart ached for the both of them because she knew how much they loved one another. She remembered how happy they had been.

It seemed all of that would remain a memory.

"You'll find someone else, someday," Vivian then said, trying to cheer her sister up.

Jo chuckled, "I don't think that's in the cards for me, Vivian. I'm not sure I believe in happily ever after anymore."

"But surely you believe in miracles. Lulu came back."

"She did. *She* is my miracle. She always was."

Eleanor gave Nick a long kiss before he finally pulled away outside of the hotel building. He stayed away for longer than he'd intended. After breakfast, Eleanor asked for a tour of the town. She wanted to see everything, which surprised him because she didn't seem to like the area that much. Perhaps since he would be living here now, Eleanor wanted to get used to all there was to see. Over time, she might grow to like it. He doubted she would ever love it. Part of him was sure she'd never come back. They would just meet up when he was traveling for his work.

"Maybe tomorrow I can come by?" Eleanor asked.

Nick inhaled sharply. "Maybe."

"Good, love you!" She kissed him once more before walking off. He said love you back, hoping she didn't notice the lack of enthusiasm in his voice.

It hadn't been raining at the hotel, but as he neared the house, it began pouring heavily. He noticed that Thomas' car was parked in the driveway and decided to park in front of the house instead. That would allow Jo's parents to park closer to the garage and not have to deal with as much rain when they arrived.

He stepped into some mud and groaned. Instead of going through the front door, he walked in from the garage, taking off his shoes before walking inside. He found Jo and Vivian talking in the living room while the children and Thomas were playing games at the kitchen table.

"This is a surprise," Nick said with a smile.

"Uncle Nick!" TJ was happy to see him. He jumped up from the table and showed Nick his Nintendo Switch. "Look at what I got!"

"Wow, lucky! That's brand new."

"Yes," Vivian said, standing from the couch. "Thomas had to pull some strings and make some calls."

"Want me to do the same for you?" Thomas asked from the table.

"No, I think I'm all right. Thank you."

He spoke for a little longer with TJ before heading upstairs to change his wet clothing. While upstairs, he tried to ignore the pang in his chest. Once he moved into the apartment, he would no longer be involved in all these family days. He was sure Jo's parents and sister would invite him to holiday get-togethers, but he wasn't even sure that would be a good idea.

Would he get Lulu for half the day and Jo the other half? Would they try to do it together for her sake?

He groaned. It all seemed complicated.

By the time he showered and made it back downstairs, Thomas, Vivian, and their children were getting their coats back on to leave. Vivian sent the children out with Thomas and remained by the door.

"Don't let her go," she said, meeting Nick's eyes.

"I think it's too late for that. Thanks for coming over."

Disappointment filled Vivian's face, but she said nothing else about it. She did, however, pull him into a hug. She held him tightly.

"Goodbye, Nick."

"I'll see you soon," he said in response. Vivian patted his arm.

"Soon."

As soon as the door closed, Nick walked toward the kitchen where Lulu and Jo were playing checkers. From what he could see, Lulu was winning by a landslide.

"She's getting the hang of this," Jo told him with a bright smile. "She's beaten me ten times."

"About to be eleven!"

"We should talk tonight," Nick said, abruptly serious. Jo's smile faded.

"Yes, tonight," she agreed.

The rain finally ended when the sun set. Puddles formed on the back porch and the yard was muddy. That made taking Butler out for his walks difficult, and now muddy footprints were leading from the back door to his bed.

Jo grabbed a towel to wipe up the muddy prints. Her mother told her she would do it, but she wasn't about to have her mother bend down with her bad back.

"I read to her, and she fell asleep mid-book," Nick said, making Jo look up from the floor. She knew what that meant. It was time to talk about everything.

She finished cleaning off the floor and stood before taking the towel over to the small basket for the downstairs laundry.

"Today with the cousins must have worn her out," Jo said. She went into the kitchen to wash her hands. Her parents had already retired for the evening. The distractions were gone.

"I saw the papers," Nick told her. "Though we'll probably need some changes after we decide how to do custody."

"Yes," Jo agreed.

Custody. It seemed like such a strange word. Not too long ago, they were childless, and now they were discussing custody of their daughter.

"Let's go outside," Jo suggested. She grabbed a large towel to wipe down the chairs on the porch. Nick took it from her and walked outside to take care of it. She followed behind him and turned on the back porch light.

She was the first to sit down. Nick waited to see where she sat before taking the seat across from her.

"So," Nick began.

"So," Jo replied. It seemed as though this should be simple enough. They both loved Lulu, and they both wanted the other involved in her life. They would be civil.

"I'm going to try to travel every other week," Nick began. "We could do one week on, one week off. Saturday-Friday," he suggested.

"A whole week?" Jo breathed.

"We don't have to do it that way," Nick said. He paused, sliding his hands to his knees. "I guess she could come with me sometimes when I travel." He stroked his chin in thought.

"What?" Jo sat up straighter. "Why... but you'll be working and she'll have school. You can't just take her off without me!"

"Jo, we're divorcing. You're saying I can never take Lulu out of the state? *Ever?*" Nick countered. "I'm keeping my place in Chicago."

Jo's eyes widened. "But why?"

"Because most of my work is up there, Jo."

"It's so you can see *her*," Jo countered. "I should have known you'd want to be there, with her." She couldn't bring herself to say Eleanor's name. "But you can't have Lulu if you plan on staying there. You'll only get to see her a few times a year then. I won't have my daughter living that far away from me."

"Jo..." Nick stood. "I'll be staying here most of the time," he said. "But sometimes, I'll want her to go with me. She is my daughter, too. And I'm sure she'll want to see my Chicago apartment. Chicago is where most of my work is, Jo. It makes sense for me to keep a place there."

"You never were happy with me, were you?" Jo asked. Nick stepped back.

"What does that have to do with anything, Jo? And yes, I was. I was *very* happy. You were the one who told me to leave, remember? You said you didn't want me near you anymore." His voice rose slightly.

"Because you weren't happy!" Jo yelled back. "I had to let you go!"

"No, you don't get to play that card," Nick disagreed. "You knew how much I loved you, Jo. And you gave up on us. No matter how hard I tried, *you* pushed me away."

"Maybe we were never really happy," Jo said with a frown. "Maybe we thought we were, but losing Lulu showed how we really were."

"Do you actually believe that?" Nick asked, incredulous.

"I don't know what to believe anymore," Jo answered.

He tightened his jaw; his shoulders felt heavy with grief. "I guess we figure out what comes next, then. We can speak with Thomas about drawing up some papers for custody.

You decide how you want it done. But we will split our time with her fifty-fifty."

"Fine."

"Fine."

They eyed one another, breaths heavy.

The next thing Jo knew, Nick had leaned forward, cupping her cheeks, and pressed a kiss against her lips. For a moment, she leaned into his kiss before shoving him away from her.

"What was that?"

"I–I'm sorry," Nick shuddered.

Jo stared at him before turning and walking back inside.

When Nick made it back to the guest room, he lifted the divorce papers.

Something came over him then, and he walked to Jo's bedroom, taking the papers with him. He couldn't believe that she suggested they hadn't been happy, because they had. They had been so very happy.

He knocked on her door.

A moment later, she showed up. She was in her pajamas, tired. Her eyes fell to the papers, and she sighed.

"What? Did I forget a signature?" She reached out to take the papers, but he pulled the papers back. "Then what? Why are you here?"

Nick turned the papers to the side and began tearing them, dropping them to the floor.

"Why are you doing that?" Jo said angrily under her breath, not wanting to wake Lulu. "Why would you do that?"

"Because we were happy," he said. "I still love you, Jo."

Jo's eyes searched his face. He didn't know what to expect from her. He almost expected her to yell at him to leave the house. But that wasn't what happened. She rushed toward him, inching herself up onto her toes, and pressing her mouth against his. He melted against her, it all feeling right. His hand moved to the back of her head to draw her closer to him.

Jo jumped up so that he had to hold her, and her legs came up around his waist. As their lips continued to accost one another's, Nick stepped forward and out of the hallway. He shut the door behind them before tugging at Jo's clothing. She did the same to him. They headed toward the bed as their clothes joined the torn divorce papers on the floor.

Twenty-Five

Late Summer 2013

"Should we come up?" Rose asked into the phone, looking over her shoulder at her husband with their new dog in his lap. Charlie, who had been adamant that he didn't want a dog, was now enamored by said dog. Butler was always with him by his side. He even slept in the bed between the two of them.

"No, Mom," Vivian said on the other end of the line.

"But she's not answering my calls or your father's calls. Have you even seen her, Vivi?"

"No," Vivian replied with a loud huff. "But her neighbor has. She said she gets food delivered to the house nearly every day. I think we should just give her some space."

Rose didn't agree with that. Just how much space should they allow for her daughter? Her husband had left her, and she hadn't spoken with them for months. They used to get updates from Nick, but now they never heard from him either. It was almost as though he had disappeared into thin air.

"I'm coming up there," Rose disagreed.

"Mom, don't," Vivian strongly stated. "Let me go by her house, see if she'll let me in, all right? Nick has only been gone for a little while. It might just take some time."

"Time..." Rose tapped her finger anxiously against the table. "Jo has been in that shell for over a year. What she needs is serious help."

"Mom," Vivian moaned. "Jo is an adult. She's been through extreme trauma and has just pushed her husband away. Let's just give her space and time, okay? You can allow that, can't you?"

Rose groaned. Her eyes moved back to her husband, who was looking to her for answers. She smiled tightly.

"Fine. But if anything goes astray, you are to call your father or me. Do you understand?"

"Yes, now, I ought to go. Callie has woken up from her nap and she's fussy. Love you!"

"I love you, too." The phone abruptly lost connection, and Rose set it down on the coffee table before sitting down beside Charlie.

"I don't like this," Charlie then said with a growl. "He just up and left her after all they went through."

"Well, Charlie, Vivi did say that Jo pushed him away. We don't know the entire story. I'm not sure Nick is entirely to blame," Rose tried to reason.

"He's been wanting a way out since the day they lost Lulu," Charlie disagreed.

"I don't think that's true. He loves Jo."

Charlie made a sound of incongruity. "He wouldn't have left if he did. Perhaps we can convince Jo to move out here.

We have plenty of space. The ocean air would be good for her."

Rose glanced out the back window, pleased to see it was a lovely sunny day.

"Perhaps."

"Here," Vivian said, placing Callie into Thomas's lap. Thomas was on his computer in the middle of working on his upcoming deposition for the next week. Ever since Nick's leaving, Thomas worked from home when he could, so he could be a support for Vivian. She very much appreciated him for it; he kept her afloat.

"What? Why are you handing me the baby?" he asked, perplexed.

"I've fed her. TJ is upstairs in the playroom. I shouldn't be gone long," Vivian explained. Thomas shifted Callie into his lap.

"Um, but where are you going?"

"To my sister's. She can't avoid me forever," Vivian said.

Thomas narrowed his eyes. "I thought you told your parents you should all give your sister some space."

"I did. I also told them I would stop by to check on her. Also, just because I told them that doesn't mean I believe it. My sister has lost it, Thomas. I'll break into her house if I have to."

Thomas let out a low chuckle, but he swallowed it when he realized the worry in his wife's voice. He bent forward, brushing his fingers along her chin.

"Maybe we should have someone to stay with the kids and I can come with you?" Thomas offered. "If you are worried, it's that bad."

"No, I can handle it. I–" Vivian paused. She hadn't expected the tears to come, but they did. Her eyes filled with them. One slipped out, so Thomas reached out to wipe it away. "I'm just a little concerned. The neighbor said they hadn't seen any deliveries today. I keep trying to call her. She won't answer." Her breath caught in her throat.

"Hey," Thomas gently said, standing from his chair. He brought Callie closer to his chest so that he had better movement with his other hand. "Take a deep breath. This doesn't all have to fall on your shoulders, honey."

"I'm her big sister," Vivian disagreed. "It is my job to protect her."

Thomas brushed his thumb over her cheek. "It isn't, but I know you will, anyway." He gave her a gentle smile.

"I won't be gone long," Vivian promised again.

"Take as long as you need."

When Vivian reached her sister's house, she searched for the spare key on her key chain. She finally found it by the mark she'd made; a little flower on the corner. She went to place it in the lock to find that the door was slightly ajar. Her heart skipped a beat. Had someone been in her sister's home?

Gently pushing the door forward, she inched her head inside.

"Jo? Are you there?"

There was no response. Vivian completely pushed herself into the house and shut the door behind her. Immediately, the stench of stale food and dust overwhelmed her. Her nose squished up, and she covered her mouth with her fingers to keep back a gag.

Slowly, she walked further inside. She stepped into the kitchen to find pizza boxes and Chinese delivery takeout boxes all over the kitchen. Forks and plates were set out everywhere, all from different weeks. Vivian was appalled. She had never known her sister to live in such a way.

"Jo?" she tried, yet again.

She turned and saw that the coffee table had a drink spilled over it. She couldn't make out what the liquid was, only that it had dried and made a sticky goo on top. Vivian bent down slightly to look at the mess. It had made a weird pattern on top, which could have been interesting and artistic if it wasn't disgusting.

She stood up and began chewing on the inside of her cheek.

"Jo?! Where are you? You can't keep avoiding me!"

With a sharp breath, Vivian went upstairs. It seemed unlikely that her sister would be outback or downstairs in the finished basement. It was more likely that she would be upstairs in her bedroom.

As she got further and further upstairs, she heard the undeniable sound of the television being on. It got much louder the closer she approached her sister's bedroom. She knocked on the door.

No answer.

"Jo, come on now," Vivian said, growing impatient with worry. She turned the knob and was grateful that it was unlocked. Opening it, she found her sister lying in bed. She was under the large comforter, turned on the side, and facing the door with one hand under her chin. She blinked, so Vivian let out a thankful breath that her sister was alive.

Vivian's eyes flew over the room. She saw more boxes of food and clothing strewn all over the place.

"This is a mess," she said under her breath.

The television was blaring and giving Vivian a headache. She walked over toward the bedside table and lifted the remote, turning the television off. Jo didn't even respond.

"You can't live like this," Vivian told her. "This isn't healthy."

It was then that Jo's eyes moved to Vivian before moving back to the now blank television screen.

"You shouldn't be here," she hissed. Vivian could hear the rawness in her sister's voice, showing how Jo hadn't spoken in weeks. Vivian swallowed hard before moving closer to her.

"Neither should you. Perhaps you should come and stay with me for a little bit. We can hire someone to clean the house. Start fresh," she tried.

Jo just closed her eyes, hiding her face deeper into the pillows.

"Jo, come on. This isn't healthy," Vivian tried again.

"Please go," Jo pleaded. "Leave me alone."

"Absolutely not," Vivian stubbornly said. "I won't let my sister live in such filth. You are coming home with me."

"Please go," Jo begged, yet again. "Please! I was so horrible to you. You should hate me, so go! Go! Please!"

Vivian frowned. She sat down on the corner of the bed and looked down at her sister, reaching over to touch her pale cheek. Despite all the food around the house, she was unconvinced Jo was eating anything. Her cheeks were sunk in and nearly gray. Part of her wondered if it was Nick sending food to the house to make sure Jo was eating something.

"Come to my house," Vivian insisted. Jo just tightly shook her head. Vivian stood up and tried to think of a way to convince her sister to leave the house for now. She needed out; she needed fresh air. This wasn't good for her. Before another idea could come to Vivian, she saw the large knife on Jo's bedside table. Her heart dropped. She moved closer toward it to find dried blood on the blade. Her stomach lurched.

"What's this?" Vivian asked, terrified. She turned to her sister. Before Jo had a moment to react, Vivian jerked the comforter off of her sister's frame. Jo only wore her undergarments. With horror stuck in her throat, Vivian stared at marks of cuts along the side of Jo's thigh and up to her hip, all at varying stages of healing. Her eyes then fell to the bloody cloth that Jo held tightly against her wrist.

"Jo...." Vivian breathed out. She fell back beside her sister, gently tugging the cloth from her arm. Beneath it was a crude cut, several inches long, which was bleeding aggressively. "Oh my god."

Jo brought the cloth back over it and closed her eyes.

"I didn't mean to cut it that deep," she said, her voice panicked from being found out. "I really... I didn't."

Vivian pressed her hand lovingly on her sister's cheek, forcing Jo to look at her.

"Listen to me," she began. "I forgive you for what you said. I'm not angry at you. I know you are angry at the world, but I love you, Jo. You are my sister and I love you. All right? Now, we're going to call an ambulance and get you seen right away. Okay?"

"Please, just go," Jo cried. "Leave me here. I can figure it out."

"No," Vivian said firmly. "This is bad, Jo. *Really* bad, but I'm here. I'll be here with you through all of it."

After Vivian called the ambulance, she called Thomas to fill him in on what had happened. As always, he was a saint, saying he and the children were fine and that he would come to the hospital if she needed him. For now, she decided it was best she was the only one there.

She felt the urge to call Nick and tell him but decided against it. That could wait until after she understood her sister's mental state better.

Finally, they allowed her back into her sister's hospital room. She walked in to find a large bandage over her sister's arm. She was awake but looked exhausted.

"Hi," Vivian awkwardly began.

"Hi." Jo kept avoiding her gaze, bringing the blanket up higher on her chest as though she could hide beneath it.

"How are you feeling?"

"Stupid," Jo answered. She went to scratch at her bandage. Vivian gently pulled her fingers away.

"Don't," she said, speaking both about how Jo felt and what she was doing. "Now, I think I should call Nick and—"

"No," Jo strongly disagreed. "No, don't call Nick!"

"He's your husband. He loves you," Vivian said, "and he would want to know."

"No!" Jo yelled. "Don't you tell him a word about any of this! He's gone. He is finally free of me."

"Free of you?" Vivian was shocked. "I don't think Nick has ever wanted to be free of you."

"You can't tell him. I won't allow it," Jo told her, crossing her arms over her chest.

"Jo—"

"If you do, I will go back to the house and refuse any type of treatment to get me better."

Vivian's brows creased in concern.

"He needs to know," Vivian weakly tried.

"He doesn't. And it's not your right to tell him."

Vivian breathed heavily. The weight of what happened sat profoundly on her chest. She blamed herself for not going by sooner. If she had, perhaps, she would have been able to notice what was happening before it got this far. She wanted to tell her sister that she could force her to get help. However, she knew it was better to meet her sister more than halfway through this. Her sister needed to want to get better.

"All right, fine," Vivian gave in. "But I am calling Mom and Dad." Jo flashed her eyes at her, but Vivian just continued, "They made me promise to give them updates."

"Fine," Jo said, like a petulant child.

"You terrified me, you know." Vivian reached across to touch her sister's hand.

Jo chewed on her lower lip. A tear slipped down her cheek. "I'm just so... tired."

"I know."

They received the call right as they were preparing to go to bed. Vivian told them how Jo harmed herself and needed to go to the hospital. Immediately, they packed and began their drive to the hospital. By the time they arrived, it was just after midnight.

Upon seeing them, Vivian stood from her seat beside Jo and pointed outside.

"What happened?" Charlie asked. Vivian had given them very few details about all that occurred.

"It's bad," Vivian said. "Jo isn't doing well. They say she'll have to stay here for at least twenty-four hours under suicide watch."

Rose gasped.

"Jo has been harming herself, but I do not think she intended to kill herself. I believe her in that regard. Her house isn't suitable for living so tomorrow, I'll hire someone to go and deep clean the place. You two are welcome to head to my house for now. Thomas has the guest room all ready."

"We're not going anywhere," Charlie said. Rose nodded her head in agreement.

"How is she?"

"Tired. Unhappy." Vivian pinched the bridge of her nose. "She's not well."

"And what comes next?" Rose asked. "After Jo leaves the hospital, what then?"

"Therapy," Vivian said. "And I think she should stay at my place for a little while. We can't let her live alone right now."

"No," Charlie agreed. "We can't. That Nick...."

"Not now, Dad," Vivian broke in. "Let's just focus on Jo right now. She needs all of us to be there for her."

"Right," he gruffly responded.

"And she doesn't want him to know," Vivian then added. "Mom, you can't tell him."

"Well, maybe not now," Rose agreed, "But in a few weeks when things are settled—"

"We need to respect Jo's wishes. She doesn't want him to know. Let's just focus on helping Jo get better."

Jo woke late the next morning to find that her parents and Vivian surrounded her. She didn't know when her parents arrived. They must have come when she was sleeping. The hospital had given her something to help her sleep. It was the first time since her daughter's disappearance that she had slept peacefully, without any sort of nightmares or dreams.

Her arm itched where they had stitched her up. She attempted to scratch at it, but the bandages were tight to keep her nails away. When she cut her arm, she honestly hadn't meant for it to be that deep. Her hand had slipped the moment it happened, and she knew it was too much. By then, it had been too late.

The cutting started the anniversary of her daughter's disappearance when she sliced the broken shard across her palm. It had been such a freeing feeling. Briefly, the pain from the cut allowed her to pull away from the pain of the loss that constantly ached within her chest. That fleeting moment was peaceful. From then on, anytime the weight had been too heavy, she resorted back to it. It didn't matter that the voice in the back of her head kept telling her it was wrong. She hadn't cared. She just wanted to forget, even if it was only for a split second.

Yet now, here she was, in the hospital. Her eyes moved to her parents, who were both half asleep. She kept quiet, not wanting to draw attention to the fact that she was awake. Then her eyes went to her sister. Vivian was curled up into what seemed like an uncomfortable ball in the chair, snoring loudly.

"Oh Jo," her mother gently said, getting up from the chair and walking toward her. Tears shined in her eyes.

"I'm all right, Mom. I really am. Or... I will be," she promised. Her mom placed her hands on either side of Jo's face and held it for a moment, eyeing her carefully.

"Don't worry, love. Your dad and I aren't going anywhere. We're staying here with you. You won't have to be alone again."

Twenty-Six

Nick contently sighed as he ran his fingers up the side of Jo's arm. It was almost as though the night before had been a reset of all they had before they lost Lulu. The two of them came together as one in a raw and passionate way. It had been rough, but full of love.

Now, he laid in their bliss. Jo still slept deeply, and the last thing he wanted to do was disturb her. He looked down her arm and gently turned it so he could see the scar etched on her skin. With his fingers, he could feel the bumpy and rough texture. He inhaled sharply.

He saw other scars along her skin too, but they weren't as visible as this one. His body shuddered, thinking of missing this pain his wife had held. He hadn't been there when she needed him the most.

A low moan made him look down to see Jo stirring.

"Jo?" he whispered. His lips lingered in her hair. "Good morning."

Yawning, Jo sat up slightly and met his eyes.

"Good morning," she whispered. Tentatively, the corner of her mouth twitched up. Nick reached up to cup Jo's cheek.

"How do you feel?"

"Like this is a dream," Jo answered.

"It's not," Nick assured her. "We're here, together, finally."

Jo pressed against his chest. Nick watched her fingers trace the path over his chest and toward his shoulders before she let out a low breath.

"Is that what you want, Jojo?" Jo placed her hand over his heart, before nodding.

"Yes. I've always loved you. I'm sorry I pushed you away. I was so -"

"Shh." Nick put his hand on top of hers, squeezing it. "That's in the past."

"And you want to be with me?" Jo asked, her eyes wide.

"It's all I've ever wanted, Jojo." Her nickname fell so easily from his mouth.

"I guess you did tear up those divorce papers," she said with a smile. "But why now?"

"I'm not sure," Nick honestly answered.

"What about Eleanor?" The question floated in the air for a moment. Jo glanced at him worriedly, furrowing her brows. "Don't you love her?" she asked.

"Not like I love you," he said. "She's someone I do care about, sure, but I don't love her in the all-consuming way that I love you, Jojo."

"All-consuming? What is that supposed to mean?"

"It means that I will always love you. It means that even when we are apart, I think of you always," Nick said. "For the past four years, I wanted to come back to you. My heart could never love someone as I do you."

Jo tucked her hands beneath the covers before sighing.

"That sounds very romantic, but it still doesn't change the fact that we became *those* people."

"Those people?" Nick asked.

"People who cheat. I never thought..." Jo glanced up her lower lip twitching. "I was never going to be that type of person."

"Oh." Nick sat up now so he could be her equal. "Well, while Eleanor and I are dating, we aren't too serious."

An incredulous laugh escaped Jo.

"You aren't pulling that, are you? Isn't that what all the cheaters say to the other woman?"

"No, I mean...." Nick shook his head. This was not coming out the way he wanted it to. "Yes, a lot of cheaters do sound that way. But Eleanor and I are casually dating."

"Casual?" Jo wrinkled her nose. "She came here to surprise you. You might think it's casual, but I'd dare say she thinks it's serious."

"I've made it clear to her that I never plan on marrying her. She and I haven't even slept together."

"What?" Jo was shocked. "But you've been together for half a year."

"And I have still been married to you. I would never have been fully intimate with someone else unless we finalized our divorce. I couldn't... I mean, I wouldn't do that to you."

Jo shifted on the bed, inching closer toward him.

"But why? We haven't been together in four years, Nick."

"Because I love you, Jo."

Jo blinked. Her face crumpled slightly, and she sobbed. Growing concerned, Nick pulled her into his embrace. He rubbed large circles over her back as he murmured sweet nothings into her ear.

"It's all right if you had someone, Jo," he whispered. Jo sat up slightly to meet his gaze. "I never expected—"

"I never – there was no one else."

A relieved sigh passed through Nick's lips. He kissed Jo's crown and then smiled. He hadn't lied; he would have understood, but he was glad there hadn't been.

"What comes next?" Jo asked.

"Hm?"

"Now? What do we do now? Are we back together? Do you move in? Was this just a night of passion?"

"I want us to be together again," he said. Jo's eyes searched his face.

"It won't be easy."

"I think it will," Nick disagreed.

"Why?"

"Because you and I were always meant to be, Jojo. Tragedy tore apart our lives. Had we never faced that, I know we would never have broken up. And now, we are thrown back together. Look at us. We knew we needed one another again."

Jo sat up, bringing one leg over so that she could sit atop Nick's lap. Her hands ran over his shoulders as she slowly bent down to give him a chaste kiss.

"I want us to be like before, Nick. I really do," she whispered in his ear.

With a smile, Nick brushed her cheek gently. He nodded in agreement. This was how it was supposed to be, him and Jo.

Nick's fingers ran down her spine before he brought them over her side, over her stomach, and into her palm. He turned her arm so that her scar was facing up. Jo shivered at his touch and her hand clenched as she attempted to pull away from him. However, he wouldn't let her go. His eyes moved from the scar up to her eyes.

"Please, tell me about this. What happened?"

Jo's lower lip trembled, and she tugged her arm away from him again. He let go of her arm, allowing her to place the scar against her chest protectively.

"It wasn't supposed to get that bad," she murmured.

"*What* wasn't?" Nick treaded carefully with his words. He needed Jo to know that she was safe and there was no judgment here in these walls with him.

"I was in so much pain," she said. Her breaths grew tight. "It was why I sent you away. I thought... I thought I didn't deserve you. I hated myself. I hated the world. I hated everything. And this.... helped."

"This? Cutting yourself?" Jo nodded. "I should have known," Nick said, touching her hand. "I never should have left you, Jo. I should have stayed. I should have –"

"I pushed you away, Nick. I pushed everyone away. Had Vivian not found me that day –"

"What day? The day this happened?" He brought her arm away from her chest and ran his finger back along the scar. Jo nodded. "Tell me about this day, please."

Jo let out a low breath. Then she quietly told him about that fateful day.

"Why... Why didn't Vivian call me or your mom?" Nick breathed. "I would have come back in a heartbeat for you."

"I know you would have," Jo said. "It's why I refused to let them tell you, Nick. You had finally gotten away."

"Finally gotten away?" Nick felt tears welling in his eyes. "Oh, Jo."

"I got help," she added. "It took some convincing, but it was the only way Vivian promised not to call you."

"I wish she had."

"I know," Jo whispered. "But you have to understand that I wasn't ready. And... I wouldn't let her, Nick. Please don't be angry with her."

"I'm not. I only wish I had done better, called more... tried to come home."

"No point in wishing for the past," Jo said. "You couldn't have known. There was one time I almost called you," Jo admitted.

"When?" Nick asked.

"About a year ago," Jo confessed. "But I was too ashamed of how I acted and my scars.... I—"

"Shh," Nick said. "It's all done now. We found our way back to one another."

Jo pressed her head against Nick's chest. He brought his arms around her. His body felt whole once more. Everything had fallen back into its place.

"What will you do about Eleanor?" Jo asked against his chest.

"I'll speak with her today. I won't lead her on," Nick said. "I never would do anything like that. Perhaps I can take her out to lunch?"

Jo looked up.

"That's a good idea," she agreed. "She is nice. I hate that she got caught in the crosshairs of all of this."

"Me too, but we belong together, Jo. I'll let her down easily. It will all work out."

Vivian heard her phone ding and lifted it. She was in the middle of making breakfast for the kids. When she saw what the message on her phone said, she childishly giggled.

"Mom? Are you okay?" TJ asked, glancing up from his tablet at the kitchen island.

"Yes, oh yes, I am just grand," Vivian said. She dropped the spatula in the pan and quickly rushed to her husband's office, feeling giddy.

Upon the door being opened, Thomas looked up in surprise. He wrinkled his forehead at Vivian's happiness. She rushed toward him, spinning side to side with a wide grin.

"What's this?" he asked.

"They slept together!"

"What? Who? Is this about some show you watch?"

"No, Thomas; Nick and Jo! They slept together!" Vivian clapped, the excitement pumping through her veins.

"Oh," Thomas said. "And you know that because...?"

"Jo texted me. It happened last night! Oh, Thomas! It's finally happened. I knew it would, one day."

Thomas smiled. He got up from his office chair and walked around to be close to his wife.

"What will you focus on now?" He asked.

"What do you mean?"

"You have been rooting for them for five years now. I know you. You always have to have something to put your focus on. What comes next?"

"A vow renewal ceremony?" Vivian asked. Her mind began to swirl with thoughts of how to celebrate. "Or... a big party? I don't know! I have to think of all the different possibilities first."

Thomas drew her closer to press a kiss to the top of her head.

"Well, whatever is planned, as long as you have your hand in it, it will be perfect. I am happy for them, truly."

"Oh me too, Thomas! So happy!"

Charlie sat on the chair by the window as he did his crossword puzzle of the day. This chair also allowed him to see into the kitchen. From this angle, he could see his daughter and Nick at the sink. Nick's touch lingered on the small of Jo's back. The two of them kept looking back and forth at one another, smitten. He tutted beneath his breath.

"Are you spying, Charlie Scott?" Rose whispered as she bent down to her husband's level and tried to see what he was looking at.

"It appears those two may be back together," Charlie answered gruffly. "I thought he had a girlfriend." He shifted in his seat.

Rose stood. Her hands clasped before her as she eyed the couple across the room.

"We can't know for sure, Charlie. Either way, it really isn't our business."

"Isn't our business!?" Charlie disagreed too loudly. Rose shushed him and hit his shoulder. Charlie looked up, but thankfully, neither Jo nor Nick noticed. "He left her at her lowest," he murmured. Though his voice was low, his anger was evident. "She deserves better."

Rose stood silently for a moment before she answered.

"I think you are far too harsh on him, Charlie. He lost his daughter too, and he was losing his wife. Jo wasn't the only one hurting."

"Even so," Charlie sighed. "I don't like it."

"You two seem... different," Lulu observed. Her eyes followed them as they finished clearing up the dishes in the sink. Her father kept reaching out toward Jo, and she would smile up at him. It differed from before, when they seemed to avoid one another.

"Different, how?" Nick asked. He turned to face her with a bright smile.

"Um, what do you call that feeling when you feel like it's happened before?"

"Oh, um, déjà vu?" Jo suggested. Lulu smiled.

"Yes, déjà vu! This feels like déjà vu, like I've been here before."

"Really?"

Lulu did not miss the happiness in her mother's voice and the smile that seemed to be always there now. Jo's eyes widened with hope.

"Yes," Lulu answered. "It's just..." She paused. Lulu couldn't explain it, but there was something familiar about how her parents were behaving, which reminded her of a time before.

"Is it how we are acting? Something that we did?" Jo asked.

Lulu hit her finger against her chin in thought. Then she shrugged.

"I'm not sure. Just you together like that."

Nick glanced down at Jo and winked. His mouth curled up into a grin before he bent down and pressed a kiss to Jo's temple.

"We do like being together," Nick said as he turned back to look at Lulu. "The three of us, that is."

"Me too." Lulu grinned.

"Good," Jo said. "Should we go outside and get some fresh air? The sun is out and I'm sure Butler would love to play."

"Yes!" Lulu agreed.

Jo stepped back inside in search of the jump rope she bought the other day for Lulu. It had been an impulse purchase. She didn't know if Lulu even knew how to use one, but she had wanted to see.

"Jo?" Her mother's voice caught her off-guard. She thought her parents had gone out for lunch.

"Yes, Mom?"

"Are you and Nick back together?" Leave it to Rose Scott to ask the hard-hitting questions without a preamble.

"We are," Jo answered. She had no reason to lie. She didn't miss how her mother smiled at Jo's confession. Her eyes looked at the back window to see Nick and Lulu playing in the backyard. "Now, I don't need to hear about how you or Dad feel about it, okay? We've only just decided. And we know there is still a lot for us to discuss and that it won't all be back how it was in just one day. It is a big day for us, though. We want to make this work. So I don't need you both telling me what a bad idea this is."

"Why do you believe I'll think it's a bad idea? *I* have always adored Nick," Rose said. "I just hope you two have thought this through."

"We have," Jo resolutely said.

"And Eleanor?"

"Nick is going to end it with her today, Mom. He wants us to be a family again. It's time for us to start over."

Rose grasped at her daughter's hands.

"I want that, too. I really do, Jo. I want you to be happy, all of you."

Jo nodded. She squeezed her mother's hands back. "We do too."

Eleanor took a cab to Nick's house. She hated taking Nick away from Lulu for long periods of time, but she had come all this way to see him. She knew they would be out for a while for lunch and that was long enough.

Stepping out of the cab, she tipped the driver and turned back to the house. She heard sounds of laughing in the backyard.

Curious, Eleanor walked over toward the sound. She touched the fence and she glanced over the top. She saw Nick chasing Lulu. The little girl's hair flew behind her as she laughed. Jo then caught her in a surprise swoop. Lulu's laughter only grew louder as Nick gathered them both up into his arms.

Jo conceded by placing Lulu down beside her. Nick gathered Jo back into his arms, nuzzling his nose into the nook of her neck. Jo glanced back up at him and their eyes met.

Eleanor swallowed hard. This was not what she had been expecting.

TWENTY-SEVEN

SPRING 2014

Jo's eyes fluttered from one corner of the room to the other. It was small, quaint. Over the past several months, it had become a room of comfort for her. In this room, judgment did not exist. She could say what was on her mind and the person before her would just listen. Sometimes the doctor offered words of encouragement or helped Jo to see things in a different light. But there was *never* judgment on anything she said.

"Tough week?" Doctor Jameson said. She adjusted her glasses on her nose before flipping the page in her notebook.

"A bit," Jo agreed. Her voice was strained and gave her away, leading Dr. Jameson to give her a solemn smile.

"We've spoken about how hard days and hard weeks are all a part of the healing process, Jo. This week, I know, is extra hard on you."

Jo nodded. A tear slipped down her cheek, and she let it fall.

"I should be planning her fifth birthday party," Jo murmured. "My daughter should be telling me what she wants and how she wants to decorate."

Dr. Jameson moved her notebook to the side and then slid forward in her chair to be closer to Jo.

"Have you spoken to Nick?"

Jo's head shook.

"I haven't...." She took a deep breath. "No. No."

"You are doing much better now, Jo. You two should speak with one another. Your daughter's birthday is in a few days. I think you should call him. You know his heart aches like yours does."

Jo chewed on the edge of her thumb. Nick had been filling her thoughts a lot lately. He did anytime she thought of Lulu. It had been nearly nine months since she had seen and spoken to him last. She was certain he wouldn't want to speak with her now.

"All right." Dr. Jameson decided not to push her on speaking with Nick. Jo was grateful. "Have you thought about declaring Lulu's death and having a ceremony for her?"

Over the past several sessions, Dr. Jameson gently pushed for her to see the facts of the case. Dr. Jameson impressed upon her how much it would greatly assist in her healing. For Jo to move forward in life, she had to let go.

"No," Jo whispered. "I can't... I'm not...." Deep within her, there was still that bit of doubt. It would scream at her that her daughter was still alive, despite what every ounce of evidence said.

"Maybe in a little while."

"Perhaps," Jo said. She tucked her hands into her lap.

"How is the part-time job going?"

"All right," Jo answered. It was a simple job of organizing folders at Thomas's office. She didn't have to speak with people, but it kept her busy. It also kept her parents from watching her every move. For a few hours each day, she could be alone and not be treated like she might fall apart again.

When the session ended, Jo saw she had several missed messages from both her parents and Vivian. With Lulu's upcoming birthday, they were all concerned that she might go back to her self-harming ways. Quickly, she texted her parents to remind them she had been in her therapy appointment. Then she called her sister.

"Ah, where were you? Mom and Dad called me about a hundred times, asking if I knew where you were," Vivian said into the phone.

"I was in therapy. Not sure how they forgot. It's on the calendar. I go the same time every week."

"Right," Vivian said. But there was something in her strained voice that made Jo think there was something else going on.

"What is it?" Jo asked.

"Well..." She paused. "Mom said there were flowers from Nick on the front porch. I think she worried you had seen them and got upset."

"Flowers? From Nick?"

"For Lulu," Vivian explained.

"Oh, of course," Jo said. "They probably came early." Lulu's birthday was still a few days away, and it sounded like Nick, to send something to her to celebrate the day their daughter was born. He had always given her a gift on that special day before Lulu went missing.

"So you *aren't* having a nervous breakdown?" Vivian chuckled, but the worry was still there beneath the surface. Jo sighed.

"No. I am not. I was in therapy, like I said. It went well. I already messaged our parents to let them know I was there."

"Okay, good. You know we just love you, right?"

"I do."

"Well, I ought to go. Love you!"

"Love you too."

Jo dropped her phone into her purse. Then she went to sit on the bench near the park. She had zero desire to head back home right now. Her parents knew she was alive and safe, so she had about an hour before they would start worrying again.

As she glanced up, she saw parents walking with their little one. The baby was tiny, maybe a few months old. She remembered when she and Nick took Lulu for her first trip to the park around that age. They had walked around the park trail and pointed out things for her to see.

Jo wondered where they would be if she'd been pregnant last winter. The baby would be around six months by now. Nick would have stayed, but she wouldn't have wanted that. Nick staying for another child would not be staying for her. No, it was best that she hadn't been pregnant.

The rain splattered on the windowpane, causing Nick to cover his head with a pillow. He didn't want to wake up. He had purposely taken the day off so that he wouldn't have to face the world today. But the rain continued to hit against the window and walls of his apartment complex with a cruel patter, patter.

His phone rang. Keeping his eyes closed, he batted at the phone with his hand. Finally, he found the button to silence the call and send it to voicemail. But it started up again. He groaned. This time, he lifted his head to see who thought it was so important to call him at eight in the morning. If it was his sister-in-law, he might scream. While he appreciated her checking in on him every so often, he did not appreciate the early morning call.

His heart stopped when he saw it was Jo's number. He quickly sat himself up and clicked to answer.

"Hello?" his voice croaked. For a moment, the line was quiet, and he was afraid that she may have accidentally called him. Then he heard the distinct hiccup on the other line; he knew was Jo crying. "Jo?"

"I just..." She took a moment to gather herself. "It's her birthday."

"I know," he murmured.

"Do you remember how loudly she screamed when she was born?" Jo asked. There was a hint of happiness in her voice at the memory.

Nick remembered that day vividly. The moment he saw his daughter, he felt this rush of love consume him. The love differed from the love he felt for Jo. It was no more or less, just different.

"I do," Nick said with a soft smile. "You were so strong that day."

"I don't know about that," Jo disagreed.

"I do," Nick disagreed further. "It will always be one of my favorite memories."

The line went silent. Nick shifted on the bed, wondering if there was something better he should be saying. Part of him wanted to ask if he should come home, but he stopped himself.

"Thank you for the flowers. They are beautiful," Jo said, a beat later. "I put them in a vase by the window in the kitchen."

Nick could easily visualize them sitting there. It was where Jo always placed any flowers he ever got her. Tears filled his eyes, and he attempted to blink them away before remembering he was alone. He allowed them to fall.

"I..." Nick stopped himself before telling Jo how much he missed her.

"I know," Jo whispered. "Me too."

Again, the two of them sat in silence. Though it was quiet, there was comfort in having Jo on the other line. Just knowing that she was there with him made the day feel slightly less stifling.

"I... I should go," Jo said, sniffling. "I..."

"Of course," Nick replied. "Thank you for calling."

"Next year?"

His heart ached. A year. Once a year, he would get to hear Jo's voice. He wanted more than that.

"Yes, next year. Goodbye, Jo."

"Goodbye."

The "I love yous" lingered in the air before the line died between them. He placed his phone back on the bedside table before laying himself back down on the bed. Again, he tugged the covers over him and hid his head under the pillow, not planning on seeing the world for the rest of the day.

TWENTY-EIGHT

2016

For the next two years, Nick looked forward to his annual calls from Jo. Though the day pained him, the calls from Jo helped ease his soul while they spoke to one another. It was the one time of the year that he got to hear her voice and to know that she was still here in this world with him.

Today, he sat anxiously awaiting the call. He'd woken up ready to hear her voice and discuss their little girl who should have been seven today. He struggled to imagine Lulu as a seven-year-old. To him, she would always be three. Always innocent. Always his baby girl.

The phone rang. Despite being prepared for it, he jumped. Nick grabbed the phone and paused for a moment before answering.

"Hello?"

"Hi." Jo's voice was soft. He tried to imagine her back at their home, sitting in their bed. His arms ached to hold her. "How are you?"

Nick's brow cocked up. There were never pleasantries like that during these calls. They usually only spoke about Lulu, about how they missed her, and about how this day would always connect the two of them.

"I miss her," he answered honestly. The distinct sound of a low sob came through on the other end.

"I do, too."

"Do you have any plans for today?"

"No," Jo whispered. "I don't...." Her words petered out. "I got the flowers. They're beautiful. I thought about taking them to the river."

"Oh, really?" Nick sat up straighter. He'd never heard Jo speak of the Savannah River as if it were their daughter's resting place. He wondered if this meant she was moving forward.

"I thought maybe...." Again, her words faded in the air. "Do you like Chicago?"

More pleasantries.

"It's all right," he said. He wanted to add it was lonely. He missed Jo every single day. Life here was only making it day to day. He'd yet to figure out how to move on without her.

"I bet you love it. You've always liked city life."

"I travel often," Nick said. "I'm going to California for a few days next week." He didn't know why he told her this.

"That's nice."

"Have you gone anywhere lately?"

"No." He heard another sob.

"Jo—"

"I miss her so much. I don't know how to be without her. I....I'm trying, but it's not right for her to not be here and I am."

"I know," Nick murmured. "That ache never will go away, but we have beautiful memories, Jo. We'll always have the memories."

Jo sniffled on the other end. He pictured her wiping the tears away. He should be there.

"I... I should go," Jo said. "I'll speak with you again next year?"

Nick wished he could figure out to make the call go on longer, but any excuse he could come up with sounded weak. He had to tell her goodbye for another year.

"Yes. I'll speak with you then, Jo."

"I...." Jo paused. "Goodbye, Nick."

"Goodbye, Jo."

A hot tear slid down Nick's cheek.

"Is this seat taken?"

Nick glimpsed up from his drink at the bar to find a woman sliding into the seat beside him. His eyes moved back to the television above the bartender, though he could not care less about the game that was on.

"Are you not eating?" the woman asked. She had a British accent, which didn't surprise him as he was at the Los Angeles airport. Many international flights came in through LAX.

"Um, I had a burger a while ago," Nick said.

"Was it good? I would kill for a good burger right now. You see, I flew from Sydney to here, and I am absolutely starving."

"Australia? I could have sworn your accent was British," Nick said. The woman smiled.

"Oh, it is. But there came an opportunity to fly to Australia, and I took it. Once in a lifetime, right? I'm a flight attendant; I'm always looking for new places to see."

"That does sound exciting," Nick said. He took a sip of his beer. He had to admit that it felt nice to speak with someone. Generally, while he traveled, he kept to himself. But he was lonely.

They spoke for nearly an hour, almost making him miss his flight.

"You know, I never got your name," Nick said as he got up from his seat.

"Eleanor Jax. And yours?"

"Nick."

He ran into her again months later at the Chicago airport. It was nice to run into a familiar face. He'd been sitting at his terminal flipping through pictures of Lulu on his phone. He did that often. The memories of Lulu were sometimes the only way to help him get through the day. He ended up on a photo of Lulu and Jo. Lulu had just started walking. Jo was standing in front of her with her hands outstretched, a bright smile on her face. He touched the screen, willing the memory to sharpen in his mind.

"Is that your wife and daughter?"

"Yes," Nick answered. He looked up and smiled. Eleanor took the seat beside him.

"I didn't realize you were married."

Nick clicked the button to make his screen dark and placed the phone into his pocket. He wondered just how much he should divulge to this woman in front of him. He never spoke about Jo and Lulu to anyone. In this world he'd created for himself, he was just single Nick working freelance. It was easier that way. When people knew the truth, they treated him differently.

"I'm—we're separated." The words came out before he could stop himself.

"Oh," Eleanor said. Her cheeks blushed. "I'm sorry."

"It's all right," Nick promised. "We've been separated for a while now. We separated after our daughter went missing."

"Oh my!" Eleanor's eyes widened. "I'm sorry; I–I had no idea."

"There is no need to apologize," Nick said. "You couldn't have known. It's been over four years now. We lost her when she was three."

"What happened?"

Nick didn't know why, but he told Eleanor everything about his daughter and his wife. He had held onto all of this pain for so long. It felt nice to speak with someone about it, someone who wasn't involved in all of it.

"It sounds like you still love Jo," Eleanor said when he'd finished.

He felt a tear slide down his chin, so he quickly wiped it away.

"I'll always love Jo. But love wasn't enough for us, not in the end."

Eleanor frowned. She tapped her fingernails against the side of the seat.

"I'm sorry."

"It's not your fault."

They spoke a while longer. Eleanor skirted around his sad past and instead spoke about her most recent travels. He appreciated how she respected that he didn't want to speak any more about it.

Two weeks later, when they ran into one another again, Nick asked Eleanor out on a date. She grinned, pleased.

"I don't want anything serious," Nick said a moment later. Eleanor's smile faltered. "I just....I don't see a serious relationship in my future, is all."

"Oh, that's all right."

"I do like you, Eleanor." It was true. He did. She was the opposite of Jo in every way and that made her safe. He could have companionship but also never have to worry about getting hurt. It was a win-win.

"But you still love Jo," Eleanor answered.

"I do," Nick said honestly. "She and I are through, though. It's time I moved forward. We get along, don't we?"

Again, Eleanor smiled. "We do. Casual and fun, right?"

Nick laughed, though he wasn't sure he had the same idea of casual and fun as Eleanor.

"Let's take it one day at a time," he settled on.

She gave him her number, telling him she'd be back in town in a week.

TWENTY-NINE

SPRING 2017

"Stop! Stop!" Jo called out, giggling as Nick twirled her around. The dog barked at his feet, while Lulu ran around the both of them. Slowly, Nick set her down. She felt dizzy, needing to blink several times. Her forehead pressed against his chest as he held onto her back to keep her steady.

When she felt the world fall back into place, Jo glanced up. Nick looked at her like he had on their wedding day. There had never been any doubt in those moments that he loved her.

"Eleanor!" Lulu called out.

Immediately, Nick's hands dropped from Jo, and she stepped back away from him. Her back stiffened. This was not how they planned for this to go down. Jo turned to see Eleanor standing at the back gate. Eleanor's lips were in a tight smile.

"She's early," Nick said under his breath.

"Well, I guess it means you can get it over with earlier?" Jo said, chewing on the inside of her lip. Though she trusted Nick and believed in him, there was still this small part of herself nagging that she was being foolish. Eleanor was beautiful and successful. Why would Nick ever choose her over Eleanor?

Jo waved. It felt superficial, and she supposed it was. Eleanor waved back while Lulu rushed over to open the gate to let Eleanor in.

"Thank you, darling," Eleanor said. She patted Lulu's head, which made Lulu grimace slightly before running back behind Jo.

"Well, I'll let you two enjoy your lunch," Jo said. "Come on, Lulu."

Once they were safely inside, Jo walked over to the window, where she could peek out to see what was going on. Even though it was not her business, she wanted to know what they said. She opened up a small gap in the blinds and looked out.

"It's not kind to spy," Lulu said.

Jo dropped her fingers. Lulu was right. "I wasn't," Jo lied. "I just wanted to make sure we hadn't forgotten anything."

Lulu giggled. "You shouldn't fib."

"All right, all right, you got me." Jo winked at her.

"Why is Eleanor here?" Lulu asked. "How long has Daddy known her?"

"Well, she's here for them to go to lunch, and I am not sure. At least six months," Jo answered.

"Oh."

Her heart hammered in her chest. Was she a fool? She and Nick had been on the verge of a divorce. They had not seen one another in nearly five years. What if their night had just been that, a night? Sure, they had missed one another, and the connection was real, but didn't all couples go through that after a breakup? Would he return and say last night had been a mistake?

Before she could psych herself out anymore, she heard her phone ring. She saw it was Vivian calling. Stepping away from Lulu's earshot, she lifted the phone.

"Hello?"

"So, tell me all about it," Vivian excitedly said.

"You want details?" Jo asked.

"Well, no, but how was it? You two are back together, right?"

"I think so," Jo said. Again, she peeked through the blinds. "He is about to take Eleanor out to lunch to break the news."

"But?"

"But what?"

"Jo, I can hear it in your voice. What worries you?"

"What if he realizes he's made a terrible mistake and that he wants to be with her? She is beautiful, and she is smart."

"Jo, you are beautiful and smart," Vivian reminded her. "And he loves you. I know he does. He would choose you in a paper bag over any other woman in the world. I bet if you had called him at any time over the past four years and asked him to come home, he would have."

"You really think so?"

"I know so. Now, get out of your head."

Nick felt awkward. He had never actually broken up with anyone before. He casually dated a few other women before

Jo. However, they had all just ended organically as they grew apart. Then he met Jo. After her, he never thought he'd fall in love again. Even though he liked Eleanor, he didn't love her, not how it counted.

They walked out of the gate. He made sure to lock it so that Butler couldn't escape when let out.

As they turned the corner, Eleanor stopped. She touched his upper arm and gave him a solemn smile. Her perfect bob framed her face. He wasn't sure he had ever seen a hair of hers out of place.

"You got your family back," she said. It was then he noticed the mistiness of her eyes. "I should have known.... This is a pleasant neighborhood. It's a wonderful place to raise a family."

"Eleanor, why don't you let me take you to lunch?" Nick offered.

"I don't think that's necessary, Nick. I just saw the three of you out back playing, and I realized it was the happiest I have ever seen you."

"I never expected it to happen like this," Nick said.

"Of course you didn't. But it's always been Jo. I've always known you loved her more than me."

"I wish —"

"Don't," Eleanor interrupted. "I don't need any of those sentiments. While I'm sad for myself, I am happy for you, Nick. I mean it."

"Are you sure you don't want me to take you to lunch?"

Eleanor chuckled.

"No, that's all right. While I am sure it would be the nicest break-up I have ever had, I should probably go now.

I needn't take you away from your family longer than neces-sary." Eleanor lifted herself on her toes so she could press a kiss on Nick's cheek. "Goodbye, Nick. I hope you have a good life. Keep in touch?"

"Sure." Nick nodded. "And thank you for understanding." Eleanor dropped her hands from his shoulders. She turned away, making Nick wonder where she would go. "Do you need a ride?" he called after her. She waved her hand, telling him she had it figured out.

He watched her until she turned a corner and he could see her no longer. That had gone much easier than he expected. He smiled. He had Jo and Lulu. He had his family back.

Jo stared at her reflection in the mirror. Her hair was stringy and beneath her eyes were dark circles from the years' worth of sleep deprivation. She ran her fingers through her hair, thinking of her sister's beautiful, thick hair that she didn't get. Jo had always thought her sister was the gorgeous one, and that she was just plain and average.

She attempted to comb her hair and give it more life, but it just fell flat. She frowned.

"What are you doing?" She jumped slightly at Nick's voice, dropping the comb onto the sink. "Sorry, I didn't mean to frighten you."

"It's all right. I just haven't had anyone in my bathroom in years," Jo said. "I mean, our bathroom. It is ours again, right?"

"It is," Nick agreed. He walked up to her, placing his chin on her shoulder. Jo raised a brow.

"Shouldn't you be at lunch?"

"Eleanor ended it right outside," Nick explained.

"What?"

"She saw us outside and knew we were back together," Nick said. Jo nervously chewed on the inside of her lip.

"Oh, was she furious?"

Nick's head shook.

"Not at all. She was happy for us, actually."

"She was?" Jo didn't know if she could believe that.

"She was," Nick repeated. "Eleanor hopes we're happy. She's always known that I love you."

"You always did?" Jo's voice was tight and full of hope.

"Of course I did," Nick said. He bent forward, kissing his wife. "It's always been you, Jojo."

Jo's heart fluttered. She reached toward his chest and adored the feeling of his heart beating. His breath was hot against her ear.

"Always," he said once more.

"And it's always been you," Jo whispered. Their eyes met, hooded over with both lust and love.

Jo slipped her fingers beneath the buttons of Nick's shirt to feel his skin against her fingertips. The warmth flooded her. Her eyes fluttered closed.

"Where is everyone?" Lulu's voice had Nick stepping back away from Jo. Jo turned back to the mirror and tried to still her rapid heart rate.

"Up here, sweetheart!" Jo called out.

She and Nick looked at one another through the mirror. They laughed.

"Reminds me of old times," Nick said.

"Yes, me too."

The sound of little footsteps came down the hallway. Jo wanted to pinch herself. How had they gotten back to this special place? It had to all be a dream. Her fingers moved to her skin, and she did a little pinch on her wrist.

"Why are you both in the bathroom?" Lulu asked. Again, Nick and Jo laughed. Jo's arm darted out to nudge Nick's. He turned his hand to grasp Jo's into his own, giving it a loving squeeze.

"I was just brushing my hair," Jo said.

"And I was helping your mother." Nick grinned at Jo, making her heart skip a beat.

"Oh, cool. What about Eleanor?"

"She had to leave," Nick answered. "She is going back to her own home."

Lulu glanced between the two of her parents. She twirled the edge of her hair with her finger before shrugging.

"You two will be together forever, right?"

Had Lulu asked that question the day before, Jo and Nick would have had to tell her they were divorcing. Today, Jo could nod.

"Always."

"Good! I like it here with you two."

Jo and Nick kept their fingers laced with one another as they walked closer to Lulu. When they reached her, Jo bent down to her level.

"We're very glad of that. We love having you back with us, Lulu. I know this is all new, and we're all learning about each other again. But we just want you to be happy, Lulu. It is all we have ever wanted."

Without warning, Lulu's arms wrapped around Jo's neck. Jo nearly cried out with joy. She slowly brought her arms around Lulu. It was only her second hug since Lulu came back home.

"We love you, Lulu," Jo whispered. "We love you so much."

"I love you too, Mama."

Jo felt a happy tear slip down her cheek. She stood, pulling Lulu up into her arms with her. Nick placed his hand on Lulu's back before bending over and kissing the top of Jo's head. Jo met Nick's eyes.

"We're back," she whispered. "We're really back."

When Jo entered Lulu's room to grab the dirty clothes that needed to be washed, she found the frame with the picture of Sally in the trash bin, turned upside down. It looked as though Lulu had placed it that way purposely. A large part of Jo wanted to leave the picture frame in the bin, but she found herself pulling it out and wiping the pieces of paper off the edges.

Jo turned the frame around so she could look at the picture. Anger still filled her when she looked at it. One day, she would have to face this woman in person. There would be a trial. She and Nick would have to testify.

She wanted all of this behind them, but it wasn't. They still had reporters everywhere. They would always be the parents whose daughter was stolen, and Lulu would always be the stolen child.

"Mama?" Jo knew she would never tire of that. She twisted to find Lulu walking into her room. Lulu spotted the frame and raised one eyebrow. "I threw that away."

"I know," Jo answered. She sat down on the edge of Lulu's bed and then patted the bed for Lulu to join her. "You don't have to throw this away, Lulu. I know that for nearly five years, you thought she was your mother. I cannot imagine how confusing all of those feelings are."

Lulu took the frame from Jo, stood, and placed it back into the bin.

"She lied to me. She took me," Lulu said.

"She did." Jo gave her a solemn look. "But you still loved her."

"I don't want it anymore. Dr. Canmore said it was up to me if I wanted to keep the picture or not. I don't."

"As long as you are sure," Jo said. "Don't do it for me or your daddy. We want our home to be a safe place for you, Lulu."

"It is," Lulu assured her. "I'm glad you're my mama. You're much kinder than she was."

Jo frowned slightly. Part of her comfort in all of it was that it had appeared at least the woman had loved Lulu while she was away from them. There had been no signs of any abuse. But those words made Jo pause.

"Was she mean to you?"

"Not mean," Lulu explained. "Just always...what was that word she would she say?" Lulu tapped her finger against her chin. "Oh! Overwhelmed. She would always say she was overwhelmed. And when she wasn't, she was sleeping or not at the house."

Jo clutched her hand over her heart.

"I'm sorry," Jo whispered.

"It's okay. I am here now with you and daddy. I don't ever have to go back, right?"

"No, never," Jo promised. She took Lulu's hands in hers. "Never. You will stay with us now. You are ours and we are yours, always."

That evening, Nick slipped into their bed. He couldn't believe that he was finally back here. It all seemed a bit too perfect. Suddenly, he felt like a shoe was about to drop. With all the trauma they had experienced, he knew they couldn't just be perfect again.

Perhaps this was a honeymoon phase. Would they be prepared for when that shoe dropped?

"Penny for your thoughts?" Jo asked. He brought his arm around her, drawing her closer. Her eyes were searching his face.

"You'd likely pay triple not to hear them."

"Why? What's wrong?" She sat herself up.

"Nothing is wrong."

Jo's fingers ran over his jawline. He still couldn't get enough of her touching him. There had been far too many years without it.

"Don't lie to me."

Nick sighed. "You're right. I shouldn't lie."

"Then what is it?"

"Everything is just a bit too perfect, don't you think?" He brought his fingers through Jo's hair. It slipped effortlessly through his fingertips.

"How so?"

"Lulu gets along with us well. You and I slipped back into place. I just... I worry that we have things to work through."

"We're still going to therapy," Jo said. His words didn't seem to concern her. "Some days will be better than others, Nick. I sincerely doubt every day will be this perfect. We have to take each day as it comes."

"That's true." He leaned forward to kiss her. "I guess we just see what the future holds."

"Exactly. And we just stay prepared," Jo added. "I think it's best we understand that we all still have trauma that plagues us, but we have one another now."

Thirty

Nick peered out the window of their home. Just the night before, there had been a special on about their family. Now, reporters surrounded the outside of their home. He didn't know how they were going to do anything today. He needed to see about a potential local job, but now he didn't want to leave the house.

He felt arms move around his middle as Jo's head rested on his back.

"What if we moved?" Jo suggested. Nick turned, not expecting her to suggest such a thing.

"Really?" he asked.

"Yes. We could start over."

"But you never wanted to move before," Nick reminded her.

"That was then," Jo said. She slowly exhaled. "That was when she was gone, but she's back, Nick. This place, it's full of hurt and pain."

"Your sister lives here and your parents."

Jo nodded.

"I know. But my parents will probably want to move back to St. Simons soon now that things are... figured out."

Nick hoped so. It was growing awkward having the in-laws living with them. He and Jo had been back together for over a month now, and his in-laws were always there. It didn't allow for much growing—and there was still so much that needed to happen. Despite all the happiness, there was still much they needed to discuss. Some days, the anger and hurt were still there beneath the surface. None of that was going to just fade away. Their therapist warned it could take years to sort through all of it and to be patient with one another.

The problem was that Rose and Charlie would step in if they were having even the smallest of arguments. So they just didn't argue and therefore those things got stuffed further down instead of being discussed.

"What about your sister? Thomas? TJ and Callie?"

"I'll miss them," Jo agreed. "But this isn't our home anymore, Nick. You have always loved to travel. We should move somewhere to start over, somewhere with things to see and do. A place where we can easily hop on a plane and go anywhere."

Nick smiled. He did like the sound of that. For the time being, Lulu was being homeschooled anyway. Eventually, the plan was to send her to an actual school. However, for now, they could easily travel as a family. He could even take them along on longer trips for his work.

"Where?" he asked.

"I don't know. Chicago?"

"You'd move to such a big city?" This surprised Nick. He had always known Jo as someone who loved living in a rural area. She never had been a fan of traffic or crowds. He, on the other hand, didn't mind it, especially if it meant he could see the world around him. He enjoyed being a part of everything.

"Why not?" Jo's smile warmed his heart.

"I don't want you to resent me, Jojo," he whispered. "Leaving your home, the only place you've ever really known...."

"I will not resent you," she promised.

That was easy for her to say now, but he couldn't know that she wouldn't change her mind once they got there. They still had so much they hadn't solved between them. And here, they had a support system.

"I think we should discuss it for a while," Nick said. "It's not that I don't trust that it's what you want. It's just that moving is a big change for all of us. Lulu has Dr. Canmore here. We have our therapist, too. I do like the idea of moving and starting over. I just want to make sure we do it in the right way."

"Oh, okay," Jo agreed. "I understand that, but this is what I want, Nick. I think it'll make us happy. And we won't have to deal with that anymore." She pointed to the window.

"They can follow us," Nick reminded her.

"Yes, but here everyone knows us, Nick. Moving, we get a chance to rebrand ourselves. Eventually, people will know who we are, but it will be different. It will be better, especially in a big city. They will have plenty of other scandals and things to focus on outside of us."

"I agree."

For the next several days, Jo researched the area of Chicago. She knew very little about the area, except that most of Nick's work came from around there.

All of it was overwhelming. They had to look at the schools, choose an area to live in, and deal with traffic. Yet despite it all, she still wanted to make this big move. All three of them were different people than they used to be. This would be a good start for them. They no longer belonged in this small town.

In many ways, they were all relearning one another. Starting over would allow that to happen more organically. A new place would keep them from expecting things to be the same.

Her only concern was pulling Lulu away from her psychiatrist. Dr. Canmore was wonderful with her, so they knew their Lulu needed to keep seeing her. She and Nick often struggled with understanding what exactly their daughter needed in moments when she felt lost, scared, or upset. The trauma had affected her in different ways, and Lulu was much too young to understand it.

With another swoop over the letters on her keyboard, Jo found a small neighborhood. It seemed promising, right outside of the city. It would hopefully be an easy commute for Nick. However, when she saw the price, her face paled. How would they afford that?

She sat back. She grabbed her water and took a few sips before chewing on her crackers.

"What are you up to?"

Jo glimpsed up to find her sister at her office door. Her sister was always doing that: popping by whenever she felt like it.

"I need to take your key to my house," Jo said.

Vivian grinned.

"Like I don't have copies. What are you up to?"

Jo looked back at her screen. She quickly closed the window so her sister couldn't look over her shoulder and see what she was researching. Both she and Nick had decided not to tell anyone yet about their plans to move. They did not need their input on their choices.

"Nothing," Jo lied.

Vivian narrowed her eyes. She glanced at the water Jo held and over to the crackers. Her shoulders bounced with happiness as she connected the pieces.

"You're pregnant!"

Jo shook her head.

"No, I am not," she disagreed.

"Yes," Vivian said with conviction. "You are."

"Vivian, I am forty years old. What makes you think I am pregnant? Do you think some miracle baby is growing inside me right now?" Jo laughed. It was absurd.

"Forty-year-olds have babies all the time, Jo. Have you and Nick used any sort of protection?"

"You know we haven't." Jo waved her hand in the air. "I can't get pregnant. You know how hard it was for us to have Lulu."

"You're pregnant," Vivian repeated.

"Oh my god. Why do you keep saying that?" Jo was growing frustrated now. She closed her laptop and stood.

"You're drinking water and eating crackers. That's all you lived off of when you were pregnant with Lulu."

"Or, I just needed a snack," Jo said. "Jeez." She thought back to the past several weeks with Nick. She hadn't had her cycle since... well, she couldn't remember. However, that was not shocking for her. It had always been unreliable. "I think you just *want* me to be pregnant. It will fulfill the rest of your fantasy of Nick and me coming full circle."

Vivian chuckled.

"I know my sister. You are pregnant. Just like how I knew you weren't pregnant back after your cruise, but I had you take the test, anyway."

Jo rolled her eyes.

"You couldn't have known."

"Oh, I did. You desperately wanted a reason for Nick to stay, so you convinced yourself." Jo shot her sister a look. "I don't blame you, Jo. That was a terrible time for you both. But now, you are. I knew the moment you were pregnant with Lulu." That was true. She had. It was like her sister had some weird sixth sense.

"I'm not," Jo argued, but her fingers lingered over her belly. "Now would not be a good time."

"When is?"

"Never, not for us. We are still adjusting as a family. We are also looking into moving." It slipped out before Jo realized it. She looked at her sister's face. Her sister smiled.

"Oh, moving? Where?"

"We aren't sure yet." It wasn't a complete lie; they hadn't made a certain choice on where they would go. "And don't tell Mom and Dad. We still have so much we need to discuss before making any decisions."

"Of course," Vivian answered. "I think it's brilliant. Fresh slate and all that."

"Thank you, Vivian, truly. Not that I need your blessing."

Vivian rolled her eyes.

"Never said you did. Now, take a pregnancy test."

"I don't have one," Jo said. "And I'm not pregnant."

"Oh, all right. I guess I cannot force you to believe me. You'll find out soon enough."

Jo wanted to wipe the smirk off her sister's face. Vivian was always so sure she knew everything. Instead of giving her the satisfaction of saying anything in return about it, she reopened her computer and ignored her. Eventually, Vivian grew bored and went home.

When Nick arrived back home, he had to maneuver around the number of people on his street. So many people wanted him and Jo to give an interview about their experiences. He refused to; he wouldn't be fodder for their showcase. He knew Jo didn't want to speak about it, either. This was a time in their lives when they were trying to find their new normal. Being interviewed and looked at with such scrutiny would help none of that.

He made it to the garage and made sure not to leave his car until the door was firmly closed. He only made the mistake once to get out before then. One time, a younger reporter had barged inside and began asking a million questions. No, he would not make that mistake again.

He stepped inside the house. It smelled amazing. He noticed his mother-in-law making dinner. He smiled at her before plopping his briefcase down by the door. His eyes scanned downstairs for Jo and Lulu. Lulu was on the floor at her grandfather's feet as he read her a story, but Jo wasn't there.

"She's upstairs," Rose said, reading his mind.

"Ah, thank you."

"Daddy!" Lulu excitedly got up from the floor. She rushed toward him and brought her arms around him for a hug. He bent down slightly to hug her better and kissed the top of her head.

"How was your day?" he asked.

"Great!" she said. "Mama's upstairs."

"Yes, that's what your grandma said. I'm going to go tell her hello." He let go of Lulu and gave her a wink before making his way up the stairs.

It took him a moment to find his wife. She wasn't in the office or any of the bedrooms. He even checked their bathroom and closets.

"Jojo?"

"Here." He heard a muffled voice. It was in her closet, but he had just opened that door. He looked again and saw that Jo was sitting on the ground, going through clothes.

"Oh, there you are." He smiled and bent down to kiss her. "What are you doing?"

"I haven't cleaned out this closet in years." Her answer was simple, but there was something in her demeanor that was off. She wouldn't quite meet his eyes.

"Is everything all right?"

"Of course. Why wouldn't it be?" Jo shrugged. Still, she kept turned away from him.

"Jo?"

"Hm?"

"Is something bothering you?"

"No."

He knitted his brows in worry before he got down on one knee.

"Have you changed your mind about the move?"

At that, Jo looked up at him. Her face softened, and she gave him a sure smile.

"No," she strongly stated. "I still think we should move. We're surrounded by reporters. That's no way for Lulu to grow up and no way for us to live. We aren't celebrities. We're just an average family, wanting a normal life."

"Then what is it?"

"I guess I am worried about how we'll afford it. It is much more expensive to live in Chicago than in this small town."

"Ah, I don't think we have to worry about that," Nick disagreed. Jo looked at him curiously, so he continued to explain. "For nearly four years, we have been managing two places and two sets of bills. Once we sell this house, we will have an easy down payment for our house in Chicago, or wherever we want to move to. We'll be able to do it."

Jo relaxed some, but it seemed there was still something else on her mind. Nick brushed his fingers over her cheek and brought some of her hair behind her ear.

"Is there something else bothering you?"

"No," Jo said.

"Are you sure?"

"I'm sure."

Before they lost Lulu, Jo would tell him anything and everything on her mind. She had never been the type to just say she was fine when she wasn't. That was not like her. But then they lost Lulu, and she had closed herself from him. Now, there was still that wall that had gone up between them all those years ago. While they were actively working together to break it down, it still had many layers to go.

"You can tell me anything," he reminded her. Jo nodded against his hand.

"I know."

Nick waited a moment longer, hoping Jo would tell him what was on her mind, but she didn't. He leaned forward to kiss the crown of her head before giving up and standing. He still had plenty to do before dinner time. He went back into their bedroom to get into more comfortable clothes. While changing, he saw a list Jo had written about potential places to live near or around Chicago. He lifted it.

"We could fly up soon and check some of these places out," he called back to Jo.

"Hm?"

"What if we flew out to Chicago in a couple of weeks? I still need to clean out my apartment there. My lease ends next month."

Jo's head peeked out from the closet.

"Yeah, that sounds like a good idea. Let's do that."

"Good."

"Your father and I have been talking," Rose began that night at dinner.

Jo set her fork down on her plate and twitched her lips. Ever since her conversation with Vivian, her stomach felt uneasy. She knew her sister had gotten into her head about this baby nonsense. She couldn't be pregnant.

"About what?" Nick asked. Jo realized she should listen to her parents. She shifted her eyes to them.

"We think it is time we move back to our home on St. Simons."

"Oh?" Nick sounded a bit too elated. Jo kicked him gently under the table. "Oh," he tried again. "Why is that?"

"Well, you two have begun this new phase of life with Lulu. It's time we allow you to be your own family now. You don't need us anymore."

"Why?" Lulu asked. She was frowning.

"Sweetheart," Jo began. "Your grandparents have their own home on St. Simons. You know, where we stayed when we went to the ocean. We will still see them."

"What about Butler?"

"Well," Charlie said. "We were thinking he could stay with you guys if you wanted."

Jo turned to look at Nick. A dog? Why didn't her parents discuss this with them before bringing it up to Lulu? How could they tell her no now?

Nick surprised her by immediately agreeing.

"That sounds great! But wouldn't you miss him?"

Jo glared right at him, but he didn't notice.

"Yes," Jo added. "Won't you miss your dog?"

"Oh, we will, but we'll still get to see him. Lulu just loves Butler so much. We couldn't dream of taking him away," Rose said.

A dog. A move. The smallest possibility of a baby. How could they possibly manage it all?

"Oh yay! Yes, please, Daddy! Please, Mama! Can we keep him?"

Nick met Jo's eyes as he tried to see what she was thinking. She gave a small, hesitant nod.

"Yes, we can keep him," Jo said, bouncing her knees beneath the table.

"Yay!"

While Lulu celebrated the fact that Butler was now her dog, Jo's worries about the future grew.

"And when will you leave?" Jo asked.

"A couple of weeks," Charlie answered. "We have our last guests scheduled and then, after they're out, we can move back."

"Oh," Jo said. She nodded. Then she stood and grabbed her plate. She needed a reason to walk away.

"What's wrong?" Nick was right behind her in a flash. She hadn't even heard him coming up behind her.

"Nothing." Jo didn't enjoy lying to Nick, but it seemed a bit overdramatic to mention that Vivian thought she might be pregnant. No, she wouldn't say anything without proof.

Thirty-One

Early Summer 2017

With a loud huff, Nick lifted the last box into the back of his in-law's car. They did not have as much stuff as he thought they would. However, many of the boxes had been heavier than they looked. This last one had nearly taken out his back.

Everything fit in his in-laws' trunk and backseat. They wouldn't need to make more visits to grab more or need a moving truck to assist them. Jo told him it was because they originally had only planned on staying for a couple of weeks.

Nick closed the trunk and stepped back. He saw his father-in-law walking up toward him with a beer in his hand. Charlie handed it over to Nick, and Nick took it from him. He hadn't expected that. Lately, he found his father-in-law to be more patient and understanding of him, which was entirely different than it had ever been.

"Thank you," Nick said. Charlie nodded. His eyes stared off within this distance. Nick wondered if he would miss it here. This town was where he and Rose had raised their two girls.

"I may have been too harsh on you," Charlie stated. He cleared his throat. "As Jo's father, I only saw her pain in all of this. I didn't see yours. You had also lost your daughter, and you were losing your wife. I cannot imagine the pain you were going through."

Nick swallowed hard. "It... it's fine."

"It wasn't," Charlie disagreed. "I can now see how much you love my daughter and my granddaughter. I now know that you didn't want to leave Jo."

"I didn't," Nick said.

"Anyway, I guess I should grab Rose. It's time for us to hit the road."

Nick watched Charlie walk inside. He hadn't expected to feel as good as he did after his father-in-law said such simple yet kind words to him.

Lulu ran out of the front door with Butler in her arms. He was yapping, wanting to be put down.

"Don't let the dog go!" Jo yelled from the doorway. She was attempting to slip on her flip-flops while chasing after them both.

"I got him!" Nick promised. He swooped over and lifted Butler from Lulu's arms. She grinned up at him.

"Thanks! He is pretty wiggly."

Nick wondered where his collar and leash were. It would be a pain to have to hold the dog while they said their good-byes. He knew how Jo's family took nearly an hour to say goodbye to everyone.

"Here," Jo said. He looked up to see that she had come with the collar and leash. He bent over and kissed her.

"Thank you."

"You're welcome."

Her words were empty. The past couple of weeks, she had become more distant with him. It felt like before when she had begun pulling away from him, except this time there was no fighting. Sometimes she would be eerily calm about something he was sure might start an argument.

Rose and Charlie were out a moment later, so Nick didn't have more time to ponder what might be going on with his wife. They instead said their goodbyes. As expected, it took up close to an hour. By the time they hit the road, it was past lunchtime.

"Your parents will have to stop for food," he said. Jo just nodded before turning and walking into the house. He wanted to follow her and demand to know what was going on, but Lulu tugged on his sleeve and he remembered he had promised to play outside with her.

Jo checked her watch. Her appointment was soon. Since her cycle still hadn't returned, she decided she would go to the doctor to find out if she was indeed pregnant. She noticed some pregnancy signs, but she also had those similar symptoms when she got overtired or when her period was supposed to begin.

She knew she could take a pregnancy test at home, but decided against it. This way, she would know for certain.

She popped her head out the back door where Nick and Lulu were playing with the dog. Nick looked up and gave her a strained smile.

"I have an appointment," she said. She had told no one about it, not even her sister.

"Appointment?" Jo could hear the clear worry in Nick's voice. "Is everything all right?"

"Yes, I'm fine," Jo replied. "I just have my basic yearly appointment. I'll be back soon."

She saw Nick frown. She pondered if she shouldn't tell him, but there was no reason to bring it up unless it was true. He'd find out soon enough either way. She waved at them both and then closed the door before there could be any more questions.

After grabbing her purse, she went to her car. The doctor's office was at the primary hospital, so it was a bit of a drive. She turned on one of her favorite podcasts and focused on it, turning off any thoughts about the past few months and what the doctor might tell her. For now, she just listened to the woman reading letters and giving love advice. It was nice to listen to someone else's worries rather than her own.

When she reached the hospital, her stomach clenched. It felt heavy and uneasy. She should have had Nick come along. She should have made this appointment when her parents were still here. Why was she insisting on keeping it this big secret?

Her eyes checked the time. It was too late to be debating any of that now. Her appointment was soon. She inhaled sharply and stepped out of the car.

She had been to this same doctor since she was a teenager. Yet, she was nervous. She was a forty-year-old woman, for Pete's sake. Her life had been turned over in many directions in the past five years. This was just the tip of the iceberg.

Immediately, they gave her a cup to collect her urine. She did as asked and sat back in the room while she waited. Time ticked by slowly. She kept reaching for her phone, wondering if she should call Nick and just tell him what was going on.

"Mrs. Anderson?"

She stood. Here was her moment of truth.

Doctor Mallory entered the room with a file in her hand and lifted it with a tentative smile. Jo sat back further in her chair.

A baby. They were having a baby.

"Jo?" Dr. Mallory said. She took her seat and rolled it closer to Jo. "I know this wasn't expected; I know you've been through a lot. There has been a time when you and Nick wanted more children. Have you been trying?"

"No. We haven't been..." She glanced around the room, looking at all the baby posters on the wall before saying, "We're much older now and there are so many changes."

"You know, there are options."

"No, I'm going to keep it. I just... well, I just need a minute to process it." She rubbed the back of her neck. *Baby*.

Dr. Mallory gave her a moment before starting their appointment.

"Do you happen to know when the date of your last period was?"

"No."

"That's no problem. Let's do an ultrasound. How does that sound? Are you ready for that? We can determine how far along you are."

Jo bit the edge of her lip, but nodded. "All right."

She hated that Nick wasn't there to hold her hand. She had taken that moment away from him with her selfishness. The fear of what might be should have been shared with her husband and not kept from him. She was still learning how to become the woman she once was; the woman who told her husband everything. She still had far to go.

Jo gasped as the cool gel hit her skin. The doctor only offered her a small smile before turning on the screen. Jo's bottom lip came in between her teeth.

"There," Dr. Mallory said. Her finger pointed at the small blob on the screen. Jo's fingers came over her lips in awe. A baby. The blob looked like a baby with a head, arms, and leg; not the little bean Lulu had been in her first ultrasound. She sat up slightly for a better view. She and Nick were having a baby.

"I'm reading you at about twelve weeks," Dr. Mallory informed her.

"Twelve weeks." Jo couldn't believe it. That would mean that she and Nick likely got pregnant the night they got back together.

"Yes. Everything looks perfect," Dr. Mallory assured her. "We will set up an appointment for a few weeks from now. Since you are over thirty-five, this is considered a geriatric pregnancy."

"*Geriatric?*"

"I know, but that's really what it's called," Dr. Mallory said.

"And the baby is doing okay? Even with my older age?"

"Yes. Plenty of women your age have perfectly healthy babies, Jo. And here." Dr. Mallory handed Jo pictures of her ultrasound. "Congrats again, Jo."

"Thank you."

Nick kept checking the clock. It felt like hours since Jo left for her appointment. He wondered if she was sick. Was that why she was being so secretive and distant from him?

The dog came up to nip at his heels, so Nick lifted him to rub his head. The dog immediately settled into his arms. Over time, they had become good friends.

Nick walked Butler into the living room where Lulu was watching some show on the television. He set the dog onto his bed before sitting down next to his daughter. His eyes kept moving to the door, hoping Jo would be home soon.

The door finally opened and Nick shot up. While walking inside, Jo had a nervous energy about her. She dropped her purse on the floor before walking over toward him.

"Hi, Mama," Lulu brightly said.

"Hey," Jo replied. She did smile, but her body was stiff. Her eyes moved to Nick. "Can we go upstairs and talk?"

"Sure," Nick answered. He took her hand. It was clammy. He swallowed hard.

When they entered the bedroom, Jo slowly let out a breath. She walked away from him and appeared to be muttering to herself. Nick watched in both confusion and amusement.

"Jojo?"

"I... I'm sorry," she whispered with a shake of her head. "I... I got some news. And—"

"Are you sick?"

"What? No," Jo said, an anxious giggle leaving her.

"Are you wanting the divorce, after all?"

"No," Jo promised. She stepped forward and pulled something out of her back pocket. Slowly, she handed him a picture. "Here."

Nick tentatively took it. He turned it around and then realized that it was a sonogram. No, that couldn't be real. For years, they had tried for another baby. Years. It was impossible that at their ages they were going to have another one.

"A baby?" he breathed.

"Yes, a baby," Jo answered. He saw she was nervously biting on her lower lip. "I.... well, I have suspected for a little while. I didn't want to say anything until I knew for sure."

"Why not?" Nick asked.

"Because everything is so new, Nick. This isn't some walk in the park. Yes, we're all back together, but we're still figuring this all out. There's still tension between us, and Lulu is still learning to trust us. We're rebuilding our lives. Now we're moving and my parents left us their dog and now... a baby."

Nick's hands rested on Jo's shoulders, giving them a supportive squeeze.

"It's a lot," he agreed.

"I know I should have told you sooner and you should have been at the appointment. I was just...."

"Scared?" Nick asked. Jo nodded. Nick used the back of his fingers to caress Jo's cheek. "We've been through a lot."

"We have. I didn't know the right way to deal with it." Jo nervously chewed on the inside of her cheek. "I handled it poorly."

"It's okay," Nick said.

"You're not angry with me?"

"Of course, I'm not." He kissed her cheek before pulling her into a tight hug. "I'm thrilled."

"Yeah?" Jo asked against his chest.

"Yes. It is a big change," Nick said. "But we are capable of this, Jo. We finally get to give Lulu the brother or sister she's always wanted."

"I am excited, too," Jo said. "I wasn't until I saw the baby on the screen. I know that sounds cliché, but it's what happened."

Nick smiled. He couldn't believe it. A baby.

"And everything is going well with the baby?" Nick asked.

"It is," Jo said. "Dr. Mallory says the baby is perfect. Though she added that this pregnancy will be a geriatric pregnancy. I'll need extra monitoring." Jo sighed. "God, I feel old. Nick, I'll be nearing sixty when this child is turning eighteen!"

Nick couldn't help but laugh. He brushed his hand along her face before drawing her chin up to him so he could give her a slow, loving kiss.

"I'll be *over* sixty," he reminded her.

"I know." She buried her face against him. He brought his arms around her to hold her closer to him. "But you've aged like fine wine. I'll be the old parent and you'll be the hot stuff dad."

"Hot stuff, huh?" Jo glanced up.

"Yeah."

"Well, I think you're hot stuff." He winked.

"You're really happy?" Jo asked. The smile had faded slightly from Jo's face.

"Absolutely."

They waited a few days to tell Lulu about the pregnancy. Jo wanted to wait longer, but she knew it wouldn't be much longer before she would begin to show. Her stomach already showed signs of her pregnancy.

To tell Lulu their surprise, they wrapped a gift for her. Jo worried it was too corny of an idea. Would Lulu just open it and look at them like they were insane? They did not know how she would react to the news of a sibling.

Jo also worried Lulu would feel they were replacing her, though Nick kept assuring her it would all work out. She hoped he was right.

"Here," Nick said, giving their daughter the present. Lulu took it and cocked up her eyebrow.

"For me?"

"Yes."

"It's not my birthday."

"Well, it's a surprise," Jo said.

Lulu shrugged her shoulders. She carefully lifted the edge of the paper. It was something Jo had noticed when they had given her birthday gifts. Lulu was delicate with the unwrapping of the paper, making sure not to tear any of it. It was so very different from when she had been a toddler; then she had ripped into the paper to get to the special surprise inside.

Once the paper was off the box, Lulu folded it and set it to the side. She lifted the top of the box to reveal a tee shirt that said Big Sister on it. Lulu's eyes didn't leave the package. She lifted the tee shirt and creased her forehead.

"Surprise," Nick said. Lulu glanced up.

"What's this?" she asked.

Jo inhaled. Instinctively, her hand fell to her belly.

"We're having a baby," Nick answered for her. He touched Jo's back and drew her close. Jo's mouth curled up into a tentative smile.

Lulu's face moved through such a myriad of emotions that it was difficult to see what she was thinking. But then she grinned.

"Really?"

"Really," Jo said.

"But I thought you couldn't have any more children."

"We thought so too," Jo answered.

"Wow," Lulu said. "I've always wanted a brother or a sister."

"We've always wanted you to have one," Nick answered.

"A baby. Cool. Um, can I play with Butler outside now?"

"Yes," Jo said.

Lulu called for Butler, and the two of them rushed outside. Nick and Jo had just begun allowing Lulu outside alone, as long as she was in the backyard and they were told she was going out there. That had come from the advice of Dr. Canmore. She insisted Lulu needed to be allowed some independence for all of their sakes. They were advised to do it in controlled ways where they knew Lulu was safe, but she could also gain that independence.

Jo walked over to the door to peek out. She felt Nick's hand on her shoulder.

"She seemed to handle that well," Nick said into her ear. He kissed the nook of her neck, causing her to happily sigh and lean into him. Her head rested back against him, glad to have him near.

It had only been a week since her parents had left to go back to St. Simons. Since then, she, Nick, and Lulu had fallen into their new routines. She had to adjust to her parents not being here anymore. For so many years, they had been a daily part of her life. However, it was nice for them to have the house to themselves. They needed this space to find out who they were now, without someone looking in all the time.

Jo turned away from the door that led outside. Her hand came up to rest on Nick's cheek. It was rough from the stubble. He hadn't shaved in over twenty-four hours. She liked when it was like this.

"I'm glad she's happy," Jo said. "That is all I want for her."

"Me too," he said.

"Do you really think we have this?"

"I do."

To tell everyone else, they invited Vivian and her family over and set up a Skype call for her parents to watch. Jo felt this was extravagant, but Nick insisted they deserved to celebrate this new life they were bringing into the world.

"I knew it," Vivian said the moment she stepped into the house. Both TJ and Callie ran around her to search for Lulu. Thomas stood behind his wife. Vivian pulled her sunglasses up over her eyes to rest on the top of her head. Jo was always so amazed by how she could make anything look elegant.

"What do you know?" Jo played innocent. Vivian rolled her eyes.

"You can play dumb, but I know what this is about."

"Oh, Thomas, come on in," Nick called from the living room. Thomas kissed his wife's cheek before walking around her and making his way to where everyone else was.

"Okay, so you were right," Jo whispered. "Just don't give it away to Mom and Dad. It's a surprise."

Vivian dramatically pretended to zip her lips and throw away the key.

"My lips are sealed, but in the future, do remember I am always right."

"I will." Jo stuck her tongue out.

When her parents were on Skype, they barely had a moment of saying anything before Lulu loudly and excitedly informed them there was a new baby on the way. At first, they looked at Vivian for clarification.

"Not me," she said, shaking her head and laughing. That's when they turned to Jo and Nick.

"Oh! We're thrilled! What a wonderful surprise!" Rose exclaimed.

"Yes, it surprised us too," Nick said.

"How far along are you?"

"Thirteen weeks," Jo answered. Her parents started doing the math and realized she was far enough along to have known while they were there, so Jo explained further. "I mistook a lot of the signs, but the doctor confirmed it. We're having a baby."

"Well, I think another grandchild sounds great," her father said. Jo smiled, pleasantly surprised to see such happiness from her father about the new baby.

"Is it now time for me to give you a penny for your thoughts?" Nick asked Jo that evening after all of the excitement had settled.

Jo wanted to say it was nothing, but she knew for her and Nick to remain in this relationship and for it to grow, she had to tell him her thoughts.

"I'm scared," she admitted. "We lost Lulu before, and we lost so many babies before her. What if...what if we lose this baby? What if—"

"Oh Jojo," Nick murmured. He slid up closer toward her on the bed, tucking her into his arms. "I'm scared too."

"You are?"

"I think it's only natural after all we've been through," he said. "But I have a good feeling about our future, Jo."

Jo nodded, closing her eyes. Nick ran his fingers lovingly through her hair and began to hum beneath his breath to soothe her. Before she knew it, she'd fallen into a deep sleep.

Thirty-Two

Before opening the door to his apartment in Chicago, Nick wondered if he should go inside first and make sure the house wasn't stuffy. He knew it wasn't dirty, though there was probably a nice layer of dust on everything.

In this apartment, he lived a relatively minimal lifestyle. He ate out for most meals, finding it easier than cooking for one. If he did eat at home, it was some TV dinner from the freezer section at the market. He couldn't recall using his stove even once while he lived here.

He opened the door, allowing Jo and Lulu to walk inside first. Then he walked behind them. The apartment smelled a little musty. He turned on the fan and opened some windows to make it smell less stale.

"So, this is where you lived?" Jo asked. Her eyes scanned the living room. Nick's followed hers. The apartment didn't have much to it: a couch, a television, and a side table. No pictures hung on the walls.

"Why did you live here, Daddy?" Lulu questioned. Nick glanced at Jo. They didn't want to lie to their daughter, but it was still a very sensitive situation. They went to

Dr. Canmore about it, who helped them explain to Lulu their separation while she was away. Yet, it seemed she still struggled to wrap her mind around what that meant.

Nick bent down to her level and gave her a small smile.

"Remember what we said about Mama and Daddy living apart for a little while when you were away?" Lulu nodded. "This is where I lived." Lulu made a face.

"Here? It's so boring here." She wasn't wrong. The place had no character.

"It's a nice place," Jo commented. "Where's the bed-room?"

Nick pointed to the small hallway. They all made the short walk to his bedroom. It was just as empty as the rest of the house, except for the one photo on his bedside table. Jo walked over toward it and lifted it. It was a photo of the three of them. Jo's fingers ran over their faces.

"You always had this here?" She asked.

"Always, yes. It was my one comfort."

He noticed her eyes glass over with tears, though he didn't know why this was such a surprise to her. He had always loved her more than life itself. His family was the only thing he had in this world. Once he lost them, he found comfort in the memories of what they had before they lost it all.

"Well," Jo said as she sat the frame back onto the table. "It shouldn't take us long to pack this place up. Does all the furniture belong to you?"

"No," Nick answered. "Just the smaller items. I think tomorrow we can get it done in a few hours. For tonight, however, I thought we might go to dinner and a show."

"A show?" Lulu screwed up her nose.

"Yes, a show. It's a play that I thought you might enjoy - *Rapunzel.*"

"I've never been to a show."

"I know," Nick said. "Your mother and I always wanted to take you to one. This one sounded fun. The show is at seven and we have dinner reservations at five o'clock."

"Oh! Yay!"

Lulu rushed back out to the living room, leaving the two of them alone. Jo's eyes kept running over the nearly empty room. He'd neatly put away all of his clothes and the waste-basket was empty.

"Maybe I should have been better," Jo whispered. Nick moved to her side. "You were here, all alone."

"Jo, we went through a lot. It was not your job to take care of me. It was mine to take care of you."

Jo made a face. "We should have taken care of each other."

"But we weren't there, Jo. We couldn't be there for one another. Now we are. Stop waiting for everything to fall apart again. It's not."

On the way back from the show, Lulu fell asleep. Jo let Nick lift her out of the back seat and they both walked her into the apartment. It only had one bedroom, so Lulu would be sleeping on the couch. They would only stay in the apartment for two nights before moving to a hotel since his lease would be up.

They would be here for over a week. Nick had a job to do for a few days and during their free time, they would search for a potential location to live.

"Is she still asleep?" Jo asked. Nick nodded. He took off his shoes and shirt before climbing into the bed next to Jo.

"I think she had fun."

"She had a blast," Jo said. "Sometimes, like tonight, I can forget for a little while. It's like we've always been together, you know?" Again, Nick nodded. "But then it comes crashing back that it wasn't like that."

"No," Nick agreed. He placed his hand on Jo's stomach and fanned his fingers over the tight skin where the baby bump was growing.

"It will be nice living closer to the city, but we'll have to find a home with a backyard. I want a play set for the kids and plenty of room for Butler."

"Of course," Nick replied. "We will find it all."

"I hope so."

"Have you told your sister or parents that we're moving?"

"Vivian knows."

"Of course she does," Nick said with a chuckle.

"But I haven't told my parents. It may upset them that we'll be farther away, but I do believe they'll support us and know it's for the best."

"Yes, I'm sure they will," Nick agreed.

Jo yawned. The tiredness that came with pregnancy seemed to be worse than it had with Lulu.

"Go to sleep," Nick said. He kissed the tip of her nose. "We'll talk more in the morning."

Packing up Nick's apartment shined a light on how lonely her husband had been for the past four years. Other than the picture of their family, there were no other mementos in his place.

Jo cleared out Nick's lone dresser, placing the pieces of clothing into a box on the bed. As she shifted through the clothes, her fingers brushed along a thick piece of paper. Curious, Jo unfolded the shirt to find their wedding photo. It wasn't framed and was frayed along the edges, clearly worn. Jo lifted it, running her fingers over their happy faces. It felt like a lifetime ago.

"I used to look at that on the particularly bad days," Nick's voice broke in. She turned to see him standing against the door frame.

"It's one of my favorite pictures," Jo said. Her eyes moved back to the photo. It was in black and white and their eyes were on one another, not looking at anyone else in the world. Nick came up from behind, bringing his arms lovingly around her and resting his head on her shoulder.

"Mine too."

"We should get it blown up and placed somewhere in our new house."

"Oh, I do like that idea," Nick agreed. His lips caressed against Jo's shoulder blade. Even though there were still kinks the two of them needed to work through in their relationship, the physical aspect couldn't be better. That had fallen right back into place.

"We're going to look at houses tomorrow?"

"Yes, but we still don't have to move, Jo," Nick said. "I don't want you to feel like this is something you have to do."

Jo turned in his arms so she could face him.

"I want to," she stated with clarity. "We need a fresh start, Nick. Chicago is where your world is now. Lulu and I are ready to start our lives here, with you."

Nick grinned.

"Only if you're sure."

"I am."

Even though it had not been the plan, Jo immediately fell in love with a house. The plan was to drive through some neighborhoods and just see what they saw. However, as they drove through the first neighborhood, there happened to be a house for sale. Jo lit up. It was gorgeous. With Nick's suggestion, they parked the car and got out to take a look.

Jo knew the moment she stepped inside the house it was meant to be theirs. She remembered from their time house hunting before that it was the worst thing to fall in love with a house off the bat. It was never a sure thing to get the house.

But it didn't matter, Jo wanted this house. It was smaller than their home in Georgia, with only three bedrooms, and was all one level. Yet, it had a large and beautiful kitchen that looked into the living room. She would be able to watch her children play as she made them dinner—well, as Nick made her dinner and she kept him company in the kitchen.

The best part was the backyard, which had a beautiful play set the realtor informed them would stay with the house.

"We should put in an offer," Nick whispered into Jo's ear as they watched Lulu play in the backyard. It was clear that Lulu approved.

"But...." She paused. "Are you sure? We haven't even sold our house yet. There's still so much—"

"Do you love it?" Nick interrupted her.

"Yes."

"Do you like this neighborhood?"

"Absolutely."

"Then let's put in an offer. If it's accepted, it's meant to be; if it's not, it's not."

"How are you so calm about this?" Jo asked him. Nick shrugged.

"I don't know. I just think we should put in an offer."

"All right. Then let's do it. Why not?"

They received a call just a few hours later that their offer was accepted. That was their sign. They were moving to this small suburb outside of Chicago. It was time for their next chapter.

THIRTY-THREE

FALL 2017

The moving truck sat outside of their house. Children's laughter filled the backyard while Jo stood in the kitchen, looking at her empty home – though it no longer was her home. In just a few minutes, they would give their keys to their realtor, who would give them to a new family.

"Hey."

Jo turned to where her sister stood. She had been out front with Nick, Thomas, and their parents talking. Her parents came up for the move. Nick joked that everything with this family had to be a spectacle. He wasn't wrong, but she knew he also secretly loved it. While away, she knew he had missed the big family atmosphere.

It would be different now. They couldn't quickly get together as a family anymore, but they would still be back to visit. Plus, her family would come and visit them, too. They had already gotten plane tickets to come up to the city for Christmas. Jo believed they were hoping for a white Christmas. They'd never had that before.

"Hi," Jo said to Vivian.

"It's so strange with it being so empty." Vivian's eyes moved around the empty kitchen. "We've had many memories in here. Some good. Some bad."

"I know," Jo agreed.

"Are you sure you don't need me coming up to help for a few days? I know how difficult a move can be, plus the pregnancy."

"Oh no, we can manage."

While Jo appreciated her sister's offer, they needed to do this next part with just the two of them. Both Nick and she had decided they would do this part alone. They had movers to help with the heavy items. But otherwise, it would just be them.

"Well, be sure to call me if you need me."

"I will," Jo promised. She then walked up to her sister and wrapped her arms around her. She held her tightly. "I love you, Vivian."

"I love you."

"I know," Jo said. She held onto her sister for a good minute before allowing her to draw away. Vivian wiped away tears from beneath her eyes.

"Allergies."

"Right, allergies."

The back door of the house opened.

"Around the house! No dirty feet indoors!" Vivian reminded the kids.

They had already had the house deep cleaned. Jo was grateful that Vivian offered to keep Butler at her house before they left. They didn't need dirty paws messing up the pristine floors.

The children paused at the doorway before shutting it and running back outside.

"I think our parents want you to head outside," Vivian said. "They want to say a proper goodbye."

"In a minute. I need a bit longer alone."

"All right."

"You saved my life, you know," Jo said. Vivian took in a shuddering breath, averting her eyes from Jo's.

"I'm your big sister; it's my job." She shook the seriousness away.

"You saved me, Vivian."

"And I'd do it again," Vivian said. "I love you, Jo. Now, I ought to get back outside before the tears come again."

As her sister walked away, Jo continued her walk through the house. It flooded her memories with moments of Lulu as a young child. She could remember her giggle and right where her first steps had been. But as she continued her journey and made it upstairs, the memories grew darker. For many months, she had remained sequestered in her bedroom. It was where *it* had happened. A shiver ran up her spine.

"What are you doing?" She jumped. "Sorry, I didn't mean to scare you," Nick said. He touched her lower back and gave it a little rub. He had been doing that more and more as her stomach grew.

"It's all right. I am just doing one last walk through the house. It's a bit bittersweet."

"I agree."

"There are things I'll miss and some more that I won't."

"What won't you miss?"

"The one stair that always makes that loud noise," Jo said. Nick's eyes brightened at the memory. When they first moved into the home, they discovered that step. It was obnoxiously loud if you stepped on it in one particular spot. They tried everything to fix it, but it seemed impossible. Over time, they just learned how to avoid that spot. Yet, now and then, they would forget and the creaking would sound.

"Ah yes," Nick agreed. "What else?"

"The terrible memories. Of course, they'll still be here." She tapped at her temple. "But I won't remember them by just walking into a room. We did a lot of yelling in this house."

"We did," Nick softly agreed.

"But we also made up in here."

Nick's mouth curled up into a wicked grin.

"We did."

"What will you miss?"

"Hm, about the same as you. I think I am more excited about our new adventure. We get to start over, Jo."

That made Jo smile. She had forgotten what an optimist her husband could be.

"To new beginnings."

"To new beginnings."

"Please be safe," Rose said to Nick. He nodded before leaning over to draw her into a hug.

"We will," he promised her.

"Thank you for coming back," Rose whispered into his ear. "You two needed one another far more than I think you knew."

As they pulled away, Nick met his mother-in-law's eyes. They were misty. He then realized his were as well. He blinked the tears away.

"Thank you for being there when I couldn't."

They continued with their goodbyes. Lulu told everyone about her new home and what they would like the most about it. Then she took an extra-long hug from her grandfather before kissing his cheek.

"Come on," Nick encouraged her when she ran toward him. He lifted her into his arms with ease and placed her into the car that Jo would be driving; he would drive the moving truck. It was going to take two days to do the journey, stopping midway for the night.

When Jo sat down in the car, he held the door open for a moment.

"Are you ready?" he asked her.

"I do wish we could ride together."

"Me too," Nick agreed.

He told her he loved her and gave her a last kiss before shutting the door. Lulu waved at him and he waved back.

Once he got into the moving truck, he saw that his in-laws were still standing and waving at them. Jo was right. This was bittersweet. He reminded himself he would see them at Christmas time as he waved back.

He waited for Jo to start her car. Then he started the truck. It was time to go.

SUMMER 2019

"**I** do love Chicago in the summer. It isn't quite so hot compared to home," Vivian commented. She was sitting with her sister on the back porch. Jo lifted her lemonade and took a slow sip.

Ever since their move here, her family visited as often as they could. They all tried to see one another every few months, if not more. It was harder for Jo and Nick to travel with the baby, but they had made it down to Georgia a few times.

When they visited Georgia, it no longer felt like home to Jo. She still loved it. It was where her family lived, but her home was here in Chicago. Here, they'd begun their new life with new friends and new adventures.

"Ma... ma!" Her son, Sam, toddled over toward Jo and hit her knee with his little pudgy hand. Jo glanced down at him and smiled. He was a happy one-and-a-half-year-old, always smiling. He looked so much like Lulu as a baby, except his hair was lighter than hers had been. Personality-wise, he was quieter and more timid than Lulu had been. He tended to take his time to figure out the world around him.

Right now, Nick was out picking Lulu up from summer camp. Over the past couple of years, Jo and Nick slowly allowed Lulu to do more and more things out of their reach. It was still something they struggled with, but they worked on it because they wanted their daughter to have a full life. Not one filled with worry or anxiety.

Any time they were out with Sam, though, he remained strapped to her or Nick's chest in a carrier. She had yet to let him explore at a playground or a mall, but that would come soon enough.

Jo lifted Sam into her lap and held him close against her. The little boy happily murmured to himself. He always enjoyed cuddles with his mama.

"So next Christmas we all go to St. Simons?" Vivian asked her.

"Yes, but we're renting a house for the week."

"Oh, us too. Four children, four adults, plus our parents and the dog? Their place would be way too small."

"Aunt Vivian!" Lulu entered the backyard. Jo glanced up to see Nick struggling with Lulu's overflowing bag from her daily summer camp. She stood, handing Sam to Vivian, and walked inside to assist him.

"Do you need help?"

"Why does she need so much stuff for art camp?" he asked. Jo just laughed and took the bag.

"Vivian wants to go out for dinner with all of us." Nick made a face. "What?" Jo asked.

"What if you and Lulu went with her and I stayed here with Sam? He does awful at restaurants." Nick wasn't wrong. Their little boy liked to yell when they were sitting. He was always wanting to be on the move. The only time he was happy while restrained was in his baby carrier.

"That's fine with me. You don't mind?"

Nick shook his head.

"Not at all."

Jo smiled up at him. They had filled the past couple of years with therapy of all sorts. They were stronger now than ever before. It didn't mean they didn't argue; they did. But they were happy.

When Jo and Vivian arrived home from dinner, Jo told her sister good night. She hugged Vivian and kissed her cheek before Vivian disappeared into the bedroom. Jo kicked off her shoes and walked down the hallway. She peeked into Sam's room to check in on the children. Lulu had decided to stay behind instead of going out to eat with her aunt and mom.

The children were sleeping peacefully. While Vivian was here, Lulu was sleeping on a padded pallet on the floor. As her eyes adjusted to the light, Jo noticed Sam was also on the pallet next to Lulu. They lay cuddled together. Jo's heart warmed. Lulu loved her little brother. From the moment Lulu laid eyes on Sam, they'd been close. Jo had been worried about the large age gap that Lulu might want nothing to do with him, but she adored Sam. She was always showing him how to do things, reading to him, and spending most of her free time with Sam.

Quietly, Jo tiptoed in. She watched her children sleeping for a few moments before she picked up the baby. He stirred slightly, so she kissed his head in an attempt to keep him from waking up. Gently, she placed him into his crib. He grasped at his small teddy and settled back down as Jo patted his back.

After Sam was settled, she made sure Lulu's blanket covered her before kissing her crown. She still pinched herself from time to time, unable to believe that this was now her life.

When she made it to her bedroom, she found Nick sitting up on the bed and reading a book. He slid his glasses up his nose and smiled at her.

"Ah, there you are."

"I didn't expect you to still be awake," Jo said. She undid the zip of her dress and slid it down to the ground, leaving her only in her slip.

"I always stay awake when you're away," Nick said.

"Well, now I feel bad for staying out so late."

"No, don't," Nick stated. "I'm glad you had a good time. You deserve it."

"I did."

Jo went into the bathroom and found her nightgown to change into. As she looked up, she saw Nick behind her in the mirror.

"Good," he murmured into her ear.

"Were the children well behaved?"

"Yes, as always."

"Good." Jo turned to face her husband.

"What comes next?" Nick asked.

"What do you mean?"

"Next?"

"I think we just get to live, Nick. Isn't that exciting?"

He smiled. "Absolutely."

Jo finished getting ready for bed. She took Nick's hand to lead him with her back to their mattress. They easily got into the bed together. As their lips sloppily came together, they knocked teeth, causing Jo to laugh.

"In our older ages, we aren't so smooth anymore," she said against his cheek.

"That's all right. We're together."

"Yes," Jo agreed. "Though I wouldn't want to have to live through that ever again."

"No, me neither." Nick's fingers ran down her arm, causing her to shiver.

Jo bent forward to kiss him again. He pressed her down slightly and leaned over her, kissing the outline of her jaw. She moaned in appreciation. Right as his hand slipped over her sleeve to pull it down, they heard a cry from the nursery.

"I guess that's my cue," Jo said. She pushed Nick away from her before running her fingers through his hair. "I wouldn't trade it for the world."

"Me neither."

"I love you."

"I love you, Jojo."

The End

A.G. Hawkins is an author, mother of two, and a military wife. She is a former teacher, who graduated with her Doctorate in Education.

Her hobbies include writing, reading, binge-watching television shows, and going to Disney. She loves spending time with her family, especially when they get to travel together. Her passion has always been to tell stories about healing.

www.ingramcontent.com/pod-product-compliance
Lightning Source LLC
Chambersburg PA
CBHW021414310726
48971CB00005B/1326